GW00496590

Flight

of

Fancy

Scottish Island Escapes

Book 6

MARGARET AMATT

Cover designed by Margaret Amatt
Map drawn by Margaret Amatt
ISBN: 978-1-914575-88-4
An eBook is also available: 978-1-914575-89-1

LEANNAN
PRESS
INDEPENDENT PUBLISHER

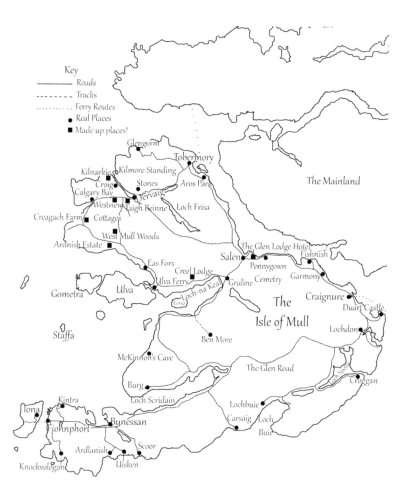

Key
—— Roads
------- Tracks
·········· Ferry Routes
● Real Places
■ Made up places!

Glengorm

Tobermory

Kilnarkie● Kilmore Standing
Croig ■ Stones
Calgary Bay ■ Dervaig
Westview■ Taigh Brinne
Creagach Farm ■ ■ Cottages
Ardnish Estate ■

Aros Park

Loch Frisa

West Mull Woods

Eas Fors
Creel Lodge
Ulva Ferry
Loch-na-Keal
Forsa

The Glen Lodge Hotel
Salen
Pennygown
Gruline Cemetery
Garmony

Fishnish

Gometra
Ulva

Staffa

The
Isle of Mull

Craignure
Duart Castle

Lochdon

Ben More

McKinnon's Cave

The Glen Road

Croggan

Burg
Loch Scridain

Iona
Kintra

Fionnphort
Bunessan

Ardlanish
Scoor

Lochbuie
Carsaig Loch
Buie

Knockvologan
Uisken

The Mainland

For Ian and Ossian

FIVE YEARS AGO

Chapter One

Taylor

Taylor sat bolt upright on the end of the couch, eyeing her therapist, who didn't return the look but flipped through her notes, pursing her lips. The soft cushion yielded under Taylor's fingernails as she clawed into it like a cat. Had she done enough? Maybe if she smiled. She relaxed her face muscles and widened her eyes.

'Ok, Taylor.' The therapist glanced up, dazzling Taylor with her white teeth. Her neon pink Chanel jacket glowed like a nuclear warning light. 'You're doing great. I know you're eager to get back to normality. That's what we all want.'

Taylor nodded.

'I'm also very conscious it's your birthday this week and a special one too.'

Taylor's lips remained curled up. Holding the expression became painful. 'Yup, twenty-one.' She was twenty-one? Her brow creased and she rubbed a finger over it before continuing to her hair and pushing a blonde lock behind her ear. She didn't want to appear confused but how could she be only twenty-one? Some days she felt about a hundred. Releasing her hand from the cushion, she placed it on her knees, jutting from beneath her short skirt. Her Hollywood tan glowed. Everything here could be bought. Otherwise, she'd be pale, freckly, and unremarkable. Her focus landed on a small silver globe on the pristine white shelves behind the desk, beside an aerial photograph of the Beverly Hills clinic. Taylor breathed deeply but silently, her gaze not leaving the shelf.

'Well, I've reviewed everything,' said the therapist. 'You can go back to your family.'

Taylor barely heard the conditions. Her inner self was air-punching and whooping. She was getting out.

'Just remember, feelings are not actions. Try to keep the two separate. You may feel like doing something but that doesn't mean you have to act on it.'

'Sure, I'll remember.' Taylor leapt to her feet, almost grabbing the door handle.

Her therapist blocked her and shook her hand. 'If you need me, you know where I am. Call me anytime.'

'Thanks.' Taylor returned the handshake as briefly as she could without being rude before hightailing it out the door.

*

The following day dawned bright, hot and dry. Taylor swapped the therapist's couch for a seat in a limo. The stereo pounded a low beat and Taylor rubbed her forehead where a dull ache blossomed.

'Is this nail ok?'

Taylor glanced across to see Skylar, her twin sister, examining an inch-long designer nail, her slim legs crossed in front of her. She turned her fingers this way, then that, so the glitter sparkled under the track lighting.

'Sure, honey.' Bianca Kane, their mother, took her hand. 'They're amazing.' Her eyes flickered from the nails to Taylor, then back. Sammy Rousse, Taylor's father, was watching too, though making a good show of pretending to look elsewhere.

Forgiveness wouldn't come quick – if ever – not from her parents and definitely not from Skylar. Skylar's grudge-holding capacity was legendary and right up there with her back-stabbing skills and her egocentricity. Taylor sighed and adjusted her up-do. In the reflection, when she was done up like this, the likeness between her and Skylar was uncanny.

'Nearly there,' said Bianca, flicking her golden hair. 'What a lot of fans have gathered.'

'I'll go with Skylar.' Sammy smoothed back his white hair. 'I'll get the driver to take the car around the back with Taylor.'

Taylor's jaw tightened and she stared out the window. Why had she thought things would be different? This was her life now. Unseen, hidden. Maybe before rehab, she'd have spoken out, but she couldn't risk being shoved back in, or worse, if Skylar had her way, being locked up and the key thrown away.

Cheers and shouts rang out as Skylar got out. Her bodyguard flanked her and ushered her up the hotel stairs. Cameras flashed and people jostled for a better view. The limo moved off. Bianca squinted at Taylor and pressed her lips together, fiddling with the hem of her short skirt.

'So, what are we going to find for you to do?' Bianca asked, her voice unnaturally high, like she was addressing a child in kindergarten. Would she whip out a colouring book and some crayons to occupy Taylor while they indulged in the weekend of birthday festivities without her?

'It's my birthday too,' said Taylor. The whole event had been planned around Skylar's wishes. *And what's in store for me? A padded cell?* Why would they bother asking if she fancied anything different from Skylar? In their eyes, only one daughter truly existed.

'Of course it is, sweetie. We just have to be careful.'

'Of what?'

Bianca resumed fiddling with her hem. 'Taylor, you're just out of rehab and therapy. I don't want to upset you or ruin your progress, so I think it's best if you keep a low profile. By all means, enjoy yourself but don't do too much and don't distress yourself.'

Like she'd have to. Everyone else distressed her without her having to try. Wasn't that their mission in life?

The back entrance to the hotel was like a different place: a grim street with graffitied walls. Taylor and Bianca got out of the limo and entered through a sliding door. A porter greeted them and led them through a warren of corridors and fire doors to the lobby.

'Skylar's gone to her room already,' said Sammy, meeting them and taking his wife's arm. 'Taylor, you should go up too.'

'You can get ready for the party, sweetie,' Bianca said. 'I'll be up as soon as I've sorted my things. I'm sure Skylar's stylist wouldn't mind giving you a hand when she's done with Skylar.'

'I'll do it myself,' said Taylor. She was done with Skylar's leftovers. She held out her hand. Her father's jaw set as he stared at the key card. Five seconds passed. Would he give it to her? With a grudging look, he dropped it onto her palm.

'No nonsense,' he said. 'You wait in your room for your mother.'

Taylor headed for the elevator. On the first floor, she jumped out, made her way to the back stairs and came down again. Sitting in her room all afternoon while Skylar had a pamper session wasn't happening.

Opportunity for entertainment knocked. If she slipped out the front door, she could pretend to be Skylar and cause merry hell. Not for the first time. The

12

punishment for pulling a stunt like that before had almost driven her to taking her own life. Then she'd been bundled into rehab and therapy. Now her family all but had her under lock and key and were hellbent on erasing her existence. Only the die-hard fans of their early work remembered Skylar Rousse had a twin sister. It was the best-kept secret in Hollywood.

As children, they'd shared roles, but that had been swept under the carpet, and anyone who asked was told the 'Taylor is ill' story. Her career had imploded while Skylar's had rocketed.

If she didn't look like her sister, she'd be cast to the dogs. But her parents couldn't risk letting her go. Taylor smiled at her reflection in a gilded mirror in the corridor; her face – like it or loathe it – was her only weapon. She could bring down Skylar with this face. All it would take was a few choice words to the paparazzi outside. Or better still, she could humiliate her sister by stripping off, acting the fool or perhaps attacking someone while pretending to be her. The possibilities were endless.

She reached the lobby and stopped. What was she doing? Two days of freedom and here she was planning trouble already. So much for not acting on her feelings. This wasn't her.

Sinking her teeth into her lower lip, she peered around. What to do? Go back to her room and behave?

Soft music drifted out a half-open door to the side of the lobby. Taylor snuck up and peered inside. Glasses clinked over the gentle murmur of chat in the ambiently lit dining area. People sat scattered about at polished wood tables, drinking either coffee or wine. A couple held hands in a raised area half obscured by a line of pot plants built into the divider. Some individuals sat alone with cells and open laptops. Taylor followed the music, humming along though she couldn't place the song, and waited by a giant fern at the door. A server dressed in black approached. 'Are you here for lunch? Or just a drink?'

'Er,' said Taylor. A drink. What irony. She could legally buy a drink. But she hadn't grown up in Hollywood without tasting the hard stuff. Her drinking binges never ended well. Was this just asking for trouble? She could stick to pop like a good girl. 'Yes, a drink.'

'Of course, follow me.'

The server led Taylor to a table close to the bar, screened off by another divider with more ferns and greenery. She accepted the giant menu and made herself comfortable. 'A Coke, please.' She passed back the menu and took out her cell. Why was she here? Why was she anywhere? Her life had little or no point. She was drifting in a sea of nothingness.

At the modern wood-panelled bar, a group of men laughed, sipping from beer glasses. Above them, copper lamps flooded the area with light, gleaming off the rows of wine glasses hanging over the bar. A beam spotlighted one of the men. His back was to Taylor, and she smirked. His white shirt and tight pants were neat, but he hadn't noticed his shirt had come untucked at the back. She contemplated it, wishing he would tuck it in. Another man slapped his shoulder and he turned away from him grinning. His gaze found Taylor and before she could stop herself, she was looking back. A rush of heat flooded through her, and, shit, she must be blushing.

'Your Coke, madam.' The server blocked her view. Taylor blinked as her drink was placed before her. Her attention lingered on the group at the bar but the man with the untucked shirt had his back to her again. She slipped her hand under her low-cut black top and traced her fingertip lazily along her collarbone. He looked like a real man, not some spotty boy with Hollywood aspirations – the type Skylar liked.

With a deflating sigh, Taylor turned her attention to her cell. No messages? Not even from her parents asking where she was. They couldn't have discovered her absence yet. The screen was blank, much like herself. She scooped it up and browsed nothing in particular. What could she do with her life? Her acting career was over. Even if she tried to revamp it, she could see Skylar shooting her down before she was airborne and her parents wouldn't allow it. But what else was she fit for? Perhaps a change of direction? She'd always loved singing. Maybe Broadway? Could she expect her name to carry some clout? It would probably be the opposite. She hadn't made friends in the biz. Her open attempt to bring down Skylar earned her cold shoulders and snidey glances from those who knew. Even with it swept out of sight, producers and directors might be wary.

She tapped the cell screen. Why was everything so complicated? There had to be a way out. Someone passed by – the man with the untucked shirt. From the fleeting glimpse of his face, he reminded her of one of the Hemsworth brothers. Well, the blonde hair and the build anyway. Her gaze followed him for a second, noting his shirt was still untucked. Still chatting to his friends, he looked her way and she caught his eye again.

Why couldn't she look away? He didn't either. A mad urge to go over and talk to him seized her. Her brain scrambled hundreds of crazy things she wanted to tell him and she felt sure he would listen intently. He ran his thumb along his lower lip, perhaps trying to erase the smile that had spread as he looked at her. She was receiving his vibes loud and clear. Maybe she should be weirded out. He could be a total creep, but that wasn't the feeling she was getting at all. Aside from being jaw-droppingly handsome, he was emitting more signals than a cell tower, and all of them were interfering with her thought process. Her insides swelled and vibrated, forcing her lips to curl into a smile. One of his friends shifted and moved between them. Taylor jerked her eyes back to her phone. *What the hell am I doing?*

Still aware of them close by, she focused on her drink, her ears pricked.

'So, guys,' one said, and Taylor squinted sideways, not moving her head. A neatly tucked shirt was level with her sightline. She flicked her glance upwards and saw the blond man grinning at the man who'd spoken. He'd fixed his shirt. Actually, none of the Hemsworths had anything on him; hot didn't begin to describe this firestorm. Her Coke sat abandoned on the table; drinking in this guy was way more appealing, even if it meant she had to ditch breathing for the next few minutes.

'So,' he repeated. 'What's the plan?'

Taylor grabbed her glass to stop her hand shaking. What a cute accent. British maybe?

'Are you going straight back to the airport?'

'No,' said the blond man. 'I'm going to the party.'

'Ooh.' The other guys jeered and laughed. 'You're going to the party. Did you get an invite from Princess Courtney herself?'

'Or the birthday girl. Has she got the hots for her rival's pilot? That would be quite a story.'

'No, nothing like that.' The blond man rolled his hand through his hair. 'I thought you guys were going too.'

'Yeah, but we're working, not partying' said a thickset man with a stubbly beard.

'You gonna try to bed Courtney?' said another.

Taylor leaned slightly closer to the gap between the tables where they were standing. Courtney Hines was *the* star Skylar was chasing for popularity. The fact Skylar had invited her to the party was typical of her phoney life. She'd kiss her cheeks and pretend they were best friends, only to stab her in the back as soon she turned around.

The blond man cleared his throat. 'Absolutely not. That's how to end my career overnight.'

'How about Skylar then? That'd be some conquest, especially on her birthday.'

'Time to shut up,' he said, putting his arm out to steer the other men away.

One of the guys coughed so loudly it sounded like he was having an attack. Taylor peeked up; the thickset man cocked his head in her direction. She bit her lip and scanned around. Oh no, he thought she was Skylar. The blond man moved away, taking the other guys with him. Taylor sipped her Coke and half closed her eyes, trying to refocus on what she'd been doing before.

As she scrolled through her cell, manically trying to prevent herself checking out the blond guy, a shadow fell over her table. Taylor glimpsed up and her heartrate quickened. It was him.

'Hey,' he said, ruffling his hair. 'Can I sit for a second?'

'Oh.' Taylor bit her lip. 'Sure.' He slipped onto the bench opposite.

'I just want to apologise for those guys. I don't think any of them realised who you were. That wasn't a nice thing for you to hear.'

Taylor opened her mouth. She had to let him know she wasn't Skylar. Her cell flashed her mother's name. *Crap.* The lookout had started. She couldn't let this guy know who she was. If he thought she was Skylar, then

Skylar she'd have to be and a well-behaved, noncontroversial version. 'It's fine,' she said.

'I guess you're used to it.'

'I guess.' She wasn't used to any of this. Guys talking to her, people paying her attention.

'I work for Courtney Hines and she'd be angry if she thought I'd upset you, so I thought I better say something.'

'Would she?' Surely the opposite was true.

'Absolutely. She's a really nice woman. The press have said stuff, but she doesn't hate you. Just like all the stuff the press say about you is rubbish. I mean, here you are.' His gaze travelled over her. She read his meaning loud and clear. The press would never believe Skylar Rousse would hang about alone in bars and they'd be right. This little stunt was going to have her locked up for the next twenty years.

'Yeah,' said Taylor, her cheeks burning as she looked into his eyes again. She had to; something magnetic pulled her. What a stunning shade of blue, clear and bright like the sea. His chiselled cheekbones and well-proportioned nose smacked of Hollywood, but he had a rugged realism about him. A butterfly storm erupted in her midriff at his smile.

'Are you having a good birthday?' he said. If he was a fan or a groupie, he was doing a great job. She should feel threatened by him and want to call security. But an overwhelming sense of calm surrounded her. The butterflies had settled and were blowing happy bubbles now, filling her with peace. She felt like she could tell him anything. Maybe that was his skill. Still, she didn't dare mention she wasn't Skylar. Her parents would have her shunted back into therapy and locked up before you could say *that's show business,* if they knew what she was doing. Not only had she skipped her room but she was out in a public place talking to people.

'Not really,' she said, hating the self-deprecation in her voice because she wanted to laugh and smile at this guy.

He tilted his head. 'I'm sorry about that. Can you just not wait for the party to start?'

'No. I don't really want that either.'

He shook his head a little. 'I thought all this was tailormade for your desires.'

Hearing him saying 'Taylor' and 'desires' in the same sentence set off the butterflies again. *How insane am I?*

'I guess you never get to show your real personality,' he said. 'It's all about the public image.'

'If the face fits.'

He leaned his arms on the table. The warmth of his smile seeped through her walls and her lips twitched. Unlike the grinding pain of trying to keep the expression plastered on for her therapist, this had the opposite effect, her shoulders relaxed and her cheeks were pleasantly warm.

'That's quite sad,' he said, and his expression filled with concern. 'What would you rather do instead if you could really choose and didn't have to put on a show?'

Taylor sucked in her lip and tried to grasp a coherent thought to put into words. 'I don't really know. I'm not sure what I like doing or even who I really am some days.'

'Aw, I'm sorry. That must be tough.' Her hand was on the table, inching ever closer to his. She wanted to shift her fingers so they touched his but she didn't dare. He looked down, then back at her, and his eyes smouldered, matching the feeling inside her completely. With a tiny laugh that was almost a sigh, he moved his hand over hers. 'You're a sad lost soul, aren't you?' She stared into his eyes, knowing he didn't require an answer. The only thing he didn't know was her true identity, but otherwise her soul was bared before him. 'I hope I haven't upset you, asking these questions.'

'No.' Her voice was barely a whimper. The warmth from his hand was overwhelming; it seeped up her arm, through her veins into every cold, dark cavity, filling them with light and hope. 'I'm good.'

He didn't speak, just looked. She did the same. Her heartrate steadied and she felt connected to him on a level so far beyond the physical it was terrifying.

A movement near the bar caught her eye. She blinked and swallowed. The man lessened the pressure on her hand.

Skylar and some celebrity friends had arrived. Skylar glared at Taylor, raised two fingers to her eyeballs, then pointed the same fingers at Taylor. The gesture said *I'm coming for you* clearer than words. She pulled out her cell. In a few seconds bodyguards would swoop in with Bianca and Sammy. They would carefully remove 'Skylar' and she'd be locked up for the rest of the day.

'Maybe I'll catch you later, at the party,' the man said.

'What?' Taylor looked back at him. Had he mistaken her distraction with Skylar as disinterest? His back was facing Skylar so he wouldn't have seen her.

'Only if you want to,' he said.

'Oh, I do.' And if she did, she needed to get back to her room quick. Her parents wouldn't entertain the idea of her going out if she was caught misbehaving. 'But right now, I have to go.'

'No worries,' said the man. He released her hand and stood up. 'I do too.' Their eyes locked again. 'But I look forward to seeing you later.'

'Yeah, me too. I'll look out for you.'

With a brief smile, he stood and headed out, apparently not noticing the real Skylar at the bar. Taylor sucked in her lip, licking the inside as she admired his backside. Once he'd left, Taylor downed her Coke and skirted around to the other side of the booths so she could leave without passing Skylar. Hopefully, if she met the man later, she'd be standing next to her sister, and she wouldn't have to explain herself.

As she slipped into the foyer, she walked straight into her father and two bodyguards. She edged back, turning around to glance at her sister. Skylar's eyes bored into her as she stirred her cocktail slowly and deliberately. Taylor swallowed. Everything about that look contained a warning. Skylar looked ready to strike, but before Taylor could think about anything else, the bodyguards seized her arms, and she was frogmarched towards the elevator.

Chapter Two

Magnus

Magnus straightened his black tie and entered the high-ceilinged room, brushing past some guys in tuxedos and almost stepping on the long dress of an older woman. 'I beg your pardon,' he said.

The woman glanced around. 'Oh, that's quite all right.'

He strode through the crowd. A band struck up a chirpy tune over the murmur of voices and the clink of glasses. A sea of unfamiliar faces swarmed around, but he didn't mind.

A booming laugh alerted him to Courtney's agent deep in chat with one of her PR guys. Magnus strolled towards them. Any port in a storm. Making friends wherever he went wasn't something he found difficult but it was easier if someone familiar showed up. The PR guy was brash and new; the one who'd made some crass suggestions in the bar earlier, before he'd noticed Skylar Rousse right beside them.

Skylar wasn't at all what he'd expected. The paparazzi had her pegged for a ruthless bitch who tore down everyone and everything, but she hadn't seemed like that. Her expression was so lost and sad. Maybe she was suffering Hollywood burnout and he'd caught her on a bad day. But she'd stirred his heart and now he wanted to see her again, check she was ok and maybe get to know her a bit better. The way she'd looked at him gave him the chills – not in a creepy way – just something he wasn't used to. Women hit on him all the time and he didn't care; most of the time he was just as bad. But that wasn't what this girl had done. How bloody confusing and unsettling. Though she was a talented actress by all accounts so maybe the whole thing was fake.

'Hi,' he said, stepping towards the guys. 'How's the work?'

'Ha, yeah, whatever. We *are* working though,' said PR guy, rubbing his scrubby beard. 'It might not look like it—'

'Too right it doesn't,' said Magnus with a grin. 'You guys have it easy.'

'Says the man who's a glorified bus driver.'

Magnus smirked. 'Yeah, remember that the next time we're thirty-five thousand feet up and we hit turbulence.'

The man laughed. A new tune started from the band and Magnus adjusted his cuffs, squinting around as he continued his chat with Jake the PR guy.

'Are you coming to the club after the meal?' asked Jake.

'I don't know,' Magnus said. 'Where is it?'

'Upstairs.' He grinned and waggled his eyebrows. 'This hotel is a one-stop shop. I guess that's why Miss Rousse chose it.'

'Wow, cool. Yeah. I might look in.'

With hundreds of guests, a hierarchy developed and Magnus was in the lower echelons. He didn't catch a glimpse of Courtney or Skylar during the meal and wondered if they had a private suite somewhere. His dinner companions were fun and he knocked back the free champagne, sharing various stories about his worst flights.

'Have you ever had anyone give birth on a flight?' asked a rotund middle-aged woman, sitting to his left.

'No,' said Magnus, 'but when I was a co-pilot on a small flight, we had a man who had a heart attack and we had to make an emergency landing with him lying in the aisle. That was quite dramatic.'

'Oh, goodness.' She raised her hand to her chest. 'How terrifying.'

As they moved through the courses, the champagne and stories flowed profusely. Magnus sat back and held his stomach. He kept fit and the occasional big dinner rarely touched him but he felt like he'd eaten the side of a cow, a twenty-pound salmon, plus half a field of vegetables, and they hadn't even started dessert.

'My god,' announced the woman by his side and he followed her sightline to see what she was looking at. An enormous cake was wheeled onto the stage. 'I guess we're doing the cake cutting before dessert,' said the woman.

'Thank goodness,' said Magnus. 'I need to fast for three days before I touch anything else. I haven't got room for another bite.'

'Oh, there's nothing on you.' The woman batted his arm.

Everyone fell silent. A drumroll was followed by raucous applause and Skylar teetered up the stairs to take her place at the mic, beaming at the cake.

'Oh my god, thank you,' she said, raising her hand for quiet then placing it on her neck. 'You're all so awesome. Thank you for coming, and check out this cake.'

The towering creation was almost the same height as her, even in her six-inch heels. How could this be the same woman he'd spoken to earlier? She must be a great actress because she was transformed into the all-glitter princess the media loved – or at least loved to hate. So much for not wanting this for her birthday. She looked in her element.

She smoothed out her tiny figure-hugging dress and flicked back a flurry of blonde hair. The perfect barrel curls reached her flat bottom. Jeez, she'd had a whole new head of hair fitted since the afternoon. Magnus tossed back a drink. This was Hollywood after all.

As she blew out the candles, cheers rang out and the room erupted into a rousing chorus of 'Happy Birthday'. Magnus joined in before withdrawing with everyone else. He joined the throng, waiting to exit.

The various areas of the hotel were opened like a theme park with something for everyone. On an upper floor, he located the club. Two thickset bouncers guarded the door. Leaving the corridor for this darkened room was surreal. Music throbbed with a modern vibe as opposed to the mellow ballroom below.

Inside, the music intensified and neon lights flickered around. Magnus slipped through the crowd of bodies, exhaling upwards, trying to cool his forehead in the stifling heat. He approached the bar and waited in line to be served. A couple beside him made out loudly. He watched in horrified fascination for a few seconds before looking away. The line got closer and eventually he had a cool cocktail in hand.

'Hey, you.'

He glanced around. From amidst a gang of friends, Skylar waved. He raised his glass.

'I wondered if I'd bump into you,' she said, breaking away from her group. 'You know who I am, right?'

'Of course.' This was getting weirder.

25

'And…' She scanned him up and down. 'We spoke earlier, yeah.'

He sipped his drink. 'Yup. I haven't forgotten.'

'Good.' She smiled her Hollywood smile – white teeth sparkling and blue eyes flashing.

'You seem a lot happier.'

'Oh, yes. Was I too morbid before? Sorry about that.'

He furrowed his brow and squinted, trying to hold her gaze and reopen the connection, but there was nothing. Maybe she'd taken drugs or something.

'You know that thing I told you before.'

'Which thing?' he asked.

'You know…' Her expression turned coy.

'The thing about this kind of party not really being your thing?'

'Did I say that? Jeez, what a case. Shoot me now.' She threw out her hands and her lips parted.

Magnus sipped his cocktail and frowned. Was this method acting? Whatever it was, she was so different, it was uncanny. Was she putting on a show for her friends?

'I don't recall your name,' she said. 'Maybe you told me, but I meet so many people, sorry.'

'I didn't tell you. It's Magnus Hansen.'

'Ooh, I like it. Handsome Hansen.'

He smirked and looked away. 'Nice.'

'Well, handsome. I don't know about you but it's a bit hot in here.' Her eyes scanned around then slipped back to his face.

'It is.'

'Come with me.' She took his hand and led him through the crowd. He'd packed away a substantial amount of alcohol that evening but, through the brain fog, he guessed a string of bodyguards and onlookers were following.

A door swung open, ushering a shift in the air, definitely cooler than inside. Holding his glass high, he made his way through the crowd circulating on the balcony. Skylar had his hand in a grip lock. Sambuca stench mingled with expensive perfumes and body sprays filtered into his nostrils, making him nauseous. The dull thump of the music pounded inside and the doors clicked open and shut as people followed them at a distance.

At the balcony edge, Skylar stopped and put her back to the railing, pulling Magnus closer. 'So,' she said. 'How do you like it out here?'

'Great,' he said, releasing her hand. He leaned his elbows on the railings and looked out, holding his glass over the street below. Skylar's eyes bored into him. Now, she was behaving like all the other women in his life. He knew what she wanted but, hell, he wasn't that easy. Not even for a Hollywood movie star. And something wasn't right. If she was drugged up, he couldn't touch her.

She trailed her fingertips over his hands and up his forearms. No shit. He almost dropped his glass over the edge. So much for his resolve. He stood tall, examining her.

Before he could think, her arms wound around his neck and he stepped back, holding his cocktail glass high; a few drops splashed from it. 'Whoa, steady,' he said as the cold balcony rail pressed into his back and the neon lights dazzled him in the soft evening darkness. He was as drunk as her if not more so. Did that even things out?

'I am steady,' she whispered. 'And ready. How about you, handsome?' She looked into his eyes as she spoke. And shit, she was beautiful. Far too perfect. All legs, tumbling blonde curls, straight teeth, and eyelashes he could hang his shirt on as soon as he could get it off. Where had the meek and mild girl from earlier gone?

Keeping her focus on him, she leaned in. Somewhere a voice told him not to, but when did he ever do what he was told? Their lips touched. Alcohol induced or not, the kiss was hot – at first. His attempt at going softly was quashed; she moulded closer until every slender curve of her long, lithe figure pressed against him. But it was fake like everything else about her. Or maybe he'd just drunk too much. This wasn't how he'd imagined kissing her earlier.

Someone wolf-whistled. Magnus pulled back, his top half over the edge of the parapet, painfully aware they weren't alone. But she didn't let go. Laughter and shouts echoed from below. Skylar anchored her fingers behind his head. He had no chance of moving. The contact deepened. Their mouths parted, and her tongue touched his. Alcohol or something on a more visceral level blocked the sensations he was expecting, instead a bland feeling barely more exciting than chewing a steak swept over him.

Still holding his cocktail in one hand, he used the other to roam over the contours of her body, barely sheathed by her tiny satin dress. Finding the small of her back, he rested his palm on it. This was insane. Maybe she wanted to get him back to her room. Would she morph back into her 'real' self if they were alone? What the hell was he thinking? The pilot from the Scottish backwoods and the glittering Los Angeles movie star, Skylar Rousse, was quite a story but he'd be lucky to keep his job if he took this any further.

Skylar grabbed the back of his shirt, hoisted it out of his jeans and slipped her hand up his back. 'Christ,' he muttered, barely breaking the kiss but spilling his drink. 'Everyone's watching. We should stop.'

She rolled her eyes in a wide arc. 'One of the perks of my life. I don't get to do anything without an audience.'

Unhooking her arm from Magnus, she swung around to face her entourage, breaking through the hoots and laughter with a loud, 'Hey!' She stamped her foot. Magnus used the moment to knock back his cocktail and ditch the glass. 'Will y'all stand back and give a girl some privacy.' She loomed larger than life, verging on dangerous, in her skyrise heels.

Adjusting his shirt collar and deliberately not looking at the assembled group, Magnus heard movements, footsteps, chatter, doors opening and the music blaring, then quietening. He needed to get out of here too.

'Oh no,' said Skylar. She took hold of Magnus's shirt and pulled him round so his back was to the door, then she slipped her arms under his and pulled him close. Leaning out from behind him, she shrieked, 'And you. Butt out.' Then she snapped at her bodyguard. 'Get rid of her, you know she's not allowed out here.'

Magnus made to turn around to see what was going on, but Skylar had pushed onto her tiptoes and sunk her lips onto his again, robbing him of the ability to move.

NOW

Chapter Three

Taylor

Taylor forced herself to breathe slowly. She gripped the edge of her reclining seat. Take-off was always the worst but that wasn't why her heart was racing. She closed her eyes and rested until the plane levelled. Peering out the tiny window, she checked they were up. Skylar's private jet pilot spoke through the intercom, telling them they could remove their belts. Taylor didn't.

'Good god, what are you fretting about now?'

Taylor slowly opened her eyes to see Skylar standing over her. 'Nothing.'

'Oh, come on.' Skylar sat beside her.

Once, it had been like looking in a mirror when Taylor looked at her sister, but not so much now. Taylor had ditched all attempts at style. Where Skylar's hair tumbled down her back in perfect barrel curls, Taylor's was shorter and straggly in comparison. Skylar's clothes were handpicked to match the latest fashions. Taylor settled for her cast-offs, which were fine even if Skylar sneered and screwed up her face at 'last year's look'. And Skylar loved make-up; she was plastered in it. Taylor settled for barely there – if she bothered at all.

'I thought you'd be leaping for joy,' Skylar said. 'You've been set free. Your first trip without Mom and Dad since… Well, forever.' Their parents had taken the first part of the journey from Los Angeles to New York, but now Taylor and Skylar were crossing the Atlantic on their own.

Taylor shook her head. 'Yeah, and why should I celebrate that? I should never have been locked up in the first place.'

Skylar burst out laughing. 'You weren't locked up. God, people say I'm a drama queen.' She laid her hand on her chest. 'We've given you a job, a home, and the therapy you need.'

'But I didn't need it. I'm not some dirty secret to be hidden away.'

'Oh, but that's exactly what you are, Taylor.' Skylar's voice turned sharp. 'What you did to me is unforgivable.'

'It was a long time ago.'

'Six years.'

Taylor closed her eyes and focused on her breathing. Arguing was futile. Skylar twisted everything. Six years ago, Taylor had been prepared to rob a high-end store disguised as Skylar. The plan to incriminate her had backfired. She'd backed out and confessed before she'd done anything. The pain and anguish at what she'd become had pushed her to the brink, she'd turned to drugs and been thrown into rehab for a year.

'Surely that's long enough. I did my stint in rehab. I've kept my head down and worked hard for you for the last five years. Can't you drop it now?'

'Maybe,' said Skylar.

'Good. Because I'm done with this job,' said Taylor.

'How do you mean?'

'I can't live my life like this, shut away, promoting you from behind the scenes.'

'Promoting me?'

'Well, yes. I do your PR.' Taylor stared at Skylar. 'Don't you even know what I do?'

Skylar examined her long glitter nail. 'It's just lip service, Taylor. Your job isn't real. It's something Dad made up to keep you busy. I don't think any of your promotions ever go anywhere. The PR manager files everything you've done in the garbage can.'

'That's not true.' Taylor bit her lip. It couldn't be true. But sometimes she wondered if she convinced herself of her own reality to stop herself from going crazy. 'And if it is, well, it just tells me that what I'm planning to do is the right thing.'

'And… What are you planning?' asked Skylar slowly.

'I'm getting out. I'm going to do my own thing.'

A flicker of fear crossed Skylar's face and she blinked rapidly. 'Taylor, that's dangerous talk. If you're using this trip to run away, then you're making a mistake. Mom and Dad won't support you if you go it alone. This is why you need to sign an agreement promising not to impersonate me again.'

'How can I do that? Sometimes people think I'm you without me even trying. I'd be breaching the agreement just living. And don't suggest surgery – I won't.'

Skylar rolled her eyes.

'I don't have to live under your thumb. I would have thought you'd have been happy to get rid of me.'

'Oh, sometimes I would, believe me. But I can't trust you. Look at you now. You got on this trip because we thought you'd changed but clearly you haven't. The minute you're on your own, you start this. I need to call Dad. If you're gonna be causing trouble, I'm not babysitting you.'

'I'm not causing trouble. I just wanted to give you the heads-up that I'm not sticking around after this trip.'

'And where are you going then?'

'I'm moving to London. With Alex.'

'London?' Skylar's lips curled upwards and she looked away, bobbing her head. 'And Alex, of course, Alex. I forgot.'

'We've talked a lot online,' said Taylor, 'and he's gonna help me out.'

'Sure he is.' Skylar winked at her. 'If that's your plan, then we're good. Nothing to worry about.'

She stood, looked around, and moved back to her own seat. Taylor frowned and shook her head. Seriously? After all her moaning, Skylar was ok with that? Wow. Finally. Taylor put in her earbuds and let calming surf sounds lull her to sleep.

*

'Will the limo be waiting?' Skylar said, as they made their way through Glasgow airport.

Liesel, her PA, nodded, running along behind, pulling both her case and Skylar's, plus carrying the holdalls with their special outfits. 'Yes, it's ready.'

The bodyguard kept pace with Skylar, scanning around as she raced along.

'And you've contacted Alex?'

'Yes, he's in the limo already.'

'He's here?' said Taylor.

'Of course he is,' said Skylar.

Taylor's stomach flipflopped. The guy who was her ticket out was here – actually here. As the location manager, he had contacts all over the UK. He'd introduced the producer to Glasgow and they were using it as the backdrop for 1950s Philadelphia after the location's success in 'World War Z'. Taylor grinned, remembering Alex's unrepeatable comments about that movie. Throughout their chats, she'd harboured the idea they'd get together and date for a bit, as well as work. She needed it. After being kept on a short leash for so long, her dating experience was pathetic.

'Great,' Taylor said. 'When we chatted, we talked about going round Glasgow together and getting to know each other a little… After we drop you off at the hotel, of course.'

Once Skylar was at the hotel and meeting the co-stars of her latest movie, Taylor and Alex could have time alone. She hummed to herself as she imagined flying free as a bird, and her veins flooded with a pleasant warmth she hadn't felt for years… Maybe ever.

Skylar's laughter cut across the overhead speakers and the chattering crowd. Her bodyguard moved in closer, shielding her as a large family group veered towards her. 'No, sorry. That won't work,' said Skylar, almost running. 'I've been messaging Alex. He and I are zipping off for an afternoon on the town. Liesel will call you a cab.'

'What?' Skylar and Alex? Seriously? 'But Alex and I—'

'Oh, Taylor.' Skylar stopped dead and both Liesel and her bodyguard crashed into her. 'You are such a sad little puppy. Alex totes thinks so too. One day your prince may come but it won't be Alex, he's not interested, not like that.'

'Ok, what?' Taylor held out her hands.

'Stay calm,' said Skylar. 'Let's not make a scene. Remember, this is like parole. You gotta behave if you wanna get a guy… So the less crazy stuff the better.'

Taylor's mouth hung open.

'Alex and I might not be back until late, so you go with Liesel and be a good girl.'

'You are kidding, right?'

'No,' she said with a flick of her long blonde hair, striding off again.

They reached the main foyer and Skylar opened her cell to ring Alex, but Taylor had heard enough. 'I'm going to the ladies' room before I go anywhere,' she said to Liesel. 'I don't feel too good.'

She whipped around and ran up the escalator. When she checked back, Skylar was stalking towards the exit, beaming from ear to ear.

Going with Skylar wasn't an option, not if Taylor could find another way. Could she catch another flight? But to where?

She was alone for the first time in years and she didn't know where to start.

Chapter Four

Magnus

'Parking brake released, and off we go,' Magnus said, pushing the throttle and easing the plane forward. If only he could push his life in the same direction and with such ease. 'Straight ahead to Alpha one. Before take-off checklist, please.'

'Config,' said First Officer Sarai.

'Checked.'

'Flaps.'

'Five green lights,' said Magnus.

'Stab trim.'

'Six point five units required and set.'

'Cabin?' said Sarai.

'Secure.' Magnus held the throttle forward, taxiing the plane towards the runway. *Secure, yup.* Randomly, being in the sky was about the most secure part of his life right now. More and more he couldn't shake the feeling he'd taken a wrong turn somewhere. Flying planes was easy compared to navigating life on the ground.

Sarai checked in with the tower. The engines rumbled steadily.

'We're cleared for take-off,' said Magnus, 'please seat the cabin crew.'

With the flick of a switch, Sarai opened communications with the cabin. 'Cabin crew, please take your seats for departure.'

'Before take-off checklist, please,' said Magnus. They worked through the list. 'You have controls.'

'I have controls,' said Sarai. 'Start timing.'

'Timing,' said Magnus. Timing indeed. His timing was immaculate when it came to planes, but it was definitely an area to work on in his private life. Breaking up with a girlfriend right before his brother's wedding was not his finest move. Possibly a catastrophic fail. This was the one time he'd been ready. He was all set to stroll in with that plus-one neatly hanging on his arm. Now he'd be sidling in alone, dancing with the old ladies, and propping up the bar all evening with everyone whispering about him. He would have to pull out his happy face and stick it on for the week.

Sarai pushed the throttle and Magnus put his hand on the base – the captain's honour, holding on in case of a need to override. 'Stabilised.'

'Take-off thrust set,' she said, pushing the throttle forward.

'Set,' Magnus confirmed, keeping his palm on the throttle base. 'Eighty knots.'

'Checked.'

'V1 rotate.' The plane eased off the ground, rising gracefully into the air. The adrenaline rush he used to get from doing this had diminished over the years and become second nature.

'Gear up,' said Sarai. 'Engage autopilot. Bug-up.'

Magnus flicked the gear lever and listened to the radio comms as he checked the flaps and flipped the overhead controls. 'Release the cabin crew.'

Sarai flicked the switch and gave the command as they cruised over Brussels, still rising. They headed north. 'So, you're off after this, you lucky sod,' she said.

'Yeah.' Magnus loosened his collar. 'I've managed to wangle ten days, though it's not exactly going to be spent in paradise.' He smiled as he pressed the cabin comms switch. 'Ladies and gentlemen, this is your captain, Magnus Hansen, and alongside me, I have First Officer Sarai Hughes. Welcome to flight 221 non-stop from Brussels to Glasgow. We have good clear weather and anticipate a smooth and uneventful flight. Sit back, relax and enjoy.' He flipped off the switch.

'I thought you were going to a wedding?'

'I am. My youngest brother.'

'Ahh.' Sarai looked forward with an all-knowing smirk. 'I get it.'

'Do you?'

'Yeah, you're the oldest and wisest and all that, but they got married first.'

He nodded sideways at her accuracy. 'Something like that.'

'I don't think I'd like it if my little brother got married first. Think of the jealousy. Ugh, having to watch him being unbearably happy all the time, pretending to be thrilled while wanting to curl in the corner and cry with a bottle of wine.'

Magnus quirked a grin. 'Ok, drama queen. I'm not that bad. It doesn't bother me. I'm not the marrying type.' Say it enough and it would become true. And it *was* true. He'd never had the need to settle. But things were changing. He felt it daily – when he passed happy couples, saw photos of his brothers and friends on social media, and discovered exes were now married or had kids. Hooking up with different women all the time was exhausting. No matter how often he tried to keep emotions out, he couldn't. Breakups hurt, hook-ups sucked. They left him empty.

'It doesn't matter what type you are,' said Sarai. 'Weddings bring out the worst in people. Even if people don't say it out loud, you can guarantee they'll all be thinking it.'

'Thinking what?'

'Why's he not married?'

'They can think what they like. It's not like I've sat around all my life wallowing in singledom, waiting for a wife to show up.'

Sarai laughed. 'Yeah, I think they'll work that much out.'

'Meaning what?'

'They'll have you branded as a playboy.'

'Yeah, great.' Maybe it was true. His love life might buy him some kudos amongst other guys but he could hardly brag about it in front of his mother. He checked the controls. 'Let's have the fifteen hundred feet checklist.'

Just as well life didn't come with a checklist. What milestones could he check off? Very few that weren't career related, and while that wasn't a bad thing, it left a gap, a huge gaping hole of unaccomplished things, and he was thirty-six. Luck had blessed him with youthful looks and good health. He kept fit and took care of himself, but it didn't alter time.

Every second brought them closer to home, closer to the moment when he would have to fess up and tell his mother he was single again. The wedding prep would be thrown at him and he'd have to grin through it, the ceremony, the feast and the reception… On his own. While everyone else had partners to fall back on, share stories, moan to, and snuggle with.

Even his 'temporary' girlfriend would have helped to ease things. Ha, who was he kidding? Temporary girlfriends were all he ever managed. Women didn't see him as a keeper. His lifestyle was flighty and easy to blame. But worse, he came with a reputation.

'Shame I didn't realise sooner,' said Sarai. 'I'd have pulled a sicky and come with you.'

'I thought you had a boyfriend.'

'I do. But I'd come as a mate, I haven't been to a wedding for ages.'

'Just wait a couple of years and you'll wish you never had to attend another one.'

'Why?'

'When your friends start hitting thirty, that's when it starts. I'm getting to the other end of it now, most of my friends are already married, some of them are on to their second. Once Carl's wedding is out of the way, I hope I won't have any more for a good few years.'

'Maybe mine.'

'Okay, apart from yours.'

'Or your own.'

He laughed and adjusted his headset. 'Yeah, don't hold your breath on that one. Oh, here, let's watch this, we could have a spot of turbulence.'

Turbulence loomed on the horizon all right. He would bring his surface calm, his smiling face and his easy temper, but underneath he would die a little more as he watched his brothers with their perfect lives and perfect wives. Sure, he didn't need that to be happy, but deep inside something was missing and with every air mile he took, he felt it more keenly than ever.

Chapter Five

Taylor

Everyone knew it was the first sign of madness – Taylor did too – but she also couldn't stop. Angry mutters escaped her lips. She ignored the funny looks from passengers. The wheels on the now four-year-old Gucci case that had once been Skylar's rattled on the floor. Taylor scanned the overhead digital monitor, searching for anything. Where could she go?

'I will never forgive her, never. Not this time. She's done it now. There's only so much a girl can take.' Forcing back angry tears, her words were drowned by a call over the intercom. 'I don't care where I go but I'm getting out of her life.' She checked over her shoulder for any sign of Liesel. *Hell, no!* There she was. Taylor dodged a queue of passengers and put her head down. Adrenaline kept her moving but tiredness crept through her limbs and she wanted to go somewhere and chill. Maybe she should stop running and return to Skylar. Would being holed up in a hotel for the week make any difference? She'd been travelling for so many hours, through several time zones, and her strength was at ground zero.

A sign for toilets loomed ahead. She could hide there and decide what to do. Maybe she could get a cab into town. She could handle that on her own, right? Ok. This was the time for sensible Taylor to kick in. She'd taken the over-emotional route out. Now she had to think. Pulling out her phone, she gaped. What? Notifications pinged in, splashing photographs across the screen. Skylar attached to Alex at the lips. Selfies in the limo as it headed towards Glasgow.

'You bitch!' Taylor shrieked at the phone. A woman in front turned around, giving her a ferocious stare, and pulled a child out of her way. 'Yes, I'm totally unhinged,' Taylor muttered. 'And I've had enough.'

In the restroom, she spent a few seconds staring at her face. 'Look at my cheeks.' They were rosy red, her eyes were puffy, and her blonde hair hung limp around her shoulders. 'Oh, god, I'm a mess.' She splashed some water on her cheeks, with no effect. *I guess it doesn't matter what I look like, who's going to see me? No one! No one ever does.*

What the hell should she do? If she returned to Skylar, she'd have to spend the week watching her and Alex. She couldn't stand it. Air. She needed air. Her chest was constricting. After so many hours on and off planes, in airports, she had to get outside. This wasn't a panic attack, it couldn't be. *Find the exit, go outside, and breathe.* Over and over, she thought the words as she left the restroom, glancing around for any sign of Liesel.

Nipping along the concourse, she followed the arrows to an escalator heading downward to the exit. The air felt too thick. She hopped on the top step and chanced a glance at her phone. Maybe she should throw the damned thing in the garbage. At the bottom of the escalator, the wheel on her case jammed. Taylor snatched at it, but as it came loose, a loud yell vibrated from behind, followed by a bang and an almighty clatter. Taylor hit the floor. With her left cheek planted on the filthy polished concrete, a crushing weight landed on her back and compressed her chest, pinning her fast. 'Oh no,' she murmured, barely able to move her mouth. Her lungs ached beneath her. She'd been caught. Who was it? Liesel? No, too heavy, too wide. A man? It must be. Their bodyguard? No, he would have gone with Skylar. Airport security?

The weight lifted. Taylor lay prone, managing to raise her hand to her nose. Was it broken? Was anything broken? Could she move? Hundreds of questions and thoughts splashed through her mind, but she didn't budge. Her vision rested on several pairs of shoes. Was she being arrested? Had they sent a hit squad to find her? Whatever was going on, it was easier to lie here, wishing the world would disappear.

'Hey, are you ok?' said a man's voice.

'I don't know.' Taylor stayed put. So what if it was cold and uncomfortable? Maybe they'd pick her up and bundle her into a squad car... or an ambulance. Would they take her back to rehab? Lock her in therapy for months on end? Send her to a commune? Maybe a nunnery?

'Can you move at all?' the man spoke again. He sounded concerned.

'Possibly.' With short, jerky movements, Taylor pushed her palm on the ground in a bid to get up. Was there anyone who could just hold her, kiss her better and tell her everything would be ok? Even her mom had never done that.

'Is anything hurt?'

'Everything,' said Taylor, gingerly pushing herself into a sitting position and wincing with a short cry.

'Jeez, I'm really sorry,' said the man. 'I thought you'd walked on. I heard someone shouting behind me and I turned round. Next thing I knew, I was lying on top of you. I'm so sorry.'

So, not a pursuer then.

'My wheel jammed, I stopped. I guess I shouldn't have.' She rubbed the side of her face. 'It's like the oldest piece of advice in the book, don't stop at the bottom of an escalator.' Taylor didn't look at the man. She couldn't. The embarrassment of the situation had started to kick in. What idiot would sit at the bottom of an escalator? People skirted around the edge of them. *Quite right. Steer clear of this madwoman.*

'No need to stare, I've got this,' said the man in a commanding tone, and the feet bustled away. 'If you can move,' he continued, 'it might be a good idea to stand up. We're causing a bit of a hazard. I don't want to make it any worse.'

'Yeah, I can move,' said Taylor. The pains erupting all over were a welcome change to the constant throb in her head and her heart. Finally, she raised her gaze to the man kneeling beside her, and her eyes widened. *Crap!* Not just any man, but a man in a black uniform with a tie, badges and wings. *I didn't just trip up a passer-by, I tripped up an airline pilot. And, oh my god.* Her jaw dropped and she stared into his clear sea-blue eyes. It couldn't be. Really couldn't be. Coincidences be damned! This was impossible. Hallucinations had been part and parcel of her life on the hard stuff, but she was clean and had been for a long time… This had to be real. She frowned. Was this the same guy she'd met on her twenty-first birthday? The one she'd felt a bizarre connection to until Skylar had spotted him 'giving her too much attention'. It had earned her a night locked in her room while Skylar did all the cake cutting and celebrating. Skylar had convinced her parents Taylor was 'out pretending to be me again'. But Taylor had escaped her room later, only to discover Skylar stuck to this guy's lips. Now the same scenario was playing out with Alex.

'Are you…?' Taylor stopped. He'd never told her his name, but Skylar had crowed about her kiss with 'Handsome Hansen' for weeks, knowing full well Taylor had spoken to him before Skylar got her claws into him. Taylor had played nonchalant, but the twin bond had been strong enough for Skylar to read Taylor's attraction, not to mention the way he'd been sitting with his hand on hers – and the way he'd looked into her eyes, kind of like he was doing now. Skylar had made it her mission to either separate them or steal him – as she always did.

'Am I what?' His brow furrowed but his stare pierced to her core.

'Handsome Hansen?' she mumbled.

'Jesus Christ,' he said, running his fingers through the blond waves atop his head. 'Is it you? Skylar?'

Taylor pressed her fingers to her throat. *Wow.* Even in this state, she resembled Skylar enough to fool him. He stared at her, his gaze roving across her face. Could he see in her eyes she was someone else? Not the woman he'd kissed? Taylor flushed. 'You remember me?' The words tumbled out and she savoured his growing smile. Now was the time to own up. *I'm Taylor, the twin no one has heard of.* She could remind him they'd met before. She'd wanted to tell him back then, but fear had blocked her brain, as it was doing now. Her chest burned when she remembered what Skylar was up to. Not only that, but all the things Skylar had done in the past. A conveyor belt of injustices at her sister's hands rolled by, taunting her with opportunities missed – or snatched away. It was Skylar he'd ended up kissing, not her. And it had looked very much like he'd enjoyed it. She'd managed a brief chat, while her sister had got the kiss, and who knew what else. An idea caught fire and she couldn't stamp it out.

Skylar's greatest fear was Taylor impersonating her and ruining her career. Taylor had sworn she wouldn't. But what about her personal life? A delicious opportunity for revenge sat up, waiting to be knocked down the fairway, and Taylor was ready. Distant words a therapist had once said wafted around: *You may feel like doing something but that doesn't mean you have to act on it.* But how could she not? This was too perfect.

'I don't think I'd have recognised you if you hadn't called me that silly name, but Magnus will do. I don't generally answer to "handsome".'

Taylor examined the floor and blinked.

'You look so different,' he continued. 'But then…'

'This is me incognito.'

'Here.' Magnus took her by the arm and helped her to her feet. A jolt of pleasure ran through her at his touch, like something she'd wanted forever, and it was finally hers. 'I'm sorry I knocked you over, but what a coincidence. Let's move out the way of this thing.' He guided her away from the escalator towards a coffee bar, his hand grazing her back. 'I'll get you a coffee.' He checked his watch. 'I can't hang about.'

Taylor's heart plummeted. Of course he couldn't. What did she expect? Rekindling a love affair from five years ago wasn't going to happen in a few seconds. It had been a fling and probably not something he wanted to repeat; Skylar was a maneater. She glanced over her shoulder, remembering what she'd been doing before the crash. Where was Liesel?

'I, er…' Taylor took a long, shuddering breath. 'I can't either. I'm in a rush.'

'No bother, but are you sure you're ok? I hope you're not too badly bruised.'

Her bones felt shaken but not irrevocably. Magnus bounced on his toes and smiled. Shit, he was good looking. He always had been. Now, he was a bit more rugged, and a lot more gorgeous. The black blazer set off his pale skin and fair hair. His tall, lean figure stood out in the crowd of passers-by. Taylor closed her mouth.

'So…' he said. 'Do you think you'll be ok?'

'I think so.' She peered around, and when she looked back, Magnus was frowning.

'Where is everybody?'

'Who?'

'You never travel alone, do you? When I worked for Courtney Hines, she didn't go anywhere without an entourage. Where's the bodyguard? The PA?'

'Oh… This is private.'

'Really? I didn't think you did private. It's not exactly my business, but are you in some kind of trouble?'

'Yeah.' Taylor pressed her lips together. 'I am in a bit of trouble. In fact, please don't say anything to anyone, but I'm kind of running away.'

Magnus frowned and let out an uncertain laugh. 'Running away? From what?'

'You know how my life is. I need space. I'm taking a vacation.'

'Here?' He smiled and raised his eyebrows.

'I'm scouting for a shoot. So… I need to get to the city centre, I guess.'

'You guess? What happened to all your PAs?'

'I'm travelling alone, and I need to make a move… in case people recognise me, you know?' She wasn't sure if Skylar was as big a name in Britain but she was pretty sure her sister would expect everyone everywhere to recognise her.

'Right.' Magnus checked his watch. 'I should get going, but I could give you a lift to the city centre if you like.'

'Oh. Aren't you flying?'

'No, I'm done for the day. I'm heading home.'

'Awesome, sure. I'd love a ride. I'll come straight away.' She followed Magnus outside into the pale late February sunshine. 'Wow, it's cold.'

'Bracing.' He grinned, and Taylor melted.

Sheesh, what an easy gal I am. One grin and I turn to goo. 'What's the hurry if you're heading home?'

'Because I've got a trip to make. I'm picking some things up on the way.' They reached the staff parking area and Magnus zapped open a flashy silver sports car.

'Will my case fit in that? Does it even have a trunk?'

'It's deceptively big,' said Magnus. 'You get in, and I'll sort your case… Eh, other side, unless you want to drive.'

'Oh, hell.' Taylor pivoted and made her way to the left side of the car. Inside, she ran her fingertips over the plush cream leather seats. Skylar would love this. She wouldn't wait two seconds. He'd get in the car and she'd start the make-out session; if they even made it back to his apartment, she'd already have screwed him at least twice. Stopping to find out if he was still single wouldn't even cross her mind if he was willing.

Taylor didn't know where to start. She'd only had the nerve to go with guys when she was stoned and those days were condemned to her deepest, darkest past. Communicating with guys online was enough for now. Alex was the latest. She'd dared cross the line and agreed to meet and look at how that had played out. The trunk slammed.

They were aiming for the city centre, but what then? Should she attempt to get to Skylar's hotel or go somewhere on her own? She'd given Liesel the slip, and she was free, but not alone.

Chapter Six

Magnus

If this wasn't surreal, Magnus didn't know what was. Skylar Rousse was in his car. He climbed into the driver's seat and caught her smiling at him. He returned it before reversing out and racing towards the motorway. Could anything top that weirdest of weird moments all those years ago when he'd kissed her? Anything other than her being here right now?

After leaving Courtney's employ, Magnus hadn't kept in touch with the celebrity world. Skylar's movies weren't exactly his thing, too much glitter, lip gloss and girl talk. But he remembered hearing at least once that Skylar had gone into rehab. Was this the result? He glanced at her as they whizzed down the slip road. She'd let go completely. Since when did she travel alone? Have her hair anything less than salon perfect? Not wear heels? Leave her room without make-up? It was a miracle he'd recognised her. Even now, the struggle was real.

'So… You're going on a trip,' she said. 'Does that mean you're coming back to the airport after?'

'No, a road trip. I'm going back home. My brother's getting married.'

'Oh, wow. That's neat. Are you a groomsman?'

'Best man.'

'Cool. And is it far away?'

'Relatively speaking, no. But it's quite a drive. It's on an island in the Hebrides called Mull.'

'An island? That sounds awesome.'

'Yeah, it's a beautiful place.'

'Wow. I've never been anywhere like that. How long will it take you to get there?'

'A few hours. At this time of year, the ferries don't run late, so I should crack on. I don't fancy a night in a hotel.'

'It sounds idyllic. And are you going on your own?'

'Yup, just me.' The words turned him cold. *Just me.* The oldest and *singlest* of the three brothers. How would his mum take it? After what he'd stupidly told her during their last phone call, she would be severely disappointed – again.

'I thought you'd be married by now.'

'Ha, yeah.' There it was, what everyone thought. 'I'm not exactly the marrying type.'

'No?'

'No. You know what I'm like.' *The kind of guy who kisses random women in nightclubs.*

'People change.'

They sure did, and the change in Skylar was the most astonishing thing he'd seen in a long time. Even her talk was so much more chilled. Where was the diva? Why hadn't she screamed or had a tantrum when he'd bumped into her? Then he remembered when they'd first met. How she'd seemed quiet and sweet. A few hours later, she'd hit him like a steam train and he'd convinced himself she'd put on one hell of a show at being genuine that afternoon, but maybe not.

'Where would you like me to drop you?' he asked.

'How about near your apartment? Are there hotels nearby?'

'Quite a few.' He whizzed into the outside lane, swooping past a line of trucks. 'But wait... You haven't booked a hotel?'

'Not yet.'

'What's got into you? Sorry, but this seems mad. Are you sure you're ok?' Had she escaped from an institution? Maybe she should still be in rehab.

'Perfectly. I'm taking time away from the craziness of my life. And ok, I admit I'm not organised. I'm used to everything being done for me, but I can handle it.' She pulled in a deep breath and rubbed her palm down her thigh.

'Ok. How about I give you some hotel names near my apartment and you can look them up.'

'Is it a good area?'

'Yeah. It's on the riverside.'

'Sounds great.'

'If I was feeling brave, I'd let you use my apartment. I won't be there all week, but…' He glanced at her. *Damn, should have kept that thought to myself.* He didn't know her. They'd had a briefer than brief kiss and he'd occasionally bumped into her afterwards. But with her reputation, he couldn't guess what she might do. His brows drew together. The girl sitting beside him didn't seem to belong to that reputation. She was the gentle, sweet one he wanted to hug and let her know everything was fine.

'You don't think you can trust me?'

'Something like that'

'I don't blame you; Skylar Rousse is possibly the most untrustworthy person alive.'

Magnus let out a laugh and tapped the steering wheel. 'Sorry, I shouldn't laugh but—'

'No, you don't have to explain. I'm not in the least offended.'

He narrowed his eyes. What was going on here? He wouldn't be sticking around long enough to find out, despite the curiosity bubbling in his chest. 'We'll be there in five minutes. So, hotel-wise, there's the Radisson RED and the Hilton Garden Inn. You could check them out.'

'Ok, thanks.'

Her stare was unnerving, but maybe she as surprised as him to have run slap-bang into someone so unlikely. If he hadn't been steering, he'd have looked back; she was calling to him without words. He sped across the Kingston Bridge and took the off-ramp onto the riverside, joining a queue of traffic. He used the time to reel off the names of more hotels close to his apartment, and Skylar put them into her phone. They passed the SEC Armadillo, and onward, he turned up a side street and zapped open the heavy gate to the parking area for his apartment. 'I'll get your case out.'

'Could I have a look at your apartment?'

Magnus chewed the inside of his lip, recalling how she'd jumped him on the balcony in LA. But that look. If she kept that up who knew what he might agree to.

'It's ok if you don't want me to. I'm just nosey.'

'You can, but I'm literally grabbing my cases and leaving.'

She beamed and followed him into the lift. As he pushed the button, he caught her eye and inhaled sharply, compressing his lips like a stopper. Nothing could happen here. Surely she was savvy enough to work that out. But was he?

With a ping, the lift stopped, and Magnus thumped the button. He turned right along the short, carpeted hallway to his apartment with Skylar hot on his heels. The key clinked in the lock and he pushed open the door.

'This place is so neat.' Skylar browsed the open-plan living area on the ground floor of the duplex. Wall-to-wall windows provided a splendid view of the River Clyde and its bridges.

'You think? It's nothing like the places you're used to.'

'Oh, I don't know.' Her eyes roamed around, landing on the baby grand. 'Can you play that?'

'I can, but we don't have time for a recital.'

'Wow, I didn't realise.'

'We didn't exactly talk before. And some things are best not discussed in the company of a world-famous movie star, especially one who's featured in musicals.'

Skylar laughed and shook her head. 'Yeah, but it's all fake. Don't you know how much technology it takes to make Sky— my voice sound good?'

'Really? If you say so. Now, I need to get changed.'

He nipped up the open stairs to the mezzanine floor, through the kitchen dining area and into his room. Everything was laid out, ready to collect, put on and get out. He hadn't expected to return with Skylar Rousse in tow. 'This is nuts,' he murmured as he pulled on a chunky knit sweater. After a quick check in the floor-to-ceiling mirror, he dashed back downstairs.

The power of her stare slapped him as his feet hit the polished wood flooring. Everything about this muted down version of Skylar was appealing in the most inexplicable way. She quirked a grin at him, then the piano, and shook her head as if she didn't believe he could play it.

'Ok, here's a quick one for you to remember me by.' He flipped open the piano lid, slipped onto the stool, laced his fingers together and flexed them. Rising to a challenge was something he never shied away from. He placed his hands on the keys and struck a few chords.

As the tune came together, Skylar laughed. 'Seriously? Is that "Any Dream Will Do"?'

'Yes.' Magnus smirked, tinkling on. 'I would sing it, but maybe another time.'

'Are you a closet Lloyd Webber fan?'

'Is that something I should be in the closet for?' He finished and closed the lid. 'He writes some first-rate music. I thought my little niece might like it and it's the perfect excuse to unleash my inner musical lover.'

'Aw man, you are funny… and cute.'

Magnus loosened his neckline and frowned. Skylar saying the cute word could be followed by any number of ill-timed scenarios. 'Yeah, thanks. Look, I'm sorry about this, but it's time to part ways. I have to make a move. You had any luck with those hotels?'

Skylar bit on her perfect lips with those amazingly straight teeth. Even without make-up, she was beautiful, in fact, maybe even more so than when she was caked in it. A light smattering of freckles gave her an elfin look. 'I had another idea,' she murmured.

'What idea?'

'How about I come with you? I could be your travel companion.'

'My what? Oh… no. Seriously, Skylar, that is not a good idea. I told you, I'm going home. This isn't just me out on a jolly.' He jammed his hands in his pockets and turned away. If he looked at her now, he'd give in. What the hell had happened to his restraint – his good sense?

'Yeah, I get it. I'm sorry.' She fiddled with the cuff of her pink hoody. Magnus watched her reflection; her expression dropped. 'I'll call one of those hotels.'

Facing her again, he gave a stoic nod. That was exactly what she had to do. Her cheeks reddened and she avoided his eyes as she pulled out her phone. Her fingers scrabbled on the case. Maybe she was in more trouble than she'd let on.

'Look, I don't want to leave you stranded.' What a stupid thing to say. What would she have done if he hadn't bumped into her? She'd have got on with things and he'd have been none the wiser. He could leave her and let her do that again. Except he *had* bumped into her and that seemed to make her his concern. 'The thing is, I don't think you've grasped what kind of island I'm going to. It's remote. There are no towns, just villages. It has no malls, no nightclubs, no amusements or anything that will interest you.'

'Does it have any hotels?'

'Hotels, yes. But not the kind of thing you like. It has country houses and seaside hotels, not your big chains or boutiques. In some places, you won't get internet or mobile, you know, cell reception. It's not a place for you.'

'You're right. Usually, I would agree but right now it sounds exactly what I need. I want to go somewhere out of the way. I need to get out of the limelight and lie low for a bit. Please, let me tag along.'

He arched his eyebrow. 'Seriously? Are you on the run? Have you done something criminal?'

'No. I swear.' She held up her hands. 'I just want to get away from my family.'

He sighed and ran his fingers over the back of his head. 'I'm not sure.'

'Think of all the things we can do on the way.' The corners of her mouth quirked up.

'Oh yeah? What you mean by that?' This seemed more like her.

'Not so long ago, you were up for anything.'

'This is exactly the kind of thing I'm afraid of, Skylar.' Magnus shook his finger at her.

A flicker of panic clouded her eyes. 'Yeah, sorry.'

'But come on.'

'I can come?'

'Only because I don't have time to argue.' He opened the main door and let her out. As they moved into the lift, he continued, 'I want to make it clear though, that once you're there, I'm taking no responsibility for you. This is your choice and on your head be it.'

'That's fine. I hear you, loud and clear.'

Her smile was inviting. There sat the opening. Was she expecting him to move in and kiss her? It wouldn't be the first time he'd made a move like that. His love life was a shitstorm and he couldn't even remember some of the women he'd been with. What kind of a bastard did that make him? But he was free; she was free – as far as he knew – and here they were alone. He'd always found her attractive, but the vulnerability added a new layer. A deep urge to protect her rose in him. Was she such a talented actress she could induce feelings like this? She'd done it before.

The lift pinged and the moment passed.

Magnus rammed his case into the tiny boot. Now Skylar's was there too, the space was almost too small. 'Get in,' he growled.

'Yes, sir.'

'I'm talking to the case.'

Moments later, they were back in the car, nipping through the city along the Great Western Road.

'I am so excited about this. I've never been to Scotland before, and now I'm gonna see so much. It's my own private tour.'

'Which you could just have paid for.'

'Yeah, but this way is better.'

Magnus stopped at the red light and swung his head around to consider her. She beamed back. 'I better not end up getting arrested for abducting you.'

'You won't.' She let out a shaky giggle, which didn't calm his nerves.

He put his foot down and they drove through the tenement-filled suburbs towards the countryside. Skylar pinned her gaze to the window. The city sprawled behind, becoming gradually more open. Not wanting to bore her with stories or details of places, Magnus kept quiet at first, but it was no use. She threw question after question at him. 'What's that? Where are we now? Loch Lomond? Like the song? Why is it called that…?' And so it went on.

'Do you want a running commentary?' He laughed and shook his head.

'Actually, yes. This is fascinating. You give air commentaries, don't you?'

'Not exactly. I just talk about the weather and what conditions we can expect today.'

'Well, that'll do. I just like the sound of your voice. I could listen to your accent all day.'

'Wouldn't you rather put some music on or the radio?'

'Not really. But speaking of music, tell me more about this musicals fetish of yours. I don't mind doing a bit of technicolour dreaming.'

'So I've heard,' said Magnus with a rough laugh.

'Meaning what?'

'Yeah, like you don't know.'

'Ok, tell you what. Let's try this.'

Magnus peered out the corner of his eye. Skylar was swiping through her iPhone. 'Can I put this on Bluetooth?'

'Sure. What is it?'

'Wait and see.' She fiddled about with the controls. The opening notes of "All I Ask of You" from *The Phantom of the Opera* flooded the car.

'Seriously?'

'Come on Lloyd Webber lover.' Skylar grinned. Magnus shook his head. The music carried on without a vocalist. 'You missed your cue,' said Skylar, flicking it back.

'You want me to sing it?'

'Come on, I bet you can.'

The intro started again and this time he did it. *Yup.* Her mouth fell open. *Yes, I can sing, and yes, I know the words.*

When she came in with her part, his eyes popped. 'So much for you needing software to enhance your voice. I think your producers need their hearing tested.'

She raised her hand to her lips as she sang, her mouth wide, displaying even white teeth and an expression of such beauty, Magnus almost forgot to look at the road. 'Love me,' she sang, 'That's all I ask…'

He poked his tongue into his mouth and shook his head. Was she using this as some kind of come on? Singing was something he'd always enjoyed but he hadn't practised for a while. Still, the opportunity to duet with a Hollywood actress was a challenge he wasn't backing down from, and his deep voice resonated around the car, shocking even himself with how powerful it sounded. Skylar equalled him, hitting the high notes with perfection.

'Oh my god,' squealed Skylar as the music wound up. 'You're utterly awesome.'

'Hardly,' he said.

'Believe me, you are.' She scrolled through her iPod. 'Do you know Rodgers and Hammerstein?'

'Not personally.'

'You know what I mean.' She gave him a playful prod. 'Can I put on "Oh, What a Beautiful Morning"?'

'Knock yourself out.'

'I mean for you to sing. I can't believe how good you are.'

'I don't know all the words to that. Can I la-la it.'

'Sure. Or we can duet. I love duetting, I just don't get the opportunity usually.'

'Why? Is no one good enough for you? The guys wear the wrong colour boxers or something?'

'Ha. Yeah. Something like that.'

Soon they were belting out classics from musicals. Magnus la-la-la-ed all the bits where he couldn't remember the lyrics. The energy was almost better than flying, nearly as good as sex and completely mad. They laughed after every song.

Midway through "One Day More" from *Les Misérables*, where they were attempting multiple parts each, a queue of red lights brought them to a standstill.

'What's going on here?' Magnus stopped singing, punched down the volume and tapped the steering wheel. 'There aren't any roadworks, I checked. And I didn't see any warning signs.'

'I could google it.'

'Do it.'

Skylar lifted her phone and woke it, turning it to face away from him as she dismissed notifications. Blue lights whizzed past and Magnus jumped. An ambulance screeched by, hot on the heels of a police car. 'I hate seeing that,' he said. 'I guess there's an accident. This is a terrible road.'

Up ahead, some people got out of their car, stretched and glanced around.

'I can't find anything on Google.' Skylar scrolled down the page.

'Try Traffic Scotland. I'm going to see if these people know anything.' Magnus unclipped his belt and got out. The wind nipped his cheeks as he approached the couple standing outside their car. 'Hey,' he said. 'Do you know what's happened?'

'Looks like an accident.'

'That's what I thought.' Magnus slung his hands into the back pocket of his jeans. 'This road is notorious.'

'If it's serious, the road'll be shut.'

'Yeah.' Magnus checked his watch, feeling like a heel. He was late, but so what? It paled into insignificance if someone was seriously injured, or worse. 'Jeez. I hope everyone's ok.' A gentle pressure on his arm caught his attention. Before he could make sense of it, he looked down to see Skylar. Ah! Those eyes, asking impossible things.

'It is an accident, according to that website,' she said. 'This road's now shut. I hope everyone's ok.' She sucked her lip, her face full of concern. The trees at the roadside swayed in the breeze and she shivered.

Magnus put his arm about her shoulder. The contact stung and soothed him equally; neither was unpleasant. 'Hey. Go back to the car. You're frozen.'

She slipped under him and wrapped her arm around his waist. He edged back a little, stopped by the people's car. Skylar hadn't backed off physical contact before, but this was more tender than her original move, which had been no more subtle than to stick her tongue down his throat. She stared into the middle distance and Magnus increased the pressure on her shoulder. How good did this feel? Like really good. Nothing like that fake balcony kiss. Here was a connection he wanted to explore at leisure, but this wasn't the right time or place – or person! He couldn't go fooling around with a Hollywood movie star. That world was in the past for him. He'd done with the glitz and spangles.

Blinking, she glanced at him with the vague imprint of a smile.

'Let's get back to the car. Thanks, guys.' He waved to the other travellers. 'What's up with you?' he asked, keeping Skylar under his wing. 'Why this burst of affection?'

'I don't like the idea someone might have died. It brings it a bit close to home.'

'Yeah, I feel the same.' He let out a sigh, then pulled her into a brief hug. 'Let's hope they're ok and it's only the cars that are wrecked.'

'What do we do now?' Skylar peeked up at him and he released her.

'I'll have to turn around and go back.'

'Back to your apartment?'

He ducked into the car. 'I'd rather not do that,' he said.

Skylar banged her door shut and raised her eyebrows. 'Aren't there other options?'

'There's another road, but it's a major detour and I doubt we'll make it to the ferry in time.' He fingered the keys in the ignition. 'I'm not sure what to do.'

'What would you do if I weren't here?'

'Go on, try to get there, and if I didn't make it, check in to a hotel, I guess.'

'Let's do that then. I don't want to hold you back. Just follow your plans and act like I'm not here.'

He started the engine and manoeuvred the car round a twenty-point turn in the narrow road, then zoomed back in the other direction. 'Yeah, I don't think there's any chance we'll make it tonight. This road isn't much longer in distance, but it's twisty and there's no way of going fast.'

'That's fine by me. I'll kick back and watch the view.' She rested her head, her gaze fixed on him.

'Then why are you looking at me?'

She gave another nervous giggle. 'Well…' She shrugged. 'You always were a handsome guy.'

'Seriously? That's cheesy even for you.' He shook his head but his ego was touched. 'Listen, if there's reception here, I should call my mum. If she hears there's been an accident, she'll panic. If there's any kind of air accident, she messages me to ask if I'm alive.'

'Get calling then. She sounds like an awesome mom.'

'Yeah.' Flicking through the handsfree, Magnus punched the call button. 'It's ringing. That's good because once we get past Arrochar, there's no chance of reception.'

Skylar raised her shoulders and put out her palms. 'If you say so.'

'Hello!' A cheerful voice filled the car and Magnus put his finger to his lips. Skylar drew her fingers across her mouth, miming zipping it shut. 'How are you, darling? Are you nearly here?'

'No, sorry. There's a road closed at Loch Lomond. We're going round via Inverary, but I don't think we'll make the last ferry.'

'Oh, darling. I'm sorry about that, but will you be able to stay somewhere?'

'We'll get a hotel in Oban. There's always something.'

'Oh, it's so nice to hear your voice. And how's your new girlfriend? Is she looking forward to coming?'

Skylar whipped her head around and stared. 'What new girlfriend?' she mouthed. 'You said you were single.'

Magnus coughed. 'Mum, about that…'

'Oh, sorry. How silly of me. Is your phone on speaker? She's listening, isn't she? Oh, goodness, I am a silly mum. Hello, new girlfriend.'

Magnus glared at the handsfree and silently bashed the wheel.

'Hey,' said Skylar.

'Nooo!' Magnus whisper-shouted so only Skylar could hear. She grinned as his mum continued.

'I hope you're well. Magnus hasn't even told us your name yet.'

He shook his head wildly and waggled his index finger, warning her not to reply. 'Right, Mum, I should go. We'll talk about this tomorrow.'

'Of course, darling, see you both tomorrow. Love you.'

'Love you, Mum.' He hit the end call button. 'But you won't be seeing both of us. Why did you reply to her?'

'She was saying hi to me.'

'Eh, no. She was saying hi to my girlfriend, and in case you haven't noticed, that isn't you.'

'You said you didn't have a girlfriend.'

'No, I said I was going to the wedding alone, which isn't the same.'

'Oh, ok.' She shuffled in her seat. 'Sorry.'

'Look, we split, ok. I haven't told Mum yet. And none of this is your business.' He started muttering to himself. Why had he used the bloody *royal we*? Having Skylar in the car had thrown him. But it didn't matter. 'Tomorrow, you're going wherever you're going and I'm going to tell my mum my lovely new girlfriend gets seasick and couldn't bring herself to get on the boat.'

'Why not tell her the truth?'

'Because… No, seriously, it's none of your business.' Cranking the gears, he sped on, keeping his eyes on the road, determined not to be distracted by his passenger – for the next few minutes anyway. Because it was a losing battle. Something about her appealed on a raw level and he didn't have the willpower to say no. What harm could come of it though? A brief hook-up with Skylar Rousse wasn't something he felt the need to pass on.

Chapter Seven

Taylor

Warm fuzziness and Taylor's life didn't usually go hand in hand. But right now, she tingled with it. Her smile almost hurt as it pushed her cheeks wide. It wasn't her business to pry into Magnus's past, but sharing his present was good enough.

This guy cared about his family, he'd hugged her in her moment of worry, they'd sung together and made beautiful music. Even when he was ignoring her, she was certain he wouldn't abandon her. She felt safe with him, like she could tackle anything. Words from the songs buzzed around her head. The duets she'd chosen were all about love and warmth. Hearing words like that and responding, even when it was just an act, felt so good.

'Why don't you get on your phone and start looking for hotels in Oban?' he muttered.

'For me? For you…? Or for both of us?' Her gaze landed on his furrowed brow and she smirked. Skylar wouldn't waste a chance like this.

'Both of us?'

'Well, you need somewhere too, don't you? I could find us both somewhere.'

'Right. But not together.'

'No?' she said, willing him to glance back. 'You don't fancy sharing?' Her heart fluttered. Skylar would do this. She had the last time. But Taylor's experience with men wasn't as widespread as Skylar's. Still, this trip had no endgame, so why should she care? She was on this ride just for the ride. She could hop off any time, or he could shove her off. None of it mattered. Her teeth brushed against her lip and she sucked it in, barely considering the impact of her words. 'I thought you might like to pick up where we left off.'

Magnus tapped the steering wheel, his jaw set. 'Oh, sure.'

'Sorry.'

'Yeah, why not. One room, one bed. Let's do it. I've waited five years to finish it.'

Taylor swallowed. Her hand trembled as she fingered the side of her phone. 'You, um, have waited five years... For me?'

'What's got into you?'

'I don't follow.'

'I'm sorry if this disappoints you, but no, I haven't waited for you. I haven't really thought about you since. And don't take this the wrong way, but it was just—'

'Sex?'

'Whoa.' He ran his hand down his face. 'Ok, I know you've had tough times in your life, but unless you've suffered some memory loss, you know as well as I do, we never got that far.'

'Oh... yeah, yeah.' Taylor fiddled with her nails. So, he'd never been with Skylar. A smile spread over her cheeks. That was good news, but her insides vibrated and she shuddered. He'd just agreed to share a bed. Had he meant it? A wicked surge fired a picture into her mind: Skylar's face when she found out. Skylar hated Taylor getting any attention. Succeeding where Skylar had failed was too – *ooh* – far too delicious. 'After the rehab, things get muddled. And you know how many guys I've been with – it all becomes a blur.'

'Seriously? That has turned me right off. I'll stick to my own room.'

'Oh. I didn't mean it like that.' Though having his own room was probably for the best. 'I always liked you. You were the guy that got away. I'm glad you never wasted time dwelling on me.'

Magnus side-eyed her. 'That's bullshit. The guy who got away? You?'

'Too much?' She drummed her fingers on her lap and smiled out the window; her reflection in the wing mirror seemed to give her a wink of encouragement. 'Maybe it's your singing. You've pulled me under your spell.'

'Get a grip,' he said, but he was grinning.

'Do you remember when we first met in the bar on my birthday? That was the real me, no pretence. You were kind and I…' She closed her mouth. Saying she'd regretted not meeting him again was stupid. In his mind, they had.

'Yeah, I remember. And you're a better actress than I thought. You really know how to play to a guy's ego. Best make it one room after all. How can I resist?'

*

Cool, clear darkness settled over the Scottish countryside. The ferry port of Oban glittered in a pool of streetlamps as Magnus and Taylor wound down the steep road. The bay curved around for some distance and in the blackness which must be the sea, the beam of a distant lighthouse flicked rhythmically.

Taylor booked the hotel with one room and one bed in her desire for wicked revenge and hoped Magnus wasn't being sarcastic when he'd agreed to it. She clenched her fingers, clawing back a growing pang of anxiety. A cold sweat clung beneath her t-shirt. What if she was a total disappointment? Would it matter? If he thought Skylar Rousse was terrible in bed, then why did she care?

But she wanted it to be good, to remove Skylar from the equation and be with him. The craving for an emotional connection wrenched deep inside. Being physically close to him might satisfy the urge. If only in the short term.

She rested back and closed her eyes. If she did a bit of method acting, she could make-believe for the next few hours that they were a real couple, heading off on vacation. Warm bubbles swelled inside and calmed her. In reality, it was never going to happen. Her world had a different definition of normal, and no matter how long she hid away, one day she'd have to return. But right now, she was a normal person on her way to a hotel with her boyfriend. The word increased her delight and she restrained a squeal.

Magnus slipped out of the car, tossed back his shoulders and took a few wide steps to the trunk. He removed the cases and adjusted the handles. As Taylor took hers, she thrust out her other hand and beamed. With a resigned smile, Magnus took hold and gently squeezed her fingertips. 'You're milking this now, aren't you?'

'Sure, honey.' She winked. Safety circled outward from Magnus's grip and the tension drained from Taylor's limbs. They strolled into the lobby of the waterfront hotel. Streetlamps cast long orange beams onto the gently rippling water. 'This place is like something from a roaring twenties mystery movie. Check out the art deco, I love it.'

Magnus looked around. 'I guess. I never really noticed before.' He headed straight for the reception desk, signed the paperwork, and took the key card. 'I'm starving,' he said. 'I kind of skipped lunch, thinking I'd be home for tea.'

'Should we go out?'

'Depends how incognito you want to be.'

'Do you honestly think people will still recognise me?'

'I don't know.' He stared at her and frowned. 'Probably not. I think you'll be safe enough unless we run into a group of fourteen-year-old *Cute Witch Academy* fans.'

'Or some more guys like you.' Taylor giggled. 'With a thing for musicals.'

'Yeah, yeah. I like the classics. I don't go in for all the glitz though. But I doubt anyone will recognise you when you're, well, all natural.' His eyes skimmed over her, sending her limbs to jelly.

'The magic of Hollywood,' she said.

'I think I like you better this way,' said Magnus. He held her gaze and a charge of desire surged inside her.

'You do?'

'You seem much more real.' He punched the button on the elevator. 'Let's offload the bags, then we can figure out what to do about food.'

Taylor let her eyelids drop briefly and stifled a yawn in the dim lights. What a long day. 'If we hit the bedroom, I might not leave.'

'I'm doing nothing on an empty stomach. I can't function without food.'

'Easy, tiger. I meant I might fall asleep.'

'I know what you meant.' He grinned and gently cuffed her upper arm.

As they entered the room, Taylor scanned the freshly made bed and the weight of her plans crushed her in a vice grip. What if he was expecting some Hollywood style moves? She didn't have a clue. She hadn't even done it with the lights on. Up against walls, stoned or paralytic was more her thing; she didn't even recall what the guys looked like or how she got there most of the time. But that had been a long time ago…

Magnus caught her eye. 'I told you, no show before food.' Stepping towards the window, he looked out over the town. Taylor joined him. Her heart leapt as he placed his arm around her shoulder. 'How about I introduce you to a British delicacy?'

'Which is?'

'Fish and chips by the seaside. I'll treat you to death by cholesterol and you can spend the next two weeks trying to regain your pre-greasy-meal body.'

'Ok, I'm not sure you're doing a great job of selling it to me.'

With a gentle tug, he pulled her round to face him. He swept her hair behind her neck, then skimmed his hands over her shoulders, leaned in and placed a smouldering kiss on her cheek. Taylor let out a whimper. 'Fish and chips' – he whispered in her ear – 'are very quick, which will leave so much more time… for whatever you want to do.' His lips returned to her cheek, moving slowly onto her neck.

What kind of thing was he expecting? Fifty shades? 'I eh…'

'That includes sleep. Come on, everybody loves chips.' He clicked her a wink and grabbed his coat from the handle of his case. 'Take a jacket, it's cold out there and we'll be eating them outside.'

'Outside? Wow, ok. You Scottish guys are men of steel, right?'

'Wait and see,' he smirked, pulling open the door.

Not far along the street, a dazzling neon sign belted out its message: Fish and Chips, from between the other more modest shops, all shut up for the day. Magnus rubbed his palms together and grinned as he joined the line that stretched outside along the sidewalk.

'The sign of a good chippie,' he said. 'When the queue is out the door.'

'If you say so.'

'I do, Skylar.' He wrapped his arm around her shoulder. 'You know, I was in two minds about you coming along, but now, I'm glad you did.'

'Are you?'

'Yeah. You're fun.'

'Am I?'

'Well, you know your Lloyd Webber. What more could I ask for?'

If that was all it took to please him, she had it in the bag.

After standing in line for ten minutes in the oil-smelling chip shop, Taylor screwed up her face at the greasy paper packet. 'It comes in paper?'

'Good old-fashioned ones do,' said Magnus. 'I hate it when you get chips in a box, they never taste the same as the ones in paper.'

Fresh air stung Taylor's cheeks and lips as they stepped outside.

'Let's get a seat,' said Magnus.

'A seat?' Taylor scanned around.

'Yup. One of the benches on the promenade. It'll be cold as ice, but it's all part of the experience.'

'You're crazy.' Taylor laughed, following him along the street. He nipped across the road and strolled on towards the sea.

'Here we are.' He threw himself down and crossed his long legs in front of him.

The slab of chilled bench numbed the back of Taylor's thighs within seconds of sitting. 'This is freezing.' She clung to the warm packet in her hands.

'Told you. But eat your chips and don't worry, I'll warm you up later.'

His words sent a buzz of excitement zipping through her. She prised open the paper and bit into the most bizarre tasting "chips". *Just as well I'm not actually Skylar;* her sister would die of shock just looking at these… In fact, she'd never have made it into the shop. 'You know these are just greasy fries, right?'

'Sacrilege,' said Magnus.

'Says you who's covered yours in vinegar and brown sauce.'

'Yup, and just wait until I kiss you. Think of the flavour.'

'Oh, please.'

He burst out laughing. The warm, rich sound carried through the still evening air. Some birds took off from the water with a noisy beat of wings. Taylor laughed along. 'I hope you have some strong mouthwash.'

'Spoilsport.'

After eating as many chips as she could stomach, Taylor tossed the paper into the nearest garbage can and held out her fingers. 'I'm covered in grease.'

'Good old grease. Lick it off, don't waste it.' He stood up and discarded his litter. 'Or will I do it for you?'

'Seriously?'

'Sure.' He took hold of her hand, drew her towards him and stared into her eyes. Taylor's knees wobbled as he lifted a finger to his mouth and sucked the end of it. 'Delicious.' He winked. The streetlamp's glow highlighted his features, showing off his well-sculpted nose, shapely cheeks and strong jaw. Handsome Hansen was the perfect nickname.

'Actually…' Taylor swallowed. His gaze was still on her, inviting her to come closer. 'The vinegar thing… I think I'd like to try it.' She rose on her tiptoes, bringing her almost nose to nose with him. He was tall but she wasn't short. Their lips touched, and Taylor relaxed, allowing every tingle to zap through her and hit all the right places. This was it, what she'd waited for, and it was so good; even the odd taste of vinegar added a pleasurable sting. Magnus took hold of her cheeks, gently holding them as he slipped closer, maintaining the kiss. Taylor edged forward until their groins pressed together. Magnus slipped his hand under her arm and pulled her against him. Taylor entangled her fingers in his hair at the same moment their tongues touched. 'Oh…' Her tummy flipped.

'Skylar,' he murmured into the kiss. 'Let's get back.'

The elevator was empty, the vinegar irrelevant. Taylor was glued at the lips to Magnus and had no intention of letting go. By the time they reached the room in a fumble of buttons and zippers, neither of them had their jackets on. Taylor's lungs spasmed as Magnus stumbled inside and turned on the light, dimming it low.

'Sure you want to do this?' He waited until she nodded, then hauled off his sweater, closely followed by his t-shirt. Could she stretch behind him and put out the light, save her blushes and her complete lack of experience? But then she'd miss that chest. It was begging to be stroked, kissed, and pressed against hers. She'd seen Hollywood guys with perfectly sculpted abs, but this was better. Magnus had muscles honed from what looked like time well-spent not obsessive body worship; a light smatter of golden hair covered him, tapering into a thin line at his navel. All real, nothing fake. 'You know, Skylar. You're so different.'

Taylor chewed her bottom lip as he stepped closer. 'Better or worse?'

'So much better.' He gently kissed her neck. 'I didn't regret not sleeping with you before. I didn't care one way or another, but now I want to. It feels right this time. It's like we were meant to meet again and to have this chance to get it right. No alcohol, no crowd.' Taylor's heart pounded. His words warmed her to the core. He wedged himself against her and she closed her eyes, accepting kisses wherever he chose to put them. If she let him lead, everything would be ok. His hands roamed under her top, grazing her nipples through her bra. 'Oh, Skylar Rousse, you are so hot,' he said with a groan that sent rocket fuel pumping into her veins.

She pounced on him, taking even herself by surprise, but it seemed as if he'd been waiting for that exact move and he lifted her off the ground. She locked her legs around his waist, kissing him deeply, their lips burning as they meshed together.

'Magnus...' Taylor pulled back, but he didn't stop, moving his attention to her neck. 'Stop,' she said. A tremor ran through her. This was too good... except for one thing.

'Are you ok?' Magnus's arms held her fast, his pupils wide with concern. 'You're shaking like a leaf. Let's not do this.'

'I want to,' she heaved. 'I'm just nervous, excited nervous, you know?' A truth she knew Skylar would never have uttered, but she didn't want to be Skylar. Not for this.

'Are you?' He raised his hand and stroked her hair behind her ear, turning her to jelly. 'I didn't expect you to be—'

'Listen.' She swallowed, her shoulders trembling. 'I wonder… Would you do something for me?'

'Sure. Name it. I'll try anything once.'

'Don't call me Skylar.'

'Wow, ok.' Still supporting her with one hand, his other slipped under her top and traced a gentle pattern along the back of her bra. 'So, what do you want me to call you?'

His cheeky smile widened. Of course, he was expecting her to say something kinky. 'My real name.'

'Because Skylar's not your real name?'

'Exactly.'

'Ok, I get it. A Marion Morrison style thing.'

'Kind of, but, you know… when you say Skylar, it doesn't feel like me.' And she needed to be herself right now. 'When we're doing this, I want to be me.'

'So, what should I call you?' A soft volley of kisses landed on her neck and he unclipped her bra inside her top.

She forced out the word, 'Taylor.'

Magnus stopped and looked at her, staying his hand. Taylor held her breath. Had she been rumbled? Maybe he knew Skylar had a sister by that name. He'd worked for Courtney Hines and she would have known.

'Taylor?' His frown grew and her heartrate accelerated. This was going to end with a bang. Her lungs closed down like the air was too thick. She clung to his neck in case he dropped her. Magnus's lips quirked into a smile and he shook his head. 'You changed your name from Taylor to Skylar?'

'I, eh… yes.'

'Even though they sound so alike?'

'Oh… Yes. I suppose they do, but, you know, with competition from Taylor Swift, it was safer to be unique.'

'You're certainly unique. Taylor.' He breathed her name onto her throat and she shuddered. Then, lowering her onto the bed, he moved on top, clamping his hands to her hips as she unlocked her ankles. She rubbed against him, a desperate ache willing him closer.

'Oh,' she moaned as he grazed her neck with more kisses, moving lower, his tongue gliding along her collarbone under her t-shirt. He pushed her loosened bra straps out of the way.

'You're sensational,' he said. 'Let's not hide it.' His palms slid up her ribs, taking the top and the bra with him and slipping them over her head. Taylor moaned. If he was super observant, he might notice her breasts weren't as perfect as her sister's surgically enhanced version, but knowing he'd never gone this far with Skylar stopped her fretting, and she forgot completely as he gently touched her. She arched back, grabbing fistfuls of sheeting and squealing in delirium as his lips worked their way down her body.

He thought she was sensational? What did that make him? Off the scale. He knew his way around a woman. She flinched, realising he knew how to make her happy more than she knew herself.

'Hey. Are you ok?' he murmured, moving close to her face again. His voice soothed and he gently stroked her exactly where she craved it.

She whimpered, 'yes,' barely able to form a coherent word among the overload of pleasure furling inside.

He kissed her again, and Taylor shoved her fingers in his hair, grinding against his hand as his lips devoured her. She spun into a daze of ecstasy. His arms slipped around her back, pulling her against the hot slab of his chest.

He groaned. 'Let's not get carried away. We have to be sensible.'

He pushed himself up, breaking her hold, abandoning her to rake about in his luggage. Taylor used the moment to regain her breath, then to lose her remaining clothes, flicking her panties from her ankle. Magnus returned to the bed, buck naked and all man. She took a moment to admire him. He lowered himself on top of her and his hot skin tickled every nerve end, sending blood surging to her ears. The virile scent of him invaded her pores, making her weightless and giddy. With a little wiggle, she positioned herself, her breathing ragged, her cheeks and neck burning, and the cells in her body pining with desperation. He moved in gently and she gasped, then exhaled in short pants.

He locked eyes with her and smiled, stroking her cheek. 'Is this ok?' His voice was hoarse.

'Yeah, all good.' She relaxed, as she accustomed herself to him, then abandoned all thoughts and gently rocked up and down. His gaze bored into her and she stared back; it scorched her until she wanted to look away or close her eyes. What did he see? Could he tell she wasn't real? *But I am.* This was Taylor and she wanted this connection so badly. He broke the look, leaning in and kissing her.

Pleasure charged in her body as they rocked, making her smile and moan. He pulled out of the kiss to draw breath, and she shook her head. 'No, don't stop,' she murmured, draping her arms around his neck and pulling him in for more. His lips parted for her and he returned her kiss lazily but crushingly intense at the same time. She nuzzled him and poured her attention onto his mouth. But she couldn't concentrate. He moved faster, breathing hard, and she slipped over the edge into shattering oblivion.

His groan of pleasure resonated like an orchestra through the blinding lights. Her heart beat frantically as he panted in her ear. The roundabout of frenzy spun, and she clung to his back, digging her nails deep until everything slowed.

She flopped back and his warm weight pressed on top of her, his shuddering breaths landing on her shoulder. She relaxed her grip on him but almost instantly tightened it. He had to stay. He would, wouldn't he? *Please, don't break this moment. Please, don't let it end yet.*

He rolled over and the chill of cold air and abandonment swept over Taylor. She pressed her lips together and covered her eyes. Had she been a terrible disappointment? He was out of bed. He flicked off the light and his footsteps receded into the bathroom. Taylor didn't dare speak; her lungs were shrinking.

After a few moments, the door clicked, then the mattress lowered like he'd sat on it and seconds later, he moved in beside her. 'Do you like to snuggle?' he whispered.

'Yes,' she said, though she'd never had the opportunity before. She curled into him. A thrill of happiness threatened to spill out as tears. He pulled the duvet over them and held her tight.

'Good, I do too.'

She buried herself in the heat of his chest and closed her eyes, unable to think of anything except the beauty of this moment. Long overdue sleep blanked out everything else, especially how many lies she'd told in the last few hours to get to this pinnacle of ecstasy.

Chapter Eight

Magnus

Something about the morning-after smell kept Magnus from opening his eyes. Skylar's, or Taylor's, perfume mingled with his body spray, their sweat and a hint of vinegar made for the perfect wake up. Her soft cheek touched his shoulder and he relaxed into it. Yes, he had to get home later, but the urgency had left him. His family would be off to work. That left… He rolled his head around to squint at the bedside clock. Three hours until checkout time at eleven.

Skylar stirred but didn't open her eyes. Her naked body moulded alongside his and he ran his hands over her, appreciating her trim figure, her smooth skin. Taylor? Seriously. If her name was Taylor, why hadn't she changed it to something completely different? But his experiences of Skylar told him she wasn't exactly a logical creature. The girl he'd met in the bar was like Taylor, sweet and gentle, but later, she'd morphed into a vamp. Now she seemed to have lost the Hollywood fakery. Had the night on the terrace been all for show? Was her whole life one phoney act after another?

With the wedding week looming, Magnus craved something to cling to. He'd grinned and smiled through the questions and comments for months, replying jovially,

'Yeah, he's my youngest brother. I can't wait, it'll be a blast. I'm so happy for him… Ah, you know me, best man duties will be great, I'll turn my hand to whatever.'

Ha! Whatever indeed. Everything except being the model son. Competing for his parents' love wasn't the issue. They were generous with their affection and didn't favour one son over the others. But when his youngest brother, Carl, had announced his engagement, a nagging sensation had chewed away at Magnus. *I'm the oldest!* And something about being the oldest and last married left an unsinkable feeling of inadequacy.

He lazed back and sighed, knowing he shouldn't care. He had a good career, a great life and he wasn't the marrying kind. All fine. But he imagined his mum's face when he turned up later, alone. She wouldn't say anything, but the look would say it all. 'Here's my eldest son, still single, still letting me down. If only he could settle with someone, I'd be happy.'

'Hey, you.' Taylor squinted out one eye and beamed.

'Hey. Welcome back to the land of the living.'

'I've been awake for ages.' She propped herself on one elbow, trailing her fingers across Magnus's chest. 'I just didn't want to open my eyes.'

'Why? In case this was all a dream?'

'Exactly.'

'Well, now you're awake, or you've opened your eyes at least, I can get up. I didn't want to move in case I disturbed you.'

'Oh, sure. So… Are you leaving right now?'

Magnus hoisted himself up. 'Actually, no. I'm not in a great rush.'

'Oh.' Taylor smirked and ran her teeth along her lower lip.

'Good news, isn't it?' He tweaked her cheek.

*

Magnus adjusted his shirt collar as he and Taylor got in the lift and headed for the breakfast room. 'I hope we're not too late,' he muttered, checking his phone. 'They stop serving at nine thirty.'

'What time is it?'

'Twenty past.'

'Oops. That was a long shower.'

Magnus arched an eyebrow as the lift doors sprang open. 'And a scorching hot one.'

She giggled.

The neanderthal part of him wanted her to stick around, but he needed her away. He had to focus on what he was supposed to be doing – being the model best man.

He made his way around the buffet, piling his plate with the remaining food, smiling at the attending staff as though he hadn't arrived with only nine minutes to spare. After finding a window table, he set up his feast. Taylor joined him seconds later, laying a neat little bowl of fruit and yoghurt on the table.

'Seriously? That's all you're having. It's hardly worth the bother.'

'After the grease-fest of last night, I'm on this for the rest of the year.'

'Wimp,' said Magnus, stabbing a sausage. His gaze left the deliciousness in front of him to look out the window. A clear February sky set sparkles dotting over the surface of the sea.

'Is that the island over there?' Taylor pointed at the hilly landmass to the left of the bay. Magnus returned to his sausage and shook his head.

'No. It is out there, but you can't see it from here. That's an island called Kerrera. Mull's much further out. The bay curves around and blocks the view. You can't see it until you're on the boat.' He considered Taylor and frowned. 'Speaking of which, are you sure you still want to go? Have you booked a hotel or what?'

'Not yet.'

'Well, you better do it, because once I've dropped you, you'll be pretty much stranded there. It's not a place you can walk about and there aren't limos on hire. In fact, you'll be lucky to get a taxi.'

'Yeah.' Taylor sat back and steepled her fingers, tapping the tips together. Her irises flashed and her expression looked impish. 'About that.'

'You've changed your mind? If you have, I'll lend my full support to the idea. I know what you're like and honestly, Mull is not a place for Skylar Rousse.'

'That may be true and I actually agree with you, but I've been thinking.'

'Yes.'

'This is an escape for me. It's like acting in a movie, only for real. Last night…' She blinked and lowered her eyes to the table. 'It was such a new experience. I was… Taylor, and I woke up beside a real guy. A nice guy, someone I like being with.' She peeked up, fluttering her long lashes.

Magnus stopped chewing and furrowed his brow. She did, did she? He enjoyed her company too, bizarre as it seemed, but what was to stop it from being one big act? He swallowed his food. 'That's nice. But it doesn't help your decision. I already told you, once I'm on Mull, I'm on best man duties and I won't have time to meet up with you. You'll be out on a limb.'

'Unless I come with you.'

About to take a sip of orange juice, Magnus stopped, his glass suspended in mid-air. 'How do you mean?'

'I could come as your date. You know, the girlfriend your mom thinks is coming with you.'

'Absolutely not. I am not lying to my family like that.' He slammed his glass down.

'Why not? You already lied to your mom.'

'No, I didn't.' He frowned, pricking a fried egg, so the yolk oozed across the plate.

Taylor folded her arms. 'Ahem. So, how come your mom thinks you've got a girlfriend coming with you when clearly you don't? That sounds like a lie to me.'

'Yeah, ok. But it wasn't a lie, I just haven't filled her in on the whole truth.'

There was the added complication of Julie, his ex, who still lived on the island. Boy, would she love a chance to snigger at him while she paraded around with a belly the size of a beachball. Julie hadn't waited three months before finding someone else, and now she was pregnant. So, yes, he'd told his mum a new woman was accompanying him, despite the fact he'd split with the woman he was seeing a few weeks ago.

'So, where's the problem? Your mom said on the phone she didn't even know your girlfriend's name. It's not even a convincing lie. If you tell her she got seasick or whatever, she'll smell a rat straight away. And I don't think that'll please her. Especially as it seems to me, you invented the story anyway.'

'Right, stop. Just stop. None of this is even remotely your business and I've already said no.' He glowered at his food, ignoring Taylor's burning gaze and the swoop in his gut. He was saying no to a week with someone who could make his life easier; someone whose company was a bit too enjoyable. He gave himself a little shake and frowned. They'd been together less than twenty-four hours and already crazy ideas were seeping through his weakened defences. That had to stop. But his mum would be thrilled if he turned up with Skylar, Julie would be silenced and Magnus could hold his head high. But no. It was a downright crazy idea.

'No worries,' said Taylor. 'I just… you know, like your company.'

'I like yours too,' said Magnus. 'But I can't risk it. You're a big star. If they found out who you are—'

'They won't. I'll ditch Skylar and be Taylor. You tell me what you want in a girlfriend and voilà' – she pinged her fingers into stars – 'I'm that girl.'

'Oh, Jesus Christ.' Magnus rubbed his forehead and sighed.

'Is that a yes?'

Magnus looked up and Taylor beamed at him. Once again, a casual jumper and jeans made up her understated fashion and she'd done her hair so it sat in a playfully messy style with loose strands twisted around her face. Her make-up was minimal and a far cry from her Hollywood style, but it gave her an all-over beauty that made Magnus want to tumble her back into bed. 'I can't believe I'm going to agree to this, but if I do, there's to be no nonsense, Skylar.'

'Taylor.'

'Yeah, and that's what I mean. You're Taylor Rousse… In fact, you're Taylor… Smith. You're absolutely not a Hollywood movie star. My mum might die of shock if she thinks I'm dating someone like that. You're just a normal girl who happens to be American. That won't bother anyone. I meet people from all around the world. But you've got to keep up the act. If you get pissed and blurt it out, I'll have all the stories I know about you round the paparazzi before you can even remember your real name.'

'Yes, sir.' She saluted him with a grin. 'I'll keep it up, no sweat.' With a cheeky wink, she smiled, holding his gaze and setting a fire in his soul.

'Right, so that's settled. I must be bloody crazy.' But more pleasant sensations were brewing inside: calmness and warmth. The satisfaction of having a companion he was at ease with, someone who could help him stay sane over the week ahead. Utterly crazy as it may be, he'd done it. He had a date for the wedding.

Chapter Nine

Taylor

Squinting between two fingers, Taylor made hundreds of wishes – most of them involving not drowning – as Magnus drove the car down the slipway. With a thump, the light was eclipsed, and Taylor shifted her hand. The cavernous bowels of the ferry loomed around.

'You do know what I do for a living,' Magnus said, side-eyeing her. 'I think I can get my car onto the ferry without any difficulty.'

'It looks scary.'

'Try landing a Boeing 747 on an icy runway, then get back to me.'

Taylor turned her face to him and smiled. 'I'd like you to fly me one day.'

'I'll give you my roster and you can book a flight because I'm not going back to private.'

A man in a fluorescent coat beckoned them so close to the car in front they were almost touching. 'How close do we have to be?' asked Taylor. The man tapped the hood and Magnus dragged on the brake.

'They pack them in like sardines. Come on, let's get out of here.' He unstrapped his belt and jumped out. Taylor followed, squeezing between the car and the ship's metal structure. 'This is where your Hollywood dress size comes in handy.' Magnus smirked.

'So I see.' Taylor edged around, following Magnus up a steep staircase. When they emerged, she drank it in. 'Oh, it's a proper ship.' Neat shelves with postcards, snacks and souvenirs lined a small store. Beside that was a restaurant. Signs overhead pointed to an amusement area and viewing deck. In the open-plan section ahead was a comfy seating area.

'Obviously. What did you expect?'

'I'm not exactly sure. I haven't been on many boats. Just a couple of yacht parties and we didn't go far out to sea.'

'Great. So there's a chance you might get seasick for real… darling.'

Taylor gave him a playful push. 'You're not actually going to call me that, are you?'

'I might if the mood takes me. Let's take a walk outside. I like to be out when we leave the harbour, it's traditional.'

'Is it? I thought you'd want to be with the driver.'

'The captain,' Magnus corrected. 'No, I'll let him do his job. I've had a go at the helm before. We did a school trip as kids and I got to steer the ship for about fifteen seconds. I love sailing. I can't believe you've never been on a boat. You haven't lived.'

A fresh wind swirled around outside, biting Taylor's neck. She drew up the collar of her soft pink jacket, shivering. 'It's freezing.' Stamping her feet, she drummed the deck with the soles of her Converse boots.

'We're not even out at sea yet. You need to get a tougher skin. I told you this wouldn't be your kind of place.'

'I can handle it. Why don't we go up front and do the Titanic pose?'

Magnus burst out laughing and Taylor's face cracked too. He shook his head and put his hand on her shoulder. 'Ok, Kate.'

In everything that had happened over the last twenty-four hours, Taylor had forgotten what she was supposed to be doing. Forgotten to worry about Skylar or even to think about what her sister, her parents and their entourage would make of the missing Taylor. She'd sent one message to Liesel, saying she'd found her own place to stay and to leave her alone. And she'd turned off all notifications.

Magnus stepped closer and wrapped his arm around her. 'You can't get to the front of these ships unless you're in the crew.'

'Shame.' But a flush of warmth filled her from the inside out. Real people did this kind of thing. They made trips home to see families, they had fun, they felt wanted.

'Though I suspect if you turned on the charm, you could bribe someone.'

'Me?' said Taylor.

'It worked on me.' Magnus took a few steps forward.

'Yeah, but I'm incognito, remember.'

'Tell you what, we could do this instead.' He leaned in and captured her lips. Taylor's tummy flipped and a bubble of contentment swelled inside her. Magnus caressed her cheekbones, holding her firm.

When they broke apart, he leaned his forehead to hers. Taylor closed her eyes, drinking in the moment.

'Come here,' he said, gently leading her to the railing and wrapping his arms around her from behind, cocooning her, his warmth shielding her from the wind. If this was part of the act, she didn't want the shoot to end.

As the boat glided away from the port, she relaxed into him. This was a view like no other and she wanted to commit it to memory. One day, when she was back in Hollywood, hidden away and trapped, this was something she wanted to pull up and remember.

Magnus nuzzled into her and she quivered. He unzipped his padded jacket and wrapped Taylor inside. 'Better?'

'Too good,' she said from her dreamlike bubble.

As the landmass in the distance grew larger and closer, Taylor experienced an out-of-body sensation of leaving something behind, something she couldn't go back and pick up. But she wasn't sure what it was exactly.

They spent the full hour on deck with no inclination to move or go inside. A loudspeaker announced for them to return to their cars and Taylor shuffled. 'Wait a bit,' said Magnus. 'There's no hurry, it's always a crush on the stairs. I like to watch the boat come in.' He chuckled and it tickled her ears. 'I've turned into my dad. He used to traumatise us as children by always waiting for the boat to dock before getting back to the car. We always thought we'd be stuck on board.'

'Yeah, so let's go.' Outside of his embrace, the wind bit, but it wasn't long before they were back on the lower deck and in the car. Then they were driving out of the darkened hull and onto the island. Magnus knew where to go, so Taylor didn't waste time looking at signs, she just tried to catch all the sights. First a little village, Craignure, then a narrow road, trees, hills, fields and glorious countryside.

'So… Where are we going?' she asked. 'Do you have a hotel?'

'Hmm, yeah. We didn't really think this through, did we? I'm staying with my parents. And they live in a small bungalow where the walls are like cardboard.' He glanced at her. 'Just saying.'

'Your parents?'

'Yes.'

Taylor's heart hiccupped. 'Ok. That complicates things.'

'Yep. And we'll be there in ten minutes.'

'Ten minutes? Magnus, we need a story.'

He frowned and gave a little shrug. 'What kind of story?'

'Well, your parents will want to know how we met and stuff like that, won't they?'

'I suppose so.' He rubbed his thumb across his chin. 'Why don't we tell them the truth. Or sort of. We could say I bumped into you in an airport, we hit it off and decided to keep seeing each other.'

'Will they believe that? Haven't you already told your mom a story about how you met your girlfriend?'

With an irritated roll of his shoulders, he replied, 'No. I just said I was seeing someone, and I'd let them know more at the time because I didn't want to jinx it. My mum knows what I'm like, so she didn't push it.'

'Ok.' Taylor drew in a slow breath. What was she doing? If she thought too deeply, her head would explode. Masquerading as her Hollywood actress twin, pretending to be Magnus's girlfriend, while actually just being herself was insane in anybody's book. Maybe the real Skylar would have the acting part in the bag. But she was Taylor Rousse and her acting career had ended at fourteen when she'd had a breakdown and been put on medication, medication that became an addiction and ended in her first stint in rehab.

When she'd gotten out, she'd hated seeing Skylar on her pedestal, doing everything she once dreamed of herself. She'd dressed as Skylar and gone out, ready to get drunk, sleep around, shoplift, or do anything which would get Skylar slapped across every gossip column everywhere. But an old family friend had 'rescued' her and the whole story had come out. Her parents weren't forgiving. Crushed by their restrictions, she'd tried to overdose and ended up with a pumped stomach and another stint in rehab. The one she'd gotten out of two days before she met Magnus for the first time. Not exactly the glowing career she'd wished for.

Since then, she'd been kept on a short leash, but now, freedom beckoned. Her gaze travelled onto Magnus. Of all the coincidences, she'd bumped into him. She'd read about stranger things but words and phrases like *destiny* and *meant to be* kept cropping up in her head. Words she'd never used in connection to herself before. No future had looked bright just one day ago.

'Here we are.' Magnus turned the car into a short drive. They passed a few widely spaced, tall pine trees before a little bungalow came into view with a wooden sign reading Tighnatraigh. 'It's pronounced tie-na-tray,' said Magnus, as Taylor frowned. Beyond a further row of trees was the sea, broad and greyish blue with the silhouette of the mountainous mainland on the horizon.

'We're here already?' *Crap.* Taylor smoothed off her clothes. Why did this not seem like a good idea anymore? What if Magnus's family hated her? She couldn't pretend they were hating Skylar, she'd know they were hating her.

'Yes. Oh, and I should tell you, my mum's aunt, Jean, lives here too. She's batty and she doesn't really like anybody.'

'Oh, great.'

'Except me. I'm her favourite. So woe betide you offend her. No woman will ever be good enough for her Magnus.'

'What?'

Magnus laughed. 'I told you this wasn't a good idea, but it's too late now. We're here and there's my mum.'

A woman stood in the bungalow door, waving and craning her neck. Before Taylor was fully out, the woman had nipped down the two steps and was upon them. She reached up and hugged Magnus. He ruffled her greyish brown bob and grinned. 'Hey, Mum. How's it going?'

'Wonderful. And who have we here?' She beamed at Taylor.

'So, here we have Taylor. And, Taylor, this is my mum, Fenella.'

'Hi.' Taylor edged forward. What now? Shake hands? Wave? Just smile? Fenella took charge, throwing out her arms and hugging Taylor.

'Wonderful to meet you, Taylor.' She patted her back. 'Now, in you come.'

Taylor glanced at Magnus. He winked and indicated with his thumb for her to follow Fenella.

'I hope the journey was ok,' said Fenella.

'Fine,' said Magnus. 'Apart from yesterday's accident.'

'I checked the news this morning,' said Fenella. 'Apparently, some people were airlifted from the crash, but they survived, so that's a blessing. I always hate to hear about accidents.'

She talked all the way into the house, through the short hall where Taylor was jumped on by three dogs: two spaniels and a retriever. They moved so fast, dotting back and forward, it seemed like a lot more. She fussed over them as they capered about, wagging their tails and rolling over.

'Into your beds,' said Fenella, shooing them into the living room. The dogs slumped into their baskets beside the radiator in the cute if a little time-warped space.

Taylor's heart filled with a happy bubble. This was a proper, cosy, homely home. Magnus had been a child here, and years of love and laughter shone through the wide-open grey curtains. Photographs on the walls and the mantlepiece showed the passage of time, three blond, curly-haired boys growing into handsome young men smiled from every frame. At the front of the room, two large sliding glass doors opened onto a beautiful sea view.

'Well, hello.'

Taylor jumped at a shrill voice.

From a little armchair in front of the fireplace, an elderly woman peered around. 'Come in so I can see you. If you stand behind me, I'll break my neck. My bones aren't what they used to be. I am ninety-two.'

'Hi, Jean.' Magnus walked around and kissed the old woman's wrinkly forehead.

'Oh, Magnus. You must stop growing. But let me see the young lady.'

With a beam and a cheeky glint in his eyes, Magnus put out his hand, welcoming Taylor for her inspection. 'This is Taylor. Taylor, meet Aunt Jean.'

'Hi,' said Taylor, pushing her hair behind her ears and trying to maintain her smile as the old woman looked her up and down.

'You're very different from the last one. Taller I think, but not as pushy.' She screwed up her nose. 'You're a scrawny one too.'

'Thank you, Jean,' said Magnus.

'She's pregnant, do you know?'

'No she isn't,' he said sharply, flicking a look at Taylor.

'I mean Julie McNabb. Your last one.'

'Oh her.' Magnus rolled his eyes. 'Yes, I knew about her.'

'She's a nippy one, looks like her grandmother, faces like shrews, both of them.' Jean rapped her fingers on the chair arm.

'Look at the sunshine,' said Fenella. 'We've had solid rain and sleet for weeks. You two have brought the sun with you. Now, sit down and relax. So, tell us, Taylor, where is it you come from?'

'California.'

'Oh, lovely, but you must be finding it a bit chilly here. Sadly, sun here at this time of year doesn't bring warmth.'

'Yeah, it's chilly.'

'California?' said Jean, tutting as she picked up some knitting needles. 'Some American place? Dear, dear.'

'But, Magnus, you don't fly to California, do you?' Fenella smiled.

'Eh, no, but we met in…'

'Amsterdam.' Taylor fluttered her lashes.

'Oh? Sounds intriguing,' said Fenella. 'Why were you in Amsterdam?'

'Flying a plane, of course,' said Magnus.

'I meant Taylor. Are you a pilot too?' asked Fenella.

'No… I eh, I'm a PA. I work for big companies. We met at the airport.'

'Yeah, we literally crashed into each other, and well… here we are.'

'Dear, dear,' muttered Jean. 'Sounds very silly. I suppose you were drunk.'

'I don't drink when I'm flying, Jean,' said Magnus.

'Wow, must be fate,' said Fenella. 'How wonderful. Now, shall I get you something to eat? Jakob's coming later, so I don't want to have lunch too early. He's stopping off here before going to Carl's. There's not enough room for me to have everyone overnight.' Fenella gave Taylor a huge smile.

'That's great, Mum,' said Magnus, 'but before we do anything else, Taylor and I should get our luggage from the car.'

'Can't you get it yourself, you lazy boy?' said Jean. 'I'm sure you can carry her case too.'

'I can, yes, but she has something fragile in it. She prefers to do it herself. Don't you, darling? Now come on.'

Taylor opened her mouth, then closed it again before following him. She took hold of his arm. 'I don't have anything fragile—'

'Shh!' He put his hand to his lips before leading her outside, then opened the trunk and leaned on it, shaking his head. 'This is a disaster. I don't know whether to laugh or cry. Some of it is making me laugh, but honestly, remind me, why did I agree to this?'

'Why? It's gone ok so far, hasn't it?'

'Are you kidding? Do you even know my brother's names? Who's getting married? Who their partners are? Their children? Do you know what I like doing? What do we do together? What do we have in common? Do you live with me, or are we in a long-distance relationship? We don't know the first thing about each other and if we start making stuff up, it'll all come out. My mum's not an idiot. She'll catch on this is fake and think I've paid someone to do it.'

'I did say we should have a story. So, tell me about your brothers and I'll remember. How about we say we both like… I don't know, music? Sailing?'

'Taylor, you've just been on a boat for the third time in your life.'

'Ok, scratch that one. Let's go with music. Now tell me about your brothers.'

'Right. I'm the eldest.'

'Are you?'

'Yes. Jakob is next, he's married to Livvi and they have a one-year-old daughter, Polly. Carl is the youngest, he's the one getting married. His fiancée is Robyn. Robyn's mother is the hotel owner at the Glen Lodge Hotel, and that's where they're getting married.'

'Right, ok.' Taylor drew in a sigh. 'Jakob, Livvi and Polly. Carl marrying Robyn, hotel owner's daughter. I think I've got it. I didn't realise you were the eldest. I thought you must be the youngest with them being married first.'

'Yeah, nice,' he said, fidgeting with the sleeve of his chunky knit sweater. 'Life doesn't always work like that.'

Taylor patted him on the arm. 'I know. And who's Julie? The shrew-faced pregnant woman. You kept her quiet.'

'Yeah, she's my ex. And even if you were my real girlfriend, I wouldn't exactly be shouting about her.'

'And the baby?'

'Well, it's obviously nothing to do with me. I haven't seen her for a year. Our relationship was a farce. I moved back here for a while last year when I was between jobs, and Julie happened. She was in the right place at the right time, but she… Well, she wanted more from the relationship than I did. I was never going to come back and live here permanently. She couldn't grasp that. If Jean mentions her again, make sure you're suitably offended. Ok, darling?'

'Of course, honey.' Taylor put her arm around his back and smacked him on the butt.

'Good.' He pulled her in for a one-armed hug.

Taylor savoured it while reciting the names of his brothers and their partners in her head. *And if I was his real girlfriend, I'd do the same. I wasn't born with the knowledge!*

Fenella bustled out of a room, a delicious smell following in her wake. Was she baking bread? A mom who actually baked was too good to be true.

'Your room's in here.' Fenella opened a door in the corridor.

'I know,' said Magnus.

'I'm telling Taylor, Mr know-it-all,' said Fenella.

'I am not a know-it-all.'

'Thanks.' Taylor ducked into the room with a smirk as Magnus frowned at his mom. The neatly decorated room promised homely comfort with its magnolia walls and long blue curtains. It bordered on old-fashioned but warmth radiated from it. Taylor clapped her hands under her chin. 'It's so cute.'

'It's probably naff compared to what you're used to,' said Fenella. 'But the bed's comfy and it has an electric blanket, that'll keep you cosy.'

'I thought that was my job,' muttered Magnus, shoving the cases into the room.

Fenella did a three-sixty with her eyes. 'That sounds like my cue to leave,' she said. 'Make yourself at home.' She smiled at Taylor and patted her on the shoulder as she left.

'Naughty,' said Taylor.

'What? Keeping my girlfriend warm is not a crime.'

'And is that all we're doing?' whispered Taylor. 'Because your mom…'

Magnus peeked out the door, then said, 'She's been married nearly forty years and she has three kids. She knows how things work.'

Taylor bit her lip.

'But we can always shove a pillow down the middle of the bed and make sure we behave,' said Magnus. 'Because I can't guarantee Jean won't be on the other side of the wall with a glass pressed against it.'

Taylor gave his upper arm a playful slap. 'You are a very bad man, aren't you?'

He sighed, opened his arms and drew her in for a hug. 'I must be. I just hope this doesn't come back to bite.'

'It won't.' Taylor rubbed her cheek into the rib of his sweater, lapping up the exquisite sensation of being wanted. The fact he thought she was Skylar was irrelevant. Right now, she was his girlfriend and part of his family, and he was doing a better impression of caring for her than anyone in her life had ever done.

Chapter Ten

Magnus

Magnus lounged into the grey chenille sofa, crossed his legs and leaned his chin on his hand. Fenella lifted a plate of cakes and offered them around the room.

Taylor's fingers hovered over the plate, and Magnus smirked as Fenella beamed at her. Her indecision wouldn't be because she couldn't decide but because she'd be trying to work out how many calories she was about to ingest.

'One cake won't hurt,' said Magnus.

'They all look so good.' Taylor lifted a slice of millionaire shortbread and Magnus raised his eyebrow. She flipped him a cheeky smile.

'So, Taylor,' said Fenella, sitting down and cradling a mug. 'What do you think of Scotland so far?'

Magnus glanced heavenward. Fenella had taught in a local primary school for almost forty years and looked like she was encouraging a diffident child to speak up.

'Oh, it's stunning but cold.'

Fenella nodded. 'Yes, this time of year is chilly. It surprised me Carl and Robyn wanted this time of year for their wedding, but it's to fit in with the hotel. They didn't want it in the main tourist season, so it didn't affect business.'

'I guess it makes sense.'

'Carl won't have a clue,' said Magnus. 'He'll do whatever Robyn says.'

Fenella peered at him over her cup. 'Do you have any brothers or sisters, Taylor?'

'I eh, yeah. I have a sister… She's um, a dancer.'

'A dancer?' said Fenella. 'Like ballet?'

'Modern.'

'Lovely, sounds very creative.' She sipped her drink and Taylor nibbled on her cake. 'And where do you work?'

'I eh… all over, you know, wherever I'm needed.' She glanced at Magnus. He sent her a little wave. Watching a Hollywood movie star sweating under his mum's inquisition was almost as delicious as the home baking. Improvisation clearly wasn't Skylar's forte.

'So, do you live with Magnus?' asked Jean.

'Jean.' Magnus growled. Jean had nosey-old-lady down to a tee.

'What? It's a perfectly acceptable question. The last one wanted to live with you, but you refused to get a house here. I wondered if this one has had any success.'

'The last one?' said Magnus quietly, with a glance out the window. Julie hadn't been the last. One girlfriend a year would really be something.

'Oh, really, Jean,' said Fenella.

Jean bit into her shortbread. 'Bunch of prudes, all of you,' she muttered.

'Now, Taylor, do you have any dietary requirements?' asked Fenella.

'Not really.'

'She doesn't like grease but she's rather partial to vinegar,' Magnus added with a wink.

Taylor narrowed her eyes at him. 'I tried fish and chips yesterday. The jury's out.'

'Oh gosh, I understand.' Fenella smiled. 'My boys are ridiculous with the amount of stuff they pour over their chips. I like some nice chips, but I'm not fussed for vinegar.'

'Except for washing the shower screen.'

'Different type of vinegar, son.' Fenella clarified, raising her hand. 'And it is very good for shining up glass. Not that he'd know,' she added to Taylor. 'Him having a cleaner and all that.'

Magnus shrugged. 'I work long hours. The last thing I want to do is come home and clean.'

'Better watch out,' said Jean. 'As soon as he gets you living there, the cleaner'll be sacked and you'll get the job.'

'Thank you, Jean,' he muttered. 'I'm not a caveman. I wouldn't do anything of the sort.'

'Thank god for that,' said Taylor. A hint of the old Skylar lingered in her teasing expression, but other than that, he barely recognised her. Now the glitz and spangle had been stripped away, she'd morphed into a sweet, sometimes nervous, and always pleasant woman. Not to mention a bloody hot one. Magnus covered his mouth in case he inadvertently said the words aloud.

When Jakob's car pulled into the drive, Fenella jumped up. Taylor breathed an audible sigh of relief. Magnus winked at her as Jean looked over. He put out his palms and mouthed, 'What?'

'You're up to something,' said Jean, waggling her finger.

'Me?' said Magnus.

'Oh, yes. You might be the most charming of my three nephews, but you're also the most trouble.'

'I'm definitely not more trouble than Carl.'

'Hmpf. You just hide it better.'

'Would you like another cake?' Taylor asked, lifting the plate and smiling at Jean.

'Is that bribery?'

'I… I'm not sure. Do I need to bribe you?'

'Maybe. If you want me to keep your secret.'

'What secret?' said Magnus.

Jean chortled into her tea. 'I have no idea but that reaction makes me wonder. I was only pulling your leg, but is there something I should know?'

'Absolutely not,' said Magnus. 'You already know too much for your own good. Now, let's go meet my brother.' He got to his feet.

'You're going to leave me all alone?' Jean grumbled.

'You'll be fine for two minutes,' said Magnus. 'Have a sherry or something.'

'Oh, you cheeky boy.'

As Magnus closed the door, Taylor slumped against the wall. 'Oh my god. Why did I agree to this?'

'Agree?' Magnus leaned over, flattening his hands to the wall and caging her in. 'It was your idea, remember.'

'Yes, I do. I must have lost my mind.'

'Maybe, but there are some perks.' He kissed her softly on the lips, holding it as long as he dared. Voices approached the front door. On the first creak, he pulled away and Taylor stood up straight. 'Hey,' he said, as his petite sister-in-law, Livvi, stepped into the hall with Fenella. 'We were on our way out to meet you, let's reverse, there's more space in the living room.'

They backed into the room, and Magnus embraced Livvi. She returned it warmly before stepping back and flicking her long mane of caramel-toned hair over her shoulder. Sensing Taylor lurking behind him, Magnus took her hand and tugged her forward. Now wasn't the time for hiding. When had she ever hidden? Actually having to drag

Skylar Rousse into the limelight was wacky, much like everything else that had happened in the last twenty-four hours. And yet, here he was, hands on her shoulders, displaying her like a trophy. 'This is Taylor. Taylor, Livvi. Aw, and what's this?' A tiny tot in a frilly pink skirt tottered in, distracting Magnus and bringing a smile to his lips. Jakob stooped behind the little princess, steering her in the right direction – though she seemed hellbent on going the opposite way. 'She can walk now?' Magnus cocked his head and his heart melted. His little niece, Polly, toddled straight for the dogs' beds, giggling as the retriever sniffed her and the spaniels swept the floor with their crazy tails. Jakob hovered about, ready to pounce before either dog or child got overexcited.

'Oh, gosh, yes,' said Livvi, adjusting a row of gold bangles. 'She's into everything. And hello, Taylor, so pleased to meet you.'

'You two will get on great,' said Magnus. Livvi had that knack of being friends with anyone and Taylor had little choice, though he wondered if the inner Skylar would rebel at some point. 'Livvi's part-American too,' he added, offering an incentive just in case.

'Yes, but I don't let on which part.'

'Ha, very funny,' said Magnus, stepping towards his brother and embracing him. 'Hey, bro.'

'You look familiar,' said Livvi. Magnus froze, wondering where this would go. Livvi was above the age bracket of the average Skylar Rousse fan, but she had the vibe of someone who would enjoy glittery shows and slapstick romcoms with heroines who tripped over their own feet and landed on their boss's shiny shoes. 'Where are you from?'

'California,' said Taylor.

Livvi perked up. 'Oh, I've been a couple of times, but my mother is from New York, so that's where we tend to go.'

'Is this the latest girl?' Jakob muttered aside and gave a half smile in her direction. Half a smile was better than nothing for Jakob. He was the reserved one.

'Yup.'

Livvi had moved onto another subject and thankfully nothing to do with Hollywood. Magnus waited for a gap in her monologue, then put his arm around Taylor and introduced her to Jakob who shook her hand.

'You're so alike,' said Taylor, smiling between Jakob and Magnus. Magnus sent Jakob 'the look' – the one they traded every time someone told them they looked alike.

'Yeah, we know,' said Magnus. 'Up until the age of about twenty, even Mum couldn't tell us apart. Even now it's touch and go, that's why he started wearing glasses.'

'Nice,' muttered Jakob.

'Oh, stop your nonsense, Magnus,' said Fenella, gently removing the dog's toy from little Polly and beaming at her. 'All my boys look alike, and very handsome. Yes, you have a handsome daddy and two handsome uncles.' Fenella tickled Polly, making her giggle.

'She knows how to make us blush,' said Magnus.

'Aw, and she's right,' said Livvi taking Jakob's arm.

Magnus looked away. *This, this, this!* This was exactly the reason he hated being the last one, the single one, the lonely one. Curse it. Anywhere else he could deal with it, but at home, it unleashed a green-eyed monster.

The last time he'd come home for an extended period he'd stupidly jumped straight into bed with Julie McNabb – not a smart move.

Catching his eye, Taylor piped up, 'Oh, definitely. There's a handsome gene in here.' She poked Magnus in the tummy and smiled.

'I know, and it's mine,' said Aunt Jean.

'Yeah, course it is,' said Magnus, but he wrapped Taylor into a hug. The knowledge this was fake tempered the heat spreading through his veins. Jean put two fingers to her mouth and pretended to wretch, more like a moody teenager than a nonagenarian. Magnus spotted his mum with her head tilted and a watery smile, and he released Taylor quickly. 'So,' he said, 'shall we go for a walk before lunch? Taylor wants to learn to sail, don't you?'

'Er, yes…' She flashed a wide grin and Magnus could have sworn a little star gleamed on her perfectly straight teeth, the Hollywood grin in action.

'I'll show you Dad's boats. He's got a sailing boat and a cruiser.'

Fenella stayed to make lunch but insisted they take the three dogs. The two spaniels and the old retriever bounded up at the sound of leads rattling. Jean grumbled about it being far too cold for anyone to walk anywhere. Taylor strolled ahead with Livvi. Magnus watched them chatting together while he discussed work with Jakob. The distraction of little Polly was difficult to ignore, especially as Jakob kept scooping her up mid-sentence, tickling her and cuddling her, then carrying her for a bit before letting her toddle off again. The dragon of envy was working overtime on Magnus, breathing hot waves of inadequacy, and lashing fear over him. Getting a cuddle from his niece and lavishing her with all the pretty things a well-off uncle could buy was fine, but he always maintained he didn't want kids of his own. They didn't fit his lifestyle, but seeing Jakob like this sent vicious surges of jealousy through his limbs. Weird and unbidden visions of being handed a tiny newborn baby reeled through his mind. The imagined pride swelled, then burst like a giant balloon when he remembered where he was. He gave his hair a determined rake.

The dogs leapt around the jetty, chasing each other up and down and back to the beach. Little Polly squirmed in Jakob's arms, desperate to get down and join in the chase, but he jollied her along safely in his grip until they were on their father's boat.

Magnus did the guided tour for Taylor and the sun lifted in the sky, casting a glittering reflection in the turquoise sea. Taylor ducked below deck and made all the right noises. Again, either her acting skills were top drawer, or her interest was genuine. The thought that it might be the latter puzzled Magnus, but he clung to a little thread that it might be the case.

After they'd exhausted their praise and interest in the boats, they trudged onto the beach and threw stones.

'You'll never beat that,' said Magnus after skimming his stone and counting twenty-two leaps.

'I wouldn't even try,' muttered Jakob, holding Polly's hand as she investigated the water's edge.

'I'm useless at it,' said Livvi.

'That just leaves me,' said Taylor, picking up a stone and slinging it forward. Everyone laughed as it plunked straight in. 'Ok. Definitely not my sport. But how about this?' She skipped towards a rope swing dangling from the branch of a tree in the wooded area.

With some jiggling, she positioned herself on it and pushed off, soaring out over the sea. She squealed with delight. Magnus saw stars and his head swam as she got higher. Flying at giddy heights held no fear for him but something about this had his heart thumping in his mouth. Taylor scuffed her shoes along the ground, bringing the swing to a standstill. 'That was awesome. Your turn.' She pinged off and passed the rope to Magnus.

'I'd probably break it these days.'

'No way,' said Jakob. 'And even if you do, will you care? You used to jump off that thing into the sea.'

Magnus smirked. 'Yeah, and so did you.'

'I think I fell off it once,' said Jakob, 'but pretending I'd jumped seemed way cooler.'

'Ok, why not? But if I break my neck, I'm suing you for damages,' Magnus warned Taylor.

'You better get yourself a mighty fine attorney then because you know who my father is.'

Magnus scrambled onto the swing with a cough.

'Who is he?' asked Livvi.

'Oh… No one. I was joking.'

Magnus rotated his shoulders, sizing up the swing, then leapt on and swung high above the sea, grinning as Jakob and Taylor took photos on their phones. As he jumped off, he leaned down to little Polly and clapped her cheeks. 'You don't do that until you're much much bigger, little lady.'

Livvi laughed. 'She's only one.'

'Exactly, never too young to learn about health and safety.'

Jakob let out a snort. 'Says the uncle who… Well, never mind.' He glanced at Taylor.

'Wise move, little bro,' said Magnus. 'Let's not tell the ladies about my youthful misdemeanours.'

'Yeah, or the adult ones.'

'Definitely not them.'

Food called and they wandered back to the bungalow. Fenella had set out a buffet-style lunch on her mismatched china, making it shabby chic and homely.

'This is gorgeous,' said Livvi.

'Totally,' Taylor agreed.

She was acing this. Magnus grabbed a plate and chatted with Jakob and Livvi. Taylor caught his eye and they passed a smile that the others would easily have taken for a loving glance but both of them knew to be code for: *we've got this in the bag*. From the sofa, Fenella checked up from the book she was reading to Polly and beamed at Magnus, her expression full of delight. Magnus sipped his coffee. Was this so wrong? Giving his mum something to smile about? Even if it was only for a day or two.

The weird clock on the living room wall whirred and clanked before striking five, and a few minutes later, Magnus's father came in dressed in his overalls. Per Hansen had given his sons his blond curls, but his had turned white. Magnus would have his head shaved if his hair ever got that wild and fluffy. His dad's eyes twinkled, couple that with the hair and he looked slightly crazed.

After greeting the assembled company, he came to Taylor and shook her hand warmly. 'So pleased you made it.'

'Thank you.'

'I'll hear all your stories shortly,' he said, still holding her hand. 'But I should get cleaned up.'

'You should have done that before you came in,' muttered Jean. 'But you Scandinavians have your own way of doing things. We warned Fenella about that right from the start.'

Fenella frowned. 'Jean, I married him nearly forty years ago, it's a bit late to change my mind now.' She rolled her eyes at Taylor and tapped the top of her forehead with her index finger. 'She's cuckoo sometimes,' she whispered.

'We should head off,' said Jakob. 'It's quite a drive to Carsaig.'

Magnus was keen to see Carl and Robyn's renovations to their new home but not enough that he wanted to spend the week there. Sure, their house was roomier than this one, but it would be nice for his mum to have at least one of her children staying with her, and Magnus was ready to take one for the team. Of course, in reality, Fenella wouldn't have given a damn where Magnus chose to stay. But watching the scenes of domestic bliss on display from his brothers was about as appealing as watching a colonoscopy on repeat for forty-eight hours while being force-fed calf's liver and pickled gherkins. *Screw it.* He couldn't handle a week of having to smile and congratulate them on their happiness at every turn while he lay sprawling on a dusty shelf like a capsized woodlouse.

Once Jakob had left and Per had disappeared into the shower, the house fell quiet. Fenella bustled around as they cleared away the plates and crockery, reliving the day and telling Taylor funny stories about children in her class. Jean fell asleep and Magnus took to brooding, only half listening. When Fenella and Taylor left the room together, he didn't follow to find out the reason, in case he was supposed to know already. Instead, he picked up one of his dad's sailing books and read it to the accompanying snores from Jean. But the words weren't going in. What might have beens and what ifs buzzed around his head like a cloud of midges. His heart lay divided between enjoying life as it was and wanting more. A more he couldn't easily achieve.

It felt like they'd only just eaten but, not long after six-thirty, Fenella pulled out the mince and tatties for dinner. Magnus could barely conceal his laugh at the expression on Taylor's face.

'It's the Scottish staple diet,' he said.

'Oh gosh,' Fenella said. 'I didn't actually ask if you liked it. Would you like me to get you something else?'

Taylor shook her head, gingerly scraping up a tiny bit of mince and placing it into her mouth. Magnus winked.

'Mmm, it's quite nice,' said Taylor. 'A lot better than greasy chips.'

'Just wait until she serves you haggis or black pudding.'

'I'm getting an education anyway.' Taylor smiled at Fenella. 'Thank you for having me and going to so much effort.'

Fenella flapped her hands, swatting away the words. 'Honestly, it's no trouble. I'm just sorry we can't offer you much entertainment. About the most exciting thing we have are a few old board games. Or you can watch TV if you'd rather.'

Magnus held in his groan – just. This was why going to Carl's would have been more sensible. At least he could have got smashed and drowned out everything else. Somehow that wasn't an option in his mum's house.

'Let's play the games,' said Taylor. 'It sounds fun.'

After they'd eaten, Fenella pulled out some boxes, including Frustration, Cluedo and about a hundred-year-old Trivial Pursuit.

'At least it isn't Monopoly,' muttered Magnus. 'I detest that game.'

'I thought you'd love it,' Taylor said. 'Don't you always win?'

'He certainly does not,' said Jean.

'This Trivial Pursuit must be at least twenty years old,' said Fenella, opening the box.

'I was six when it came out then.' Taylor giggled.

'Are you only twenty-six?' said Fenella, shooting Magnus a look.

He adjusted his neckline. Yeah, she was young. But the Hollywood lifestyle gave her maturity beyond her years. Though he'd seen her youthful vulnerability too. Or was he being an out-and-out idiot? He reached for the quiz box. 'Actually, I think this game is older than twenty years. You should know all the answers,' he said to Jean. 'You're the only one who was alive when these things happened.'

Fenella pulled out a card. 'The first question is about Aristotle.'

'My point in a nutshell,' said Magnus.

Taylor's laughter increased as the evening went on and she relaxed. Magnus rested his hand on her thigh and squeezed it with a little wink. Twenty-six or not, she was his, at least for the week, and her smile made his chest swell with warmth.

When they finally wound up for the night, they let Taylor use the bathroom first.

'Sorry, the perils of a small house,' said Fenella. 'Only one bathroom, though we do have a little cloakroom if you're desperate.'

'I don't mind, it's all so cute. And thanks, thank you so much.'

'Oh, you're so welcome,' said Fenella. 'I'm sorry if it seems a bit primitive.'

'Not at all, it's so cosy and such awesome fun.' Taylor beamed as she left the room and Magnus finished putting away the quiz cards.

He heard the bathroom door click shut.

'She's a sweetheart,' said Fenella. 'I like her a lot. Even if she is very young.'

'She's not that young,' muttered Magnus.

Fenella lifted the games boxes. 'I'm not criticising. She's a lovely girl. I hope she's the one this time.'

'Mum, let's not do this,' said Magnus. 'We've only been together a very short time, let's not get ahead of ourselves.'

'I'm not. I just want you to be happy.'

'I am. I don't need anyone else to make me happy. I can be perfectly happy on my own.'

'Oh, fiddlesticks,' said Jean. 'You talk a lot of nonsense, young man.'

'Right, well, I'm off to bed. You two can talk about me amongst yourselves once I'm out of the room.'

'We wouldn't,' said Fenella as he leaned in a placed a kiss on her forehead.

'Goodnight, Mum.'

'We will,' said Jean.

'And goodnight, Jean.'

'Sleep well,' said Per.

'And you,' said Magnus, stretching and heading for the bedroom. He scrolled through his phone, answering some messages and laughing at some silly videos on his friends' WhatsApp chat. The door dragged across the carpet as Taylor came in, wrapped in a towel. Magnus imagined unravelling it and coiling her into his arms. But he didn't want to waste time. Snooze too long in this house and someone else would nip into the bathroom first.

He took a quick shower but didn't linger. Keeping Taylor waiting was just rude. He rubbed his hair dry and dragged a towel around his waist before slipping across the corridor into the dimly lit bedroom. Taylor was at the window in a pair of short pink pyjamas with a strappy top, peering through the curtains into the darkness.

'Hey,' he said, raiding his case for some PJs. She didn't reply or turn around as he discarded the towel from his waist and pulled on his shorts and t-shirt. 'Are you ok?'

She backed away from the window, wiping her fingers under her eyes.

'What's wrong?'

'I just feel so bad. Your mom, your dad, everyone. They're so kind, so nice. And I'm deceiving all of them.'

He closed the space between them and put his arms around her, resting his lips on her hair. 'Taylor, you don't have to do this. If you want to leave, it's ok. I'll tell them things didn't work out. I don't want you to be hurt by this. I never thought it was a good idea. I wish I'd stuck to my guns.'

'But that's the problem. I don't want to leave. I want to be here. I like being with you. It's the deception I don't like.'

'So... what are you suggesting? That we come clean?'

'No. Not that. Everything will change if they think I'm some big star. I like things being cosy. It's such a shock to my system to go somewhere and be so warmly accepted. And it's hard to stomach because it isn't real.'

'The feelings are real. My mum and dad are like this. Even when the week is over, and sometime down the line, I tell them we've split up, you'll still have these memories.'

'I guess.' She withdrew from his hold, pulled back the grey check covers and got into the bed. 'Oh, wow. It's so warm.'

'The electric blanket,' he grinned. 'You won't want me warming you too.'

She raised her watery gaze. 'I do.'

He got in and she curled into a ball, nestling in his arms. His cheek rested on her soft forehead and he closed his eyes. This felt like home. Not just the room, the house, or the island. But Taylor at his side.

Chapter Eleven

Taylor

Taylor pushed the kitchen door closed as the kettle roared to the boil. She didn't want to wake anyone. She flung her arms around herself and rubbed them. Never had she lived in a house this small. Once or twice she'd visited small apartments in LA and New York, where modern designs had been put into play to use every space, and sure, this house was bigger than that, a comfortable family home. But the Rousse family was used to grandeur, and size was everything. This kind of living was alien. Taylor opened a couple of cupboards and located a mug. She poured boiling water into it and clung to the hot china. Odd as this lifestyle may seem, so much of it appealed to her. Mostly abstract sentiments Taylor couldn't pin down, but they floated around her like unseen guardians, keeping her safe in a place that should be alien. She cradled her mug, watching a flicker of light rising in the distance from the small kitchen window.

Truly, it was just as well she was Taylor and not her twin sister. Skylar wouldn't have lasted ten minutes if she'd got in the door. Even if she'd been acting, she'd have demanded a team of cleaners, not because the place was dirty, but she needed an utterly sterile environment. The furniture, which was cosy and had wear and tear born of

118

family love, would have been thrown out and replaced with pristine new stuff before Skylar got within three metres of the place.

Taylor wouldn't change it for the world. The only thing she would change was the situation. All the plans had turned to dust overnight. What had seemed like a good idea was now a nightmare. So much for gate-crashing a wedding and Magnus's life, she hadn't stopped to consider the emotions involved. Not just hers, or his, but his whole family. Deceiving people as genuine as this felt all wrong.

The door opened behind her and she spun around. 'Good morning,' said Fenella, stretching her hands behind her head, making her look like a fluffy pink bear in her giant house robe.

'Hey,' said Taylor. 'That looks cosy.' She'd settled for a hoody over her short pyjamas, but her feet and legs were like ice blocks.

'Yes, it is. Carl got it for me for Christmas. I didn't like to tell him it's about six sizes too big for me. I might not be as trim as I used to be, but this has room for two more people.'

'You look great to me.'

'Thank you,' said Fenella. 'I've tried to be good for the last few months. It wouldn't do for the mother of the groom to spoil the wedding photos by not fitting her dress.'

Taylor laughed. 'You'll look great.' She covered her mouth at a sudden thought. A dress! She'd come on the pretence of being Magnus's date for the wedding, but she had nothing to wear. Skylar's wardrobe was full of so much glitz, she could change three or four times for an event, but Taylor didn't even have one of her red-carpet hand-me-downs. How could she explain this away? And where could she get a dress?

'Is everything ok?' asked Fenella, putting her hand on Taylor's shoulder. 'You look away in a dream.'

'Sorry, yes. I think it's the travelling catching up with me.'

'Didn't you sleep well?'

'I did for a while.' Being in Magnus's comforting embrace had made dozing off easy. But once she'd woken, harsh reality crept in, making falling back to sleep impossible. The whole thing sucked, but at the same time, each second of this life was precious. 'I think I'm still jetlagged.'

'Oh, did you fly over this week? Magnus doesn't say much, but I thought you were living together.'

'Er, no. Not yet, you know,' she fudged, uncertain what Magnus had already told her. 'I work all over and I flew in the day we drove here. We met in Glasgow.' A fragment of truth remained amidst the sea of ever-growing lies.

'Oh dear, it'll take your body time to adjust. Go and sit in the living room, it's warmer. Just mind the dogs, they'll jump all over you. In fact, I'll let them out, that'll keep them busy.'

Taylor followed her along the hall; the carpet was lovely and soft on her bare feet after the cold lino in the kitchen. She held back as Fenella calmed the dogs and pulled the sliding door wide to let them out. A gush of chilled air filled the room before Fenella slammed it shut. 'They can potter for a bit. I'll walk them later. Oh, you look frozen. Hang on.'

She left the room and Taylor curled into the squashy sofa, cradling her mug. Everything was so surreal. Her eyes half closed, but when she opened them again Fenella had come in and was holding a fleece blanket and a hot water bottle in a furry case. 'This'll help you keep warm for a bit.

I'll make some breakfast and coffee. Would you like anything?'

'I'm ok, it's a bit early for me.'

'Yes. No problem. Per's getting ready for work. I always get up with him, just from habit. I only work part-time these days, and I'm off today, thank goodness. I'm getting too old for classroom capers.'

'Don't you enjoy teaching?'

'I do mostly, though some days, I feel more like a negotiator for the UN, the number of times I have to keep the peace.'

A few moments after she'd left the room, the door opened a fraction and Per Hansen put his head round. 'Good morning, and goodbye,' he said. 'I hope you enjoy your day and see some more of the island. I'll catch up with you and Magnus later.'

'Oh, sure.' Taylor gave him a little wave. As he closed the door, she heard him speak in the corridor and Magnus's low voice answered. He came in, yawning and stretching.

'There you are. I wondered what happened to you.'

'I woke up and couldn't get back to sleep.'

'Really?' He flopped down beside her. 'I went out like a light.'

'Magnus.' She sat up, placing her mug on a side table. 'I remembered something.'

'What?' He lounged back, flipping his head to the side. 'That you're the most beautiful girl this side of the Atlantic?'

Taylor opened her mouth to reply as Fenella walked in. Magnus coughed into his arm to hide a laugh and Taylor threw him a dirty glance. Fenella smiled serenely as she carried a plate and mug to the dining table by the window and sat down. 'So, you're driving to Carsaig today,' she said.

'Yup,' replied Magnus.

'Oh, you'll love it down there, Taylor,' said Fenella. 'Stunning place. The road can be a bit dodgy at times, but Carl and Robyn have the most beautiful cottage.'

'Yes, it's very nice,' said a shrill voice from the door. Jean hobbled in. 'I think Magnus fancied it himself last year, didn't you? When you were dating that other one.'

'No, I didn't.' Magnus raked his fingers through his hair. 'Julie fancied it, but not me. I'm glad Carl got it.'

'About time,' said Jean. 'He lived in a shed before that.'

'Did he?' said Taylor.

'Sit down, Jean,' said Fenella. 'It wasn't a shed, it was a lovely log cabin.'

'Lovely?' said Jean. 'I've seen nicer dog kennels.'

Magnus winked at Taylor. 'I'm going to shower. We can head down early, there's lots to do apparently, though god knows what. I hope they haven't left anything important this late.'

'You have to try on your kilt suit,' said Fenella, 'in case it needs adjusting.'

'I don't see why it would. I haven't changed height or weight in the last few months.' He got to his feet. Taylor sat for a moment after he'd gone, then got up.

'I just remembered something.' She hurried out and opened the bedroom door. His naked back filled her vision.

He grabbed a towel and spun around. 'Shit,' he said. 'I thought you were Jean.'

Taylor laughed. 'Does she often walk in on you when you're dressing?'

'Don't joke. I wouldn't put anything past her.'

'Listen, there's a major problem.'

'What?'

'I don't have anything to wear to the wedding, and I don't suppose there are any women's partywear stores on the island.'

'No.'

'Well, what should I do? I can't ask to borrow a dress from your mom because why would I come to a wedding without bringing one?'

Magnus folded his arms and cocked his head. 'Would you borrow one from my mum anyway?'

'Why not?' *Oh, of course!* Skylar wouldn't borrow clothes from anyone, and definitely not a middle-aged woman.

'You've had some kind of bonkers personality transplant,' said Magnus. 'I didn't think you'd travel anywhere without at least six party dresses… per day. What's going on? This is just a friends and family affair. If you have any kind of dress, it'll be fine. You don't need to go all out on the red carpet, they won't mind, really.'

Taylor compressed her lips, holding in her breath, her words, and her panic. After slowly exhaling, she nodded. 'Yeah, the thing is, I didn't bring anything like that. This is an escape. A week without my Hollywood twin.' Her heart raced as she said the words, though Magnus wouldn't get the significance. 'This week I'm Taylor, and I want nothing to do with Skylar. So, I don't have any dresses.'

Shaking his head, Magnus looked around. 'You sound like you have split-personality disorder, but I get what you mean. Ok… How about we tell my mum you must have forgotten to pick up your dress bag at one of the airports and see what she comes up with. Honestly, my mum has a solution for everything.'

'Ok, ok.' Taylor rubbed her temple. 'Yes. Let's do that.'

Just as Magnus predicted, Fenella came up with not one solution but several, and all of them without even a hint of panic. 'I can think of at least three lovely ladies on the island who are about your size and will probably have something they can loan you. Or we could take a trip over to the mainland, there are shops in Oban where we could get something. Leave it with me. I'll call Robyn first. She's the bride, so I don't want to stress her out. I think you're about the same height. If she has something, you can always pick it up when you're there today.'

The tension gone from her shoulders, Taylor jumped in the car, and Magnus put his foot down. 'You're not on the runway,' she said, clinging to the handle above the passenger door.

'I like to put in a bit of speed here, it's the only straight and flat bit on the island.' They rounded a bend and the road twisted away into the distance. 'See what I mean? It'll be a crawl for the next hour. You may as well sleep.'

'No way. This might be my only trip to Scotland, I want to remember it.'

'Well, good morning Ladies and… Lady.' Magnus glanced at her and continued in a smooth voice. 'Sit back and enjoy your flight to Carsaig. I'm your pilot, Magnus Hansen, and conditions for today's journey look good. I don't envisage any problems, so—'

'Oh, shut up.' Taylor slapped his thigh and he burst out laughing.

The drive through the island was like a private tour, with Magnus relating the stories and passing on his first-hand memories. Taylor would have been happy with the scenery but his delight and energy gave her an added buzz. With clear cold weather, the sea views and rocky glens filled her with ideas for films. Not ones Skylar would ever star in; she baulked at period drama. But Taylor could see historicals set here, with dashing highlanders and island girls.

'Is there anything I need to know about your brother before we arrive?'

'Not really,' said Magnus.

Taylor didn't push the question. Even a real girlfriend couldn't be expected to know everything about everyone. She just hoped they hadn't overlooked anything blatant.

The road to the cottage was as narrow and twisty as Fenella had described. Taylor could drive, but this road scared the shit out of her. 'Seriously, what do you do if something comes the other way?'

'Find a passing place,' said Magnus.

'And if there isn't one?'

'Someone has to reverse.'

Taylor massaged her temples. 'I don't think I could take the pressure. Who can reverse that far on twisty roads like this?'

'Me.' Magnus laughed.

'Yeah, but not all of us are trained pilots. I guess that's why you took up that career.'

'I always enjoyed navigating, so maybe. Originally, I wanted to work on ships, but I got a flying lesson for my birthday one year and that changed everything. I don't think my parents expected the gift to have such a dramatic effect on my choice of career.'

'And they didn't object to it?'

'No. I'm not sure they thought I was serious at first, but when they realised I was, they were great about it. It isn't the easiest career to get into so I was glad to have their support.'

'Wow,' said Taylor, 'that must be a great feeling.'

'Surely you know how it feels. Your parents must have supported you. They're in the business, aren't they?'

'Oh… Yes, sure.'

'Or didn't they want you to follow in their footsteps?'

'Yes, but…' Taylor sank her teeth into her lower lip. Oh yes! Her parents had wanted both her and Skylar to follow them into acting, perhaps even rival the Olsen twins, but Taylor had fallen off the rails. She'd been the better actress but she suffered from nerves. When the big break came, she'd decided to go for it and brave Skylar's fury. But before she could accept, the producer changed his mind. Skylar got the role. Taylor couldn't prove it but she was convinced Skylar had got her drunk then masqueraded as her. She'd gone to the producer under a false pretence, saying she was too nervous to do the role. Skylar denied it. All Taylor remembered was waking with an aching head. But Skylar insisted Taylor had done the talking herself. Her parents started to doubt her sanity and she'd turned to drugs for comfort. 'It's always hard to live up to parental expectations, especially when they're so big in the biz in their own right.'

Magnus pulled a quizzical expression. 'I don't know anything about them. I guess they're not as famous over here.'

You should google them. The words teetered on the edge of Taylor's tongue and almost fell out. She stopped just in time. No way did she want that. If he googled them, he'd see their bio and possibly discover they had two daughters, one of whom was named Taylor! Why had she told him her real name? That was a question she knew the answer to. When they were close, that was the name she wanted to hear Magnus call out, not something fake, and definitely not Skylar.

Taylor devoted the rest of the journey to filling in Magnus on her parents' filmography, TV credits and life, in the hope of diverting him from a google search. As they pulled up the drive beside a long, low seashore with spindly, tangled winter trees alongside it, Taylor wondered if she should tell him the truth. But would that make things better? What if he banished her and she was stuck out here in the wild? Friendless and lost. He parked the car beside the gorgeous little seaside cottage. This was the stuff of dreams, a single-storey building with a stunning timber extension, looking out over a perfect view. Taylor exited the car and gaped around, sucking in the sea air and adding the view to her memories.

'Come on, darling.' Magnus smiled, taking Taylor's hand and leading her to the door. 'Let's go and meet the lovebirds.'

'And they can meet the lovebugs.'

His blue eyes twinkled as he considered her. 'Are you in love?'

The door swung open before Taylor could reply, revealing a broad-shouldered man with a mass of sandy curls tucked behind his ears. Carl, the third brother; the resemblance in the eyes and the smile was uncanny.

'Hey!' The two brothers clapped each other on the shoulders.

'Not getting a haircut for the wedding?' asked Magnus.

'Robyn likes it,' said Carl.

'Verging on TMI,' said Magnus.

Carl glanced at Taylor. 'Hi.' He beamed.

'This is Taylor,' said Magnus. 'Let me bring her into the light so you can see how beautiful she is.'

'Seriously?' said Taylor.

Carl laughed. 'Yeah, he's serious. We know how shameless he is.'

'Thank you,' said Magnus. 'And you're right, I'm not ashamed of how beautiful Taylor is.'

Carl chuckled and stepped aside, ushering them out of the entrance hall and into a stunning open-plan living area. Taylor drank in the vision of the long rambling garden stretching down a modest slope to the sea. A boat moored at a jetty glinted in the early spring sunlight. The whole thing looked straight off a postcard. Her mouth fell open.

'And Taylor…' Magnus coughed and she turned around. Magnus was mid introductions and she hadn't heard a thing.

'Sorry, I was so entranced by the view, I forgot myself.'

'Well, you met Jakob and Livvi yesterday.'

They were together in the living area with little Polly and an elegant woman, tall and slim with a sheet of long ice-blonde hair.

'And this is Robyn, the beautiful bride-to-be.'

'Nice to meet you,' said Taylor.

'And you,' said Robyn. 'Fenella phoned and said you'd had a bit of a dress disaster.'

'Yes, totally ridiculous of me. I mean to come to a wedding and not actually pick up my dress.' She raised her palms upward.

'You did have a long way to come. It must have been exhausting,' said Robyn. 'And we appreciate you making the effort.'

'Yeah, we don't want Magnus to be left on the shelf,' said Carl.

'Shut up. It was you for long enough.'

'Why don't we let them fight it out,' said Robyn. 'I'll show you some dresses I have. I laid out a couple. If you don't like them, it's ok, but you can try them on.'

'Great,' said Taylor, determined whatever Robyn had, she'd accept. She wasn't Skylar Rousse, and she was happy to beg, steal and borrow when necessary.

Chapter Twelve

Magnus

'So, where did you meet her?' asked Carl as soon as Taylor and Robyn had left the room.

Magnus relayed their part-true story.

'That's cute,' said Livvi. 'Falling for someone you literally fell over.'

'Yeah,' said Magnus, adjusting his shirt collar.

'She seems nice,' said Carl, 'but after Julie, even a banshee would seem friendly.'

'Yeah, yeah,' said Magnus. 'I know you didn't like her, but she had her moments.'

'Now it's your turn for TMI. None of us want to know.'

Smirking, Magnus turned away. Jakob stood near the glass doors, holding Polly's hand and letting her lead him around.

'Taylor reminds me of someone,' said Livvi. 'I think it's someone I was at school with. I just can't put my finger on it.'

Magnus hoped she hadn't grown up watching Skylar's shows.

The door opened and Taylor returned wearing a beautifully understated dark purple dress.

'Gorgeous,' said Magnus and she beamed.

'It's a miracle, Robyn's shoes fit me too.'

'Great,' said Magnus. 'You're sorted. Is it my turn now?'

'Sure, let's get you togged up,' said Carl.

'What? You're going to dress me? Er, no thanks.'

'No way,' said Carl. 'But I laid the clothes out in the new guest bedroom at the end of the corridor. I'm sure you can get into them yourself.'

'I'll try my best.'

'I should change back too,' said Taylor. With a rustle of satin, she led the way into the hall.

'Keep it on,' he said. 'Let's see how we look together.' Pushing open the door at the end of the corridor, he let Taylor go in first.

'Oh, this is a neat room,' said Taylor.

'Yeah, maybe we should have stayed here.'

'No, I like your mom's place. It's so homely and warm.' Taylor swished around, admiring herself in the long mirror.

'I feel a bit warm right now,' said Magnus, stepping towards her and sweeping her into a kiss. Even the glitz didn't return her to brazen Skylar. She was all Taylor. Being at liberty to kiss her whenever he liked, as long as she was into it, was a luxury he didn't want to waste. The ardent pressure of her lips and her fingers sliding through his hair told him she was good. He guided her back towards the door and hallelujah! He grappled with a knob below the handle. What a considerate and sensible brother installing locks. Magnus clicked it around without breaking the kiss, grinning through it as Taylor started on his buttons. 'Leave them,' he said, stepping back and hauling off his shirt.

'What about the window?'

'Shut the curtains. I don't want to risk my sisters-in-law walking past and seeing me undressing.'

'Is that what you're doing?' Taylor smiled, sweeping the curtains across the window.

'For starters. Let's hope the walls here are thicker than the ones back home because I don't feel like holding anything back.'

'Me neither. I really want you.'

She wrapped her arms around his neck and he rolled up her dress, pulling her close. Her fingers plunged into his hair and her lips locked with his. Knowing they didn't have much time before someone came looking doubled the tension. He pulled his wallet from his back pocket.

'Are you going to pay me?' asked Taylor.

'No, I'm getting covered.'

Taylor watched everything with wide eyes. For all her Hollywood experience, she had an unexpected innocence about her. Magnus wouldn't put it past her draconian father to have censored her love life. He turned her around so her back was to him and he gently pulled down her dress, touching her softly and kissing her neck. 'You really are gorgeous,' he whispered in her ear.

'Can I look at you?' Her voice echoed with uncertainty.

'Sure.' He released her and stepped round to face her. 'Here I am.'

She stroked a curl of his hair behind his ear. 'Handsome Hansen.'

He took her hand and held it tight. 'Magnus will do.' Resuming their kiss, he led her to the bed and sat her down. 'This will have to be quick.'

'I'm ready.'

He grinned and moved in slowly. She arched against him, closing her eyes. 'Is this ok?' he whispered.

'Yes,' she murmured, wiggling a little. He let her find her place with a dreamy smile on her lips.

'Good,' he whispered in her ear as they rocked together. 'You're good. Very good.' He was going to lose it soon. 'Good for me.'

She whimpered as he plied his attention on all her sensitive spots, her gaze slipping out of focus. He snaked his hands around her, supporting her back as she tripped out. He couldn't hold on much longer. Nope. Not one more second. He groaned, burying his head in her neck and let go, losing his mind to the waking world.

After a few moments locked together, Magnus rolled to the side and threw back his head. 'Short, but oh so damned sweet.' Taylor nuzzled in beside him and he put his arms around her. She melted into him, dress and hair rumpled, skimming his over-sensitive neck with kisses. 'Taylor, no. No more. It's too soon. And we can't anyway. Jesus. They'll be wondering what the hell we're doing.'

'I know, but I like you,' Taylor muttered into his ear, making him twitch.

'Let's save it for later.' With an effort, he pushed up into a sitting position. Taylor didn't budge. 'Thank Christ there's an en-suite.' He made his way to it, gave himself a quick wash and a towel dry before returning to the room and pulling on the wedding kilt suit. Taylor swapped places, taking her turn in the bathroom. When she emerged, Magnus was fully dressed, and she'd straightened herself out. 'Don't we look like quite the pair?'

'You're so hot it that kilt. Totally hot. I want to have you all over again.'

'Save that thought. Go and throw cold water on your face. You can have me in the kilt on the wedding night and do whatever you want with me.' He adjusted his tie in the long mirror.

'Promises, promises.'

'I mean it. Now, get back to the other room and change. I'll parade myself for the others.'

'What will you tell them?'

'I'll think of something.' He gave her a quick squeeze on the shoulder before making his way back to the living area. As he stepped in, the collective stare greeted him. 'So, how's this?'

'Neat,' said Livvi.

'Does it fit ok?' asked Carl.

'I think so.' Magnus tugged the edges of the black formal jacket.

'And there wasn't a problem?' said Carl. 'You were ages.'

'Sorry, Taylor came along. We were posing.'

'Posing?' Carl coughed onto the back of his hand and muttered aside to Robyn, 'Is that what we're calling it these days?'

She nudged him to be quiet.

Livvi laughed. 'You should have come in here for the show, we could have taken pictures.'

Magnus straightened his tie. 'Yeah, I didn't think about that.' A laugh almost burst out. Cameras and audiences were the last thing required for what had just occurred.

After they'd decided he looked fine and the kilt fitted, Magnus changed back into his normal clothes. Quickly checking his reflection, he shook his head. 'Seedy git, so I am.'

Had they guessed the truth? How crass did they think he was, having a quickie with his girlfriend at any opportunity? But it was far worse than they could know. Taylor was a woman he'd picked up a few days ago. Sure, he'd known her before, but hardly. They'd shared one Hollywood kiss he'd been almost too drunk to remember and now he was parading her as his girlfriend. This was a new depth even for him. If his brothers knew. *Jeez. Great example, Magnus.* A frigging teenager would behave better.

Chapter Thirteen

Taylor

Taylor smoothed the dress one last time, hoping she hadn't irrevocably crushed it. Her cheeks flushed pink with friction burns from grazing against Magnus's stubble and the memory of what they'd just done. She trailed her fingers across her pink lips, swollen and tender from the kissing.

That kind of quick experience wasn't unknown to her. What was completely new was a man who cared, who considered her needs and showered her with attention like she was someone worth having.

She tossed off the dress and turned in the mirror, seeing herself anew. Not a soulless shell, but someone worthy. Her skinny jeans and slim-fit top transformed her into Taylor again, but valued Taylor. Not someone to be hidden. Magnus was a few doors away, waiting for her. Wanting her. *No.* Wanting Skylar. Her expression dropped as she pulled on her hoody. Would he feel the same if he knew who she really was? Was he doing this because he wanted to notch up a Hollywood movie star as well as have a date for the wedding? This was just for a week anyway. She had to quit getting so involved. Act. Just act. Pretend like it didn't matter and go through the motions, but whichever way she stacked it, her heart was too full to let go.

The door to the living area opened silently. Taylor slipped in and sidled up to Magnus as he chatted with his brothers. Casually, he slid his arm around her shoulder, gently rubbing her with his thumb.

'Would you like to go for a sail?' he asked.

'Now?'

'Yeah, Carl's cool to take the boat out. She's a beauty. I haven't been on her yet.'

'Well, sure.'

Taylor borrowed a warm coat from Robyn and they trooped towards the jetty. The white cabin cruiser gleamed ahead. A tarp flapped in the light breeze and water slapped its hull. Magnus clutched Taylor's hand as they climbed aboard.

'Are you driving?' she asked.

'If Robyn and Carl let me have a go, I wouldn't mind taking the helm.' He darted up the stairs after his youngest brother, leaving Taylor alone until Livvi and Jakob climbed aboard. Jakob clung to Polly, keeping her close and only passing her to Livvi when his feet were firmly on deck.

The engine fired up and water churned at the stern. Livvi chatted quietly to Polly about what was happening. Taylor rested her back on the rails, watching the view on the far side and keeping an eye on the cabin. Magnus popped his head out, smiling and throwing her a half wave. She took the wave to mean he'd be down in a minute after he'd overseen the 'take-off'. This must be tough for him having to sit out the action. The engine noise increased and Magnus hopped down the steep stair.

His jacket was off and he rolled up his sleeves, jumped off the boat and untied a rope. Taylor couldn't drag her gaze from him as he leapt back on board, coiling the rope with his muscular forearms.

'Hey.' He scooted along and rested beside her, leaning his elbows back. 'This is the life.'

'Aren't you frozen?'

'You Californians have no bottle,' he said.

'Oh yeah?' Taylor unbuttoned the borrowed coat, slipped it off, and dropped it on the bench.

'Eh, what are you doing?' whispered Magnus. 'Is this appropriate? We have children present.'

Taylor folded her arms. 'I'm showing you some Californian bottle.' The wind caught her and she shuddered.

'Oh, yeah,' said Magnus. 'Very convincing.'

'Yeah, actually.' She grabbed the jacket. 'There's no way.' Across the deck, Livvi smirked and Jakob shook his head. 'Does anyone ever beat him at anything?' Taylor asked them.

'No,' said Jakob. 'And if you do, he'll say you cheated.'

'Rubbish,' said Magnus and Jakob cocked his head. 'Ok, maybe partially true.'

Taylor pinged his arm. 'You are a bad boy.'

'Come see this,' he said. 'You can get up front here if you still want to indulge your Kate Winslet fantasies.'

She slipped around the deck after him until they reached the triangular area at the prow. Wind buffeted her cheeks and tangled her hair; the long coat flapped around her. 'Oh, my god, it's so cold.'

Magnus turned to her and his lip curled into a wolf-like grin. 'I'll keep you warm.' He stepped back and wrapped his arm around her. 'I think it's my lot in life, keep Taylor warm.'

Her teeth chattered together. 'Just wait until we're in California. It'll be my job to cool you down.' Their eyes met. It was crazy. They weren't going to California. In a few days, they'd never see each other again. Magnus would walk away, thinking he'd had a secret affair with a movie star while Taylor would… She bit her lip, still in an eye-lock with Magnus. What would she do? Where did she go from here? How did she coax her heart into forgetting this and throwing it into the memory pile?

'Nice touch,' he whispered, stroking his thumb over her cheek and melting her. 'You're a bit too believable.' He ducked forward and kissed her cheek.

Once she'd been a talented actress, but none of this was an act anymore. Everything she felt was genuine. It made keeping up the pretence easy, but the fall would crush her unless… Was it possible? Was there the tiniest, dimmest flicker of hope? What if she fessed up and came clean? Maybe they could keep going, be a real couple?

'Magnus.' She slipped her fingers around his neck. 'Do you think—'

'Hey, Magnus!' Carl shouted from above, drawing back as he saw them. 'Sorry, I didn't mean to interrupt.'

Magnus shrugged it off. 'What do you want?'

'I thought you might like a shot up here.'

'Sure.' He winked at Taylor. 'Come on, darling. Let's take control.'

At the top of the ladder-like stair, Taylor entered the cabin and glanced at the plush seating and table area. Skylar might even approve of this, though she'd want it all to herself.

'This is so neat,' said Taylor, sitting at the table while Magnus took over the steering. 'Can you sleep on it?'

'Yeah,' said Carl. 'It has a bedroom below deck. We hope to travel in it this summer.'

'It's perfect. I think I want one.'

'Magnus will be pleased to hear that. Won't you?' He turned to his brother. 'You've found yourself a girl who likes sailing.'

'Ha, yeah.' He didn't turn around but raked his hand through his hair.

What was he thinking? Maybe wondering how to tell his family in a few weeks that they'd split. He hadn't found a girl who liked sailing. He hadn't found a girl at all, not for real. Taylor smiled at Carl. 'I'd love to try it.' If he was willing to try, she was.

She took out her phone and snapped photos of the rocky cliffs and scenery as they sailed by. Hundreds of notifications sat on her messenger apps. She dismissed several missed calls and checked it was on silent. Whatever anyone wanted could wait. She guessed the gist. Where was she? When was she coming back and had she dared cause trouble? Well, she'd impersonated Skylar again, but this time it wouldn't harm her sister. Just herself.

Magnus sat at the helm, his shoulders back and his chest out. Taylor sidled in behind and leaned over his shoulder so her cheek pressed on his. 'Hey,' he said, raising his hand to cup her face. 'Are you enjoying this?'

'It's great.' She held out her phone. 'Let's get a selfie.'

Magnus leaned in and smiled. One corner of his mouth raised higher than the other. Taylor could see this picture having a devastating effect on her in the future. Already that smile could make her come undone and when he was nothing more than an image on her phone… What then? She turned her head and pressed her lips to his cheeks. Desperate words wanted to come out, but she didn't dare say them.

Drizzly rain rolled in as the afternoon progressed and they sat around the table in the cabin, except for Jakob, who stayed outside, wrapped up to the nines, walking up and down with little Polly as she got sleepier and sleepier on his shoulder.

'He's great, isn't he?' said Taylor. 'He's so patient.'

'He's the best,' Livvi said, peering out and smiling. 'I can't imagine a better dad for my children.'

'Are you having another one?' asked Carl.

'Someday, I hope so,' Livvi replied.

Taylor glanced at Magnus still at the helm. He seemed resolute in looking forward and not taking part in their conversation. Jakob signalled to Livvi and she opened the door. He nipped up the stairs and flopped onto a seat, Polly fast asleep zipped into his jacket, resting her head on the crook of his neck – too adorable for words. Taylor started to understand how difficult this trip would have been for Magnus to make alone. She got to her feet and moved in behind him again, slipping both her arms around his neck and linking them at his chest. 'You're awesome,' she whispered in his ear, rubbing her cheek against his stubble.

'What's brought this on?'

'I just wanted you to know.'

'Thanks.'

She stayed stooped over, holding onto him until they were back at the jetty. 'Have you taken over driving completely?'

'Yeah. I think Carl wants to chill.'

Taylor let go as Magnus manoeuvred the boat into place. Carl leapt out and tied her up.

As Fenella was expecting them home for dinner, Taylor and Magnus said their farewells. Taylor wanted to talk to Magnus all the way home and words tumbled around her head, but none came out. He turned on some gentle music and Taylor's eyelids grew heavy. Her forehead touched the window's cool glass and the exhaustion from the past few days finally caught her.

Chapter Fourteen

Magnus

It seemed a shame to wake her. Magnus tapped the steering wheel, looking between the bungalow and Taylor. If he could carry her as gently and carefully as Jakob had done with little Polly, he would. But even with her Hollywood figure, he'd never get her out without waking her.

'Hey.' He ran the back of his hand down her cheek. 'Taylor.'

She stirred, closing her mouth and blinking slowly.

'We're back,' he said.

'Oh, god.' She sat up and pressed her fingers to her forehead. 'I didn't mean to fall asleep.'

'It's ok, you're allowed to.'

'I know. I just… Oh, I'm sorry. I wanted to chat.'

'You needed the rest more.' He stroked her cheek again. 'Are you ok to go in or do you want to sit for a minute?'

'I'm ok.' She yawned. 'Would you listen to me? I think it must have been the sea air. What a great day. Your family are so cute. I love being part of this.'

'Do you? Isn't all this beneath you?'

'Not at all. I swear.'

Magnus flipped her a sceptical look, then undid his seatbelt. He hopped to the far side and helped her out; she wobbled. As they strolled to the bungalow door, he slung his arm around her shoulder. 'This is a crazy thing we're doing, but if we take out the fake stuff, I do like you being here with me.'

Her eyebrows peaked in the middle and the corner of her lips turned up. 'Thank you.'

'On a human level, I want you to know that.'

'I like you too.' She leaned in. 'And Magnus—'

He clasped her face and kissed her before she could say anything else. Something was brewing and he wasn't ready for it. He wanted to cling to this moment. Taking it long and slow, the way he liked best, he intensified the friction with teasing flicks of his tongue, peppering her lips, then sliding in to taste perfection.

The bungalow door clicked. 'Oh, there you are, sorry,' said Fenella

Magnus broke off and stared into the middle distance before turning to his mum. 'Hi, Mum,' he said.

'Hey,' said Taylor, glancing at her feet and brushing her palm on her thigh.

'Come in, it's so cold out here.' As they passed, Fenella said to Taylor, 'Sorry to butt in like that.'

'It's ok,' said Taylor, her cheeks pink and flushed.

'No, Mum, it isn't,' said Magnus.

'How was I to know what you were up to? I didn't want you getting cold.'

I was quite warm enough. He clamped his mouth shut.

'I think you're an amazing mom and you've raised three great sons,' said Taylor.

'Aww, thank you.' Fenella opened her arms and hugged her. Magnus smiled as he took off his jacket and hung it inside the hall cupboard.

A long evening, which Magnus would have found tedious on his own, seemed to delight Taylor. She beamed, soaking up the family chat and joining in with the stories, though not telling any of her own. It was easy to forget none of this was real.

With a huge grin, she allowed Fenella to fix her a bath. 'I have these wonderful bath bombs,' said Fenella. 'Choose whichever one you like. I get them from the island soap shop and they're truly amazing.' Winking at Magnus, Taylor disappeared into the bathroom and Fenella said, 'Take your time, just relax. Make the most of your break.' She emerged, drying her hands, and closed the door. 'Are you going in with her?' she asked Magnus.

'No, Mum,' he said defensively.

Fenella chuckled and patted him on the arm. 'Come and get a cuppa.' Bypassing the living room, Magnus glimpsed his father watching the TV and Aunt Jean lost behind a ball of wool, knitting pins clacking manically together.

'Taylor's a lovely girl,' said Fenella as they reached the kitchen and she set the kettle to boil.

'Yeah, isn't she?'

'She told me about her family yesterday.'

'Did she?' Magnus shuffled his feet. Had she fabricated some story to tug at Fenella's heartstrings? 'What did she say?'

Fenella opened the cupboard and pulled out two mugs. 'About her parents being public figures in America and how she grew up in the spotlight. I think it's been hard for her, she's always been in their shadow. And I think her sister is big in the dance world. Taylor's been pushed out of sight and had very little confidence until recently. It's been a steep learning curve. She's still young.'

'I know, and don't start getting at me about that.' He frowned at the half-truths blending with Taylor's fiction and wished he could lessen Fenella's sympathy without sounding callous.

'I don't mind. Age is just a number, as Jean keeps reminding me. But it does worry me.'

'Why? I'm not taking advantage of her.' No. This had been her idea and everything they'd done was perfectly consensual.

'I'm glad to hear it. I didn't raise my boys to behave like that, but she's young enough to be impressionable. Your relationship has worked well for her. She told me…' Fenella lowered her voice '… she's never felt so strongly about anyone. And I can see how much she means to you. I'd hate for her to get hurt.'

Magnus shook his head and leant back on the work surface. 'Look, she's a bigger girl than you think.' *Shit, double shit and bloody hell.* His mum had fallen hook, line and sinker for the act. He'd have to leave it several months before he dropped the 'we've split up' bomb. Otherwise, she'd think he was a cold-hearted monster who'd dumped a woman who truly loved him. Of course, when this woman was a seasoned actress, she could pull off that trick without any bother.

Fenella put her hands on her hips. 'Magnus.' Her voice was stern. 'Why do you do that?'

'Do what?'

'Act as if nothing will come of it. You were the same with Julie, and in some ways that turned out for the best. She has a mean streak and she can be difficult. But it was your lack of commitment that drove her away.'

Magnus poured himself a cup of tea. 'Look, she wanted impossible things from me. She's committed to living here; I'm not and I never was. She wanted to house hunt with a view to me settling back here, but that wasn't what I wanted. Sometimes, she changed it to wanting a holiday house, but that was to appease me. She had no intention of leaving and I had no intention of giving up my job. It wasn't because of commitment fears.'

'Wasn't it?' Fenella looked askance.

'Even if it was, you said it yourself, I was right in that instance.'

'Well, I hope you'll at least give Taylor a chance. I'd hate to think she's put in all this effort only for you to dump her in a few months.'

'What effort are we talking about?' He frowned. Was it that obvious she was putting on a show?

'She's flown all the way from America to share your brother's wedding with you. That's a pretty grand gesture and it tells me she cares a lot about you.'

'Hmm, yeah.' He cradled his mug, not looking at his mum.

'It's plain to see, Magnus. Maybe this time, instead of thinking you're in it for the short term, why not flip your mindset and imagine what things might be like long term. If you would let them.'

'Yeah, we'll see.'

'Promise me you'll try, for both your sakes.'

He nodded but didn't promise. How could he? Because he and Taylor were as incompatible as ever. Come the end of the week, she'd be back in Hollywood, starring in films, and Magnus Hansen, the man from the island, would be a tiny dot in the multi-coloured painting that was the life of Skylar Rousse.

Had Taylor fallen asleep in the bath? Ages passed. Magnus got himself ready for bed and brushed his teeth in the tiny cloakroom near the door, using his travel toothbrush.

As he passed the bathroom door, he heard water splashing and a thud as feet hit the floor. He returned to his room and switched on the bedside light before perching on the edge of the bed, rubbing the soft hairs on his thighs. He grabbed the control for the electric blanket and lowered it a notch. The heat was too much.

The door opened with a slight creak and Taylor slipped in wearing her skimpy nightwear.

'What kept you?' he said. 'Did you fall asleep?'

'No. I was just thinking.'

'Oh.' He ran his hand over his forehead. 'Can I turn off the blanket? It's too hot for me.'

'Sure.' She deposited her clothes and hopped into the bed. 'I thought it was you who was too hot for me.'

'Yeah. Funny.' He clicked off the blanket and shuffled under the covers. 'But I will keep you warm if you like.'

'Ok. But I might start thinking you only love me for my body.'

'Who said I loved you at all?'

'Well, you're my boyfriend, so you're supposed to at least pretend, aren't you?'

Leaning out the bed, he turned off the light, rolled over and found Taylor. She nuzzled in close. 'Yeah, I guess.'

'How about we tell each other some things we love about each other…' Taylor ran her fingertips along his cheekbone.

'But—'

'Shh. Let me start. I love your hair and how soft it is on top.' Her fingertips slipped into his curls. 'And I love your eyes, they're so bright. And I love your arms.'

'My arms?' He huffed but tightened his grip.

'Because they're strong, and I love the way they hold me and make me feel safe.'

'Right.' What was she doing? This was like some kind of kinky talk, but lust wasn't the only thing rushing through his veins. Whatever it was, it strengthened him.

'And I love your voice; your Scottish accent is so charming. And your laugh, and your wit. I love your family and the way you value them and respect them.'

'Ok, Taylor.' He stroked her hair and kissed her forehead. 'You're making me blush. This is all lovely but—'

'Shh. Don't spoil it. I love the way you make me feel like me. I love how you kiss me and how you make love.'

'Taylor—'

'I mean it.' She slipped her fingers under his shirt and ran them over his back. 'Now, it's your turn.' Magnus closed his eyes. 'Tell me,' she whispered.

'This is just you acting, right?'

'Tell me.'

'I love…' The word choked him for a second. 'I love… how we share the same taste in music.'

Her laugh fell as a breath on his neck and he twitched.

'And I love it when we sing together; it's exhilarating. I love your talent. Not just the singing but the way you're making all this feel a lot more real than it should.' Why was he playing along? Now he'd started he couldn't stop. He gently stroked her back as he whispered, 'I love how wanted you make me feel, and how you're doing this not just for your own benefit but also for mine. It's helping me so much. I love how natural you are. None of this feels forced, and the way you've adapted to everything here is amazing.'

Taylor sniffed and Magnus smoothed his hands over her face before anchoring his fingers in her hair.

'Taylor, what is it?' The damp edges of her eyes betrayed her.

'I don't want this week to end. I can see it being the best and worst week of my life.'

'Let's just ride it out and see what happens.'

'But what happens after that?'

'I don't know, Taylor.' He placed another lingering kiss on her forehead. 'I guess you go back to Hollywood and I go back to the air.'

'Yeah, that's what I thought.'

Well, that was the deal after all, wasn't it?

Chapter Fifteen

Taylor

Taylor woke early, dazed by the memory of the words that had passed between her and Magnus. Acting or not, those words had a powerful impact on her soul. She'd discovered what being loved felt like. Pale yellow light crept through the slight crack in the curtain, casting a dim glow around the room. Where was Magnus? Had she scared him off?

She sat up. No. Had she blown it completely? Somewhere in the house came the sound of a toilet flushing and moments later the door creaked open.

'There you are,' she said, relief washing over her.

'Bathroom break,' he muttered, rubbing his eyes. 'That's all.'

'Actually…' Taylor, suddenly aware of her own need, leapt up.

'Are you ok?' he asked.

'Bursting.'

The bed was blissfully warm when she returned. And super hot when Magnus rolled closer. 'Are you naked?' she whispered, her hands finding the answer before he spoke.

'And ready,' he said, kissing her. 'Let's risk it.'

'Are you sure?'

'After your talk last night, I hardly slept.'

'I meant it.' With every fragment of her soul.

He ran his finger over his cheek. 'I'm not so good at talking about stuff like that. Let me show you.'

His words were good enough for her but she wasn't going to pass up an opportunity. She sat up and pulled off her top. 'Ok.'

With a broad grin, he lowered her to the mattress the moment she was in the bed and sealed his mouth on hers. She kissed him with more force than she intended. Her hips ground against him, the soft fabric of her pyjama shorts adding friction, making her ache. Magnus rolled his palms over her, softly but powerfully. Taylor arched into him as his lips found her sensitive spots and drowned them in his attention. When she was satisfied and drunk on pleasure, Magnus positioned himself between her thighs, and Taylor let out a sigh as they became one again, as they were meant to be.

'Is this ok?'

She loved the way he always asked. No other man had ever cared. 'Sure,' she replied. She'd always be ok when they were together – when he was hers and no one else's.

She brought her hands to his chest, down his abs and slipped them under his arms, digging her nails into his back and savouring every second. The mattress was wonderfully soft and not at all creaky.

Taylor's eyelids dropped as she concentrated on the charge building inside. Magnus's heavy breathing filled the room and she guessed he was trying not to make a sound.

'Jesus, Taylor,' he whisper-growled in her ear.

Her eyes rolled back and she let go, holding back nothing except the cry she wanted to let rip. She gripped his shoulders and together they held their breath until everything calmed. He flopped onto her, panting.

As he rolled over, he took her with him. She rested her cheek on his warm shoulder and her fingers touched his skin above his racing heart. All the week's happiness flowed through her: the family love, the warmth, the acceptance and this. A tear pricked and she rubbed against his neck to push it away.

'Holy mother,' whispered Magnus. 'We should get an Oscar for this.' His chest rose and fell. Taylor moved with it. 'The best silent performance for a century.'

'Yeah,' said Taylor, tracing a circle on his pecs and making him twitch. She let out a faint moan and Magnus gently rolled his palm over her back, causing her to melt into a pool of perfect nothingness. The warmth sent her into a stupor and she closed her eyes, drifting off for an unknown length of time and only waking when the covers moved above her. Magnus was up and tucking her in.

'You sleep for a bit. I should shower and get ready, I'm leaving soon.'

'Ok.' Taylor nuzzled into the pillow but still watched out the corner of her eye as he pulled his pyjama bottoms back on.

He was due off on a secret stag event that day, and Taylor was going to help Fenella, but she grudged the time away from Magnus.

Before he left, he tucked away a strand of her hair and kissed her goodbye. 'I hope it goes ok today. I'll miss you.'

'I'll miss you too.' She slipped her arm around his neck and kissed him full on. He responded but when they broke apart, he looked a little uncertain. She wanted to repeat the words of the night before in daylight. *I love you.* But something stopped her; the timing wasn't quite right.

'I better go.'

Loneliness and emptiness rolled over her again – back to the default state, where no one saw her or knew she existed. He'd flipped her world. The way he looked at her, the words he said, how he made love to her, and the warmth they'd shared all belonged to her. Whatever lust he'd had for Skylar for a few minutes was nothing compared to this. *Would it be the same if he knew who I was though?* Maybe his feelings developed because Skylar was who he wanted.

After she'd fully woken, she showered and traipsed into the kitchen to fix herself a coffee. Someone touched her shoulder. Taylor turned round. Fenella placed her arm around her. 'You look lost. Are you ok?'

'Yes, just… You know.'

'Missing Magnus?'

'It's strange without him.'

'Oh, you've got it bad,' Fenella said. 'But don't worry, I'll look after you. How would you like to walk the dogs with me before we head off?'

'Yeah, sure.'

Taylor didn't have a jacket warm enough for the wilds; she'd planned to spend the week indoors or viewing the City of Glasgow from the warm interior of a limo. Magnus had helpfully left a polar fleece and she pinched it, despite it being far too wide for her. Fenella took her on a beautiful walk through a woodland of spindly bare trees with the sea on the left, lapping at rocks close to the beach where she'd come with Magnus and the others on her first day.

At first, she listened as Fenella held the conversation, but after a while, she asked questions about what was planned for the day. 'I know we're going to a hotel to help set up for the wedding but Magnus was sketchy on the details. He just said I was to go with you and help out.'

Fenella shook her head. 'He's a man, arrangements like this go in one ear and out of the other.'

Taylor giggled.

'So, the wedding is taking place at the Glen Lodge Hotel. The bride's mother owns it, but Robyn and Carl were heavily involved in doing up the place last year, so it's special for them. But Maureen, that's the owner, she's a bit flaky. After she lost her husband, she struggled a bit with the responsibility. So, we're all going to pitch in and make sure everything looks wonderful. I might add,' said Fenella with a frown, 'Maureen and Robyn haven't always had the best relationship and I feel duty-bound to make sure Maureen doesn't skimp on anything. I shouldn't gossip and it's a long story, but really, I keep my eye on Maureen. Robyn's like a daughter to me now and I want to make sure she has the best day tomorrow.'

'Wow, it sounds complicated.'

'It is a bit, but don't worry. Stick with me and you'll be fine.'

*

With nervous excitement, Taylor got out of Fenella's car at the Glen Lodge Hotel. This was more the kind of place Skylar would like, as long as the interior had been made over completely. She liked an old building, especially one as grand as this two-storey grey stone mansion, but only if it had ultra-modern interiors. Period-chic was fine, assuming it wasn't over a year old. Taylor expected a bit of a museum piece inside but she couldn't have been more wrong. 'This is gorgeous, it's so tastefully Scottish.' She admired the array of wildlife paintings.

'Yes, it is,' said Fenella. 'These pictures were done by a local artist, Georgia Rose. She's one of the bridesmaids and a close friend of Robyn and Carl.'

'And a top artist too.'

'Definitely. She's a very talented young woman.'

A skinny middle-aged woman with short white hair came out of a back room at the reception desk. 'Oh, hello,' she said.

'Hello, Maureen.' Fenella pulled off her gloves. 'This is Taylor, Magnus's girlfriend. I've brought her along to help.'

'Hi,' said Taylor.

'She works in PR so she's good at organising.'

The door to the backroom lay open and Taylor noticed another woman lingering about. When she caught Taylor's eye, she stepped into view. She was a head taller than Maureen and wore her shoulder-length dark hair very sleek with super-straight bangs. Leading the way like a cannon aiming at Taylor was her bulging tummy. She patted the bump and smiled serenely. 'Hi, Fen,' she said. 'I thought I heard your voice.'

'Oh, hello, Julie. How are you?' Fenella stiffened, and Taylor remembered Julie was the name of Magnus's ex. Was this her? Jean had said she was pregnant, it would fit.

'I'm well, thanks,' said Julie, cradling the bump. 'Tired, but it goes with the territory. I only have six weeks to go.'

'Oh, yes, it's exhausting.'

'Did I hear you mention Magnus?' Julie asked, smiling a red-lipped smile.

'Yes, he's back for Carl's wedding.'

'Of course. And…' Julie screwed up her face at Taylor. 'Are you?'

'I'm Taylor R— Smith. Magnus's girlfriend.'

'Lucky you,' said Julie, her nose crinkling.

'Isn't she?' said Fenella. 'Are we decorating the dining room?'

'Er, yes…' Maureen glanced at Julie. 'You go right through.'

Fenella beckoned Taylor to follow her down the corridor, where she pushed open a set of double doors. No sooner had they closed behind her than she muttered, 'That was Julie McNabb, Magnus's ex.' She rolled her eyes.

'Sorry about that. Julie makes a nuisance of herself at times and she's been beastly to Robyn in the past. Maureen promised she would make sure Julie wasn't working over the wedding weekend, but as she's here, I wonder if that's changed. I certainly don't want her here tomorrow, spoiling Robyn's big day. There's Robyn over there, I'll ask her, and I'll introduce you to everyone.'

Taylor followed, wanting to sneak into the background. People all around were laughing and joking like old friends. This was way out of her comfort zone. She didn't fit or belong here.

'Hi, everyone.' Fenella smiled.

Amongst the assembled group, Taylor saw Livvi with little Polly on her hip. Other than them and Robyn, a sea of unrecognisable faces swam before her.

'So, this is Taylor. Magnus's new girlfriend. I want to introduce you all, but the poor girl probably won't remember. So, very quickly, Taylor, I'll tell you who everyone is, but feel free to ask them again. Over here we have the talented Georgia I was telling you about; she did the wonderful paintings.'

A young woman with a tousled blonde bob gave Taylor a wide smile and a wave.

'She's a bridesmaid, as are these two lovely ladies, the McGregor sisters. Beth is the tall one, and Kirsten, sorry, she's the short one, but it doesn't make her any less wonderful.'

Taylor smiled at them both.

'And over there putting up the stage is Blair.'

'The one with the blond dreadlocks,' said Georgia. 'He's famous all over the island because he looks like a Viking.'

'He's a super joiner, from what I've heard,' said Fenella.

Georgia grabbed another woman with gorgeous long red hair as she walked past. 'And this is Autumn.'

'Hi,' said Autumn.

'She's like Blair's half-sister type thing. Well, their parents are together.'

'But we're not actually related,' said Autumn.

Taylor blinked. 'I don't see myself remembering half of this.'

'Ask Georgia if you need to know anything,' said Autumn. 'She knows everything about everyone – in the nicest possible way of course.'

Everyone dispersed back to their own business and Taylor flexed her fingers. What was she supposed to do? Everyone seemed friendly, but they were busy. Livvi migrated towards them and Fenella took Robyn by the hand. 'I need to ask you about Julie,' she said. 'I see she's working today, but I thought Maureen had arranged for her to be off this weekend.'

'Yes, she isn't meant to be here,' said Robyn. 'She's just doing a couple of hours to help out while we do this.'

'Well, if she's here tomorrow, I'll be booting her out myself,' said Fenella.

'Thanks.' Robyn glanced at Taylor. Taylor twiddled her fingers in front of her. 'Julie and I were at school together. That was obviously a long time ago, but she never liked me and to be honest, I don't particularly like her either, though I've tried my best while she's here. I'm really glad she's not with Magnus anymore.'

'Yes, I quite agree,' said Fenella, giving Taylor's arm a squeeze. 'And hello there, Princess.' Livvi had sidled up close and Polly was tugging on Fenella's sleeve. Livvi passed her over and Fenella gave her a cuddle. 'This is a job for me. How about I look after you and let your mummy do the jobs.'

'Suits me.' Livvi smiled. 'I'm doing some flower arranging with Joanne, the florist. Would you like to help, Taylor?'

Another person to remember. 'Yeah, ok, but I've never tried it before.'

Livvi led her to a table covered in beautiful bouquets of elegant blue and white flowers. A woman in her early forties with long dark curly hair was unwrapping flowers from clear plastic packages. 'Hello,' she said. 'I'm Joanne.'

'Taylor,' she said with a brief waggle of her fingers.

'Well, girls, let's carefully unpack these and arrange them around the tables. I'll do one and show you, then if you can do the rest.'

'We'll try,' said Livvi.

'Great.' Joanne gave them a brief demonstration and made sure they were happy with what they were doing, then said, 'I'm going to hang the wreaths outside. I hope Blair can help me, he's better on a ladder than me.'

'These are gorgeous.' Taylor ran her finger over a table centrepiece with a candle and ribbons mixed with the flowers.

'Thank you,' said Joanne. 'I have a few more of them to do. I can show you how when I come back.'

Taylor lifted one of the packages, glad of something to occupy her. Blair appeared behind Joanne and tapped her.

'Are you ready for the hanging?'

'That sounds a bit scary,' said Joanne.

He grinned and Livvi giggled. Taylor joined in. His Viking air wasn't as intimidating when he smiled, in fact, he looked almost cuddly.

'I meant the hanging baskets.'

'Wreaths, Blair.'

'Them too.'

Taylor watched them leave before returning to her flowers. 'He's cute,' said Livvi, consulting a hand-drawn diagram. 'So, these are for the tables in here.' They set to work organising the vases with the flower combinations in the pictures. Both the tables and chairs were covered in white cloths and the chairs had a pale blue sash that matched the flowers.

Joanne returned after a while and smiled at what they'd done. 'This is great.' Blair peered over too, his expression nonplussed.

'Have you heard the story about how Taylor met Magnus?' said Livvi, as she poked in a tall blue flower.

'No,' said Joanne.

'I'm not sure I know who Magnus is,' said Blair.

'Carl's brother,' said Livvi. 'They literally fell over each other in an airport.'

'Amazing,' said Blair. 'One of these fate type things.'

'Yeah, it was lucky. Of all the people I bumped into, it just happened to be a super-hot, single pilot.'

They all chuckled.

'That tells me it was meant to be,' said Joanne. 'I love the idea of everything happening for a reason.'

'Exactly,' said Livvi. 'Like I believe I was meant to meet Jakob. He came to my rescue at a wedding when I needed a shoulder to cry on... quite literally. And now I see it was perfect. I couldn't ask for a better husband. I was all over the place before that.'

'Absolutely,' said Joanne. 'I had a terrible life before I met my husband. I have so many regrets about that time. I had an awful partner. His daughter was like my own child and when we split, he banned me from seeing her. I still hope I'll see her again one day. But apart from that, I've been happier than ever.'

Blair rubbed his chin. 'Well, you ladies can chat on. I have to finish the stage.'

'I feel a bit sad for him,' said Joanne. 'He's a bit of a lonely sort.'

'I don't know why,' said Livvi. 'He seems really nice.'

'He is. I just don't think he's had any luck yet. But he's young, so he doesn't need to worry.'

Taylor had become so immersed in the discussion, she started to feel sorry for Blair too, even though she didn't know him and probably wouldn't see him again.

'So, have you and Magnus been together long?' asked Joanne.

'Em, not too long.'

'But it'll work out,' said Livvi. 'I can feel it.'

Wouldn't that be a thing? A wholly impossible but wonderful thing. 'The distance will always be an issue.' Taylor plonked a flower into the next empty vase.

'Maybe,' said Livvi, 'but I travelled so much as a child, I don't see it as a barrier. My father is Lebanese and my mother is American. Magnus is a pilot; he knows how to get from place to place. It might not be as big a problem as you think.'

As Taylor lifted another flower, her heart did crazy flips. Livvi's words set off the thoughts she'd touched on the previous day. What if she could stay with Magnus and give this a go for real? It would mean coming clean, but they'd grown so close, he'd understand, wouldn't he?

She'd love to throw the towel at Skylar and their parents and tell them where to shove it. This week proved she was fine on her own. What if she moved to Glasgow? She had experience in PR from working for Skylar. Magnus's apartment was the perfect spot. It could work.

The centrepieces were perfect in the middle of the tables, unlike Taylor's vision. What a piece of nonsense.

Move to Glasgow? Who was she kidding? Until a few days ago, she barely knew its name. And she didn't know Magnus, not the real Magnus. Did he even want someone living with him or being with him in the long term?

All of which left Taylor deflated as she finished off putting the vases on the tables and returned to Joanne for further instructions. Being part of this was fun and made her feel involved and worthy, but what was the point?

Aware of a commotion of voices, Taylor strolled to a corner where Fenella and Robyn were talking with Maureen. Robyn looked pink-cheeked and even a little tearful, which didn't seem to fit with the cool, collected woman Taylor had seen so far. Fenella pulled Robyn into a hug and patted her back. 'It'll be all right. We can sort this. It won't be the same, but we can have CDs, and all my boys are good musicians. I'm sure between them, they can beat out a live tune or two.'

'Is everything ok?' asked Taylor.

'The wedding singer has cancelled,' said Maureen. 'They can send the band but their vocalist is ill and can't make the trip.'

Taylor bit her lip, remembering the days she was considered a talented singer. 'I used to sing a bit, for, em, you know... parties,' said Taylor. The sickening nerves she'd suffered years ago bubbled below the surface, but this was an emergency. 'I'd be happy to help out. Maybe a few easy numbers so at least you get some live stuff.'

'Would you do that?' said Robyn.

'Sure.'

'There,' said Fenella, beaming between Robyn and Taylor. 'We'll tell the band to come. Taylor can sing a few numbers and we can see if Magnus will do some too.'

'Of course,' said Taylor. She didn't need to do it alone.

'You've heard him sing?' said Fenella.

'Yeah. We duetted in the car on the way here. He has an amazing voice. And what a vocal range.'

'I couldn't agree more,' said Fenella. 'But I'm not sure how confident he is about doing it in public though. Carl is good but he can't perform at his own wedding.'

'I'll keep him company,' said Taylor. This she couldn't wait to see. They could nurse their nerves together. A buzz of excitement tingled in her veins because they could also make more beautiful music together.

Chapter Sixteen

Magnus

At the top of Ben More, Magnus huddled together with his two brothers, using their backpacks as a wall to stop the biting wind.

'Whose bloody idea was this?' he said.

'Shut up, this is a great pre-wedding stag-do type thing,' said Carl.

'Yeah, I'd have settled for a weekend getting pissed in Budapest,' said Magnus.

'This is a good idea, but it's a bit risky,' said Jakob.

'So's drinking in Budapest,' said Magnus.

'I mean if you fall, Carl, you might have an interesting look for the wedding.'

'I won't.' Carl grinned. 'Though this will deaden the pain if I do.' He pulled out a bottle of beer for each of them.

'You're serious? You want to drink on top of a 3000-foot mountain the day before your wedding,' said Magnus, shaking his head.

'Yeah, why not?' Carl pushed the bottle into his hand.

'Ok, well, Jakob, you're the responsible one, what do you make of this?'

'I think he's a stupid idiot, but you're the pilot, would you risk it?'

'If I get caught with even the slightest dash of the stuff in my system, that's my job up the spout.'

'And have you been caught yet?' said Carl.

'Of course not. Oh, screw it. Crack it open.'

'You read the bottle?' said Jakob.

Magnus glanced at it. 'You little shit.' He squinted at Carl. 'Alcohol free. You tosser. Who drinks this kind of muck?'

Carl burst out laughing. 'You do today.'

'Moron,' muttered Magnus, as Carl chucked him the bottle opener.

Carl stood. 'Right, I'm going to toast my beautiful bride-to-be and wish her health and happiness.'

They drank to her. 'Do you want to hear what I'm going to say in my speech tomorrow?' said Magnus.

'Probably not,' said Carl. 'I'm more worried about what Maureen will say. She can be weird sometimes.'

'Do you remember what Livvi's father said at our wedding?' Jakob said. 'Something that sounded like he'd sold her to me.'

Magnus knocked back a sip and chuckled. 'Jeez, yes. That raised an eyebrow or two. He's a character that guy, and wasn't Livvi's mother throwing herself at all the men?'

'Yeah, they're a right pair to have as in-laws,' muttered Jakob.

'Your choice, little bro.'

'Not really. I didn't actually choose *them*.'

'You know what I mean. You chose your wife and she came as a package.'

'You have all this coming to you,' said Jakob.

'Do I?' Magnus downed some more of the yucky stuff. 'Says who?'

'Surely you're going to get married one day,' said Carl.

Magnus shrugged.

'So, what's Taylor then? Some girl you picked up at an airport and bribed to come with you?' asked Jakob.

Almost choking into his drink, Magnus wiped his mouth. 'Of course not, dumbass.'

'Well, you don't seem very serious about her.'

'And?'

'Well, she must be quite serious about you,' said Jakob, 'or she wouldn't have come all this way. Are you stringing her along?'

'None of your business.'

'I think we all know what you were doing when you disappeared yesterday,' said Carl. 'Is that what's keeping you together? She's good in the sack?'

'Right, shut up. This isn't your business. I can conduct my life as and how I like. If I don't want to get married and be in the perfect family bubble, that's my choice. I'm not stringing Taylor anywhere she doesn't want to go. She knows the deal, so you can stop worrying your virtuous little heads about it.'

Magnus ignored the look they gave each other. Smug gits the pair of them. Always the same. Even when he showed up with a girlfriend in tow, it still wasn't enough, they'd always be the perfect boys.

'Wanna try knocking these babies over?' said Carl, lining up the empty bottles.

'Stupid question.' Magnus grabbed three rocks and hurled them one at a time, not even bothering to aim properly. The bottles dropped like sitting ducks, and Magnus turned to Carl with a self-assured smirk. 'Beat that, why don't you?'

*

'Carl is insane,' Magnus told Fenella, Per, Aunt Jean and Taylor when he finally arrived home late that afternoon.

'Well, we all know that,' said Jean.

'I can't believe that's what he had you doing,' said Fenella, rolling her eyes at Jean. 'Just as well he didn't tell me. Climbing a mountain! The day before his wedding!'

'And they were fine.' Per laughed. 'It sounds like the best idea I've heard in a while.'

'While the women slaved away,' said Jean.

'Exactly.' Taylor grinned. 'You were off having the time of your life and we were working.'

Magnus snorted and shook his head. 'That'll be the first in a while.' The words were out before he realised how dreadful they sounded. With his parents not knowing this was in fact a Hollywood movie star who made barely two films a year and spent the rest of her time being famous, their frowns were justified. 'Just kidding,' said Magnus. 'Taylor is run off her feet with all that PR work.'

'Oh, if you only knew,' she muttered. 'But you've got some work to do yourself.'

'How do you mean? Do the guests want a flying lesson?'

'Oh, better than that,' said Fenella, smiling along with Taylor.

'Ok, put me out of my misery. Why are you looking at me like that? What am I to do?'

'We're going to sing at the wedding tomorrow.'

'We?' He glared at Taylor. 'What do you mean?'

'Well,' said Fenella, holding her hands up in front of her, 'the wedding singer cancelled and Taylor volunteered to step in.'

'You did?'

'Just for a few songs, ones that we know.' She winked at him.

Fenella patted her arm, beaming. Magnus drummed his finger on his chin. This was more like Skylar, the showgirl. He almost scoffed aloud; so much for keeping her cover.

'Right.' He took a deep breath. 'I might manage one or two as long as I can read the lyrics, I never remember all the words.'

'I'm sure that will be fine,' said Fenella. 'I'll go and call Robyn. She'll be thrilled.'

'Do you fancy a walk to the beach before dinner?' Magnus asked Taylor.

'Haven't you had enough walking for one day?' said Fenella.

'Kind of, but I haven't had a chance to show Taylor very much and we only have a couple more days.'

'Sure, let's go,' said Taylor, jumping in before Fenella could object again. 'I could do with some fresh air. Today was great. Thanks, Fenella, for letting me tag along.'

'Oh, you're very welcome, and so well organised.'

Wrapped up to the teeth again, they left through the French doors and trudged towards the shore. Magnus whipped his arm around Taylor's shoulders. She had on his fleece but it didn't seem to be warming her enough.

'What's going on?'

'How do you mean?'

'My mum thinks you're well organised. What's that all about? Who are you and what have you done with Skylar Rousse?'

Taylor coughed and looked away. Her hood blew down and her shoulder-length hair tangled around. 'I'm actually her evil twin, and I've locked her in a cellar for a week while I initiate my plans for world domination.'

He laughed and, stepping in front of her, snaked his arms around her waist, pulling her in for a long soulful kiss. 'Does that also involve volunteering yourself to sing?'

'I wanted to help.'

'Not just show off?'

'No. Robyn was upset. She'd obviously set her heart on having at least a few live songs.'

Magnus smiled and ran his fingertips down her cheek. 'You're a revelation. Who knew you could be so kind? Thank you.'

'Any time.'

'I missed you today,' he whispered onto her mouth, pressing against her so their bodies touched in all the right places, even through their layers of clothing.

'And I missed you too.' Taylor slung her arms around his neck, looping her hands behind him, and sealing her lips with his. Their tongues met, sending a frisson through him. 'Do you think they can see us from the house?' whispered Taylor.

'I don't care. I'm kissing my girlfriend, what's wrong with that? This is exactly what my mum wants, for me to be in love.'

Taylor grinned broadly. 'And are you in love?'

'Of course I am. Come on.' He started walking again. 'Why don't we run?'

Before Magnus could reply, Taylor took off across the scrubby grassland, towards the sea. Magnus followed, surprised at her turn of speed but catching her eventually.

'Took you a while,' she said, still running.

His feet fell heavily in his thick walking boots as he kept pace with her. 'I've climbed 3000 feet today and back. Cut me some slack.'

'I would have thought that would be easy for you. Your stamina is legendary.' Putting on a burst of speed, she reached the edge of the beach and bent double, resting her hands on a ragged boulder as she caught her breath. 'I am so out of training.'

'You look pretty fit to me.' Magnus eyed her over, then made his way through the barnacle-covered rocks to the small sandy section beyond. He jammed his hands into his pockets and looked out to sea, inhaling the fresh clear air. 'This is like our private beach.'

'Is it?'

'It doesn't belong to us but no one ever comes here. Hardly anyone even knows about it. We used to play here every day as kids.'

'It's a beautiful place to grow up.'

'It had its ups and downs, like anywhere. But this was definitely a plus point.'

'Look at this.' Taylor stopped and picked up a small dappled stone. 'I've never seen a stone this colour, it's bright pink.'

'This island has some amazing stones. That is a beautiful one.' Magnus squinted at it before Taylor placed it back on the ground and inched closer to the water.

Not sure exactly why, he retrieved the little stone, turned it over in his hand, then put it in his pocket. On one side of the beach was a wooded area full of gnarled bushes and spindly winter trees. Magnus walked towards it and grabbed two sticks. 'This is a ritual we have,' he said, handing Taylor a stick.

'What? Do we have to fight with it?'

'No.' He laughed. 'Write your name in the sand. We always do it. I think my mum has a photo of the first time I ever did it when I was about four, the *S* looks like a number *3*. I must have made her so proud.'

'I'm sure you still do.'

'Ah, maybe.' Magnus bent over, dragging the stick through the sand until his name emerged. With a little smile, Taylor did the same, writing hers a few feet below his and adding a little love heart at the end. 'Aww, isn't that sweet?' said Magnus.

'It's all for you.'

'Haha,' he said. 'All for me indeed. What am I? The love of your life.'

'Up until a few days ago, you were a pilot I met briefly long ago who always intrigued me, then you became, well, someone special.'

'Ok, how's this then?' He bent over again and added the word *loves* between their names and stepped back to read, 'Magnus loves Taylor.'

'Aww, what a romantic you are, but this is even better.' Taylor dragged her stick through the sand underneath her name, writing out the word *forever.*

Magnus burst out laughing. 'Ok, that's a good one. Let's get a selfie. Then I can blackmail you with it on social media for the rest of your life.'

She squinted at him. 'I might have to get you to sign something to say you won't.'

'Come on, trust me. I'm an honourable guy.' He raised the phone as she snuck under his arm. After some adjustment, he got them both in with the wording behind. 'It's not like anyone would recognise you anyway, and it isn't even your name.'

'Don't move yet. Take another one,' said Taylor, 'only this time, kiss me.'

'Ok.' He held up the phone again, turning his head to Taylor. The angle was impossible, but Taylor took his face in her hands and pulled him into a kiss so deep concentrating on getting a picture became irrelevant. Her soft lips were like a drug he couldn't get enough of.

Flinging the phone in his pocket, he abandoned the photo, wrapped Taylor in his arms and joined the kiss.

'It's freezing.' Taylor giggled. He unzipped his jacket and pulled her inside, then leaned her back. She pressed against him as he lavished his attention on her mouth.

'No matter what happens, this is special,' he whispered.

Her eyes closed as his lips touched her again and he kissed her into the oncoming wind.

Chapter Seventeen

Taylor

Taylor peered through the gap in the curtains of the little bedroom. Trees swayed in the distance beyond a ridge of gnarled bushes. In the pale sunrise, she could make out the little beach she and Magnus had been to the day before.

Had the tide washed away the messages they'd left there? He'd immortalised it in a photo and sent it to her. She had proof that once in her life someone had professed to love her – forever!

The whole thing was fake, but those kisses were real. Weren't they? *I'm just a desperate fool.* Yes. All she was doing was clinging to the wish someone would notice her, but Magnus would never have seen her like this if he didn't think she was Skylar. All these phoney dreams were built on a framework of lies.

Warm hands touched her shoulders. 'Are you ok?' Magnus's words were soft, seeming to come from far off though he was right there.

'What are we doing here?'

He sighed and pulled her into a warming hug. 'We've taken it to a whole new level, and it's probably not healthy.'

'If it was real, it would be amazing.'

'That's true and this might be a stupid thought, but…'

'Tell me.'

He swallowed and his Adam's apple brushed against her forehead. 'Maybe this is just a beginning for us. Could we carry on seeing each other? I'm not crazy, I know about your lifestyle, but I wonder…'

Taylor peered at him, hardly daring to believe her ears. This was exactly what she wanted, but these words were for Skylar. 'I do want that, Magnus, but there are things we need to talk about.'

'Sure, sure, I get that. Maybe after today, when the wedding is done, we can talk.'

'Yes.' She pushed forward and pecked him on the cheek. Yes. She had to confess, that was all. Confess to the truth and hope beyond hope he could see her for the girl inside.

He hugged her and the strength of it almost brought her to tears. She squeezed her eyes shut. 'I'm so glad I crashed into you.' He patted her back.

'Me too.' Her lower lip trembled and she buried herself in him, hiding all her weakness and insecurity in his broad shoulder.

Magnus was on best man duties and couldn't hang about. He left early, giving Taylor an extra kiss before he headed off. Taylor stuck with Fenella, Per and Aunt Jean.

'I can do make-up and hair,' Taylor said as Fenella flapped about, looking flustered. 'I learned back in Hollywood when…' She froze, hoping Fenella was too preoccupied to have noticed but, worse luck, she glanced at Taylor in the living room mirror as she fixed an earring.

'Hollywood?' said Fenella. 'What did you do there? Is that where you learned to sing?'

'Kind of. I just did this and that and make-up was part of my job. I picked up some great tips. Would you like me to do yours?'

'I'd love that. Maureen is getting hers done with the bridal party today. Robyn invited me too, but I think it's better if I don't. I'll probably cry, which I will do anyway. I love Robyn, I just feel she should do this with her mum, not me, and I don't want Maureen thinking I'm pushing in where I'm not wanted.'

'I'm sure you'll always be wanted,' said Taylor, indicating Fenella should sit at the table. 'You're such a caring mom. Magnus still wants to please you. If you weren't a mom he loved and respected, he wouldn't try so hard.'

'Oh dear,' said Fenella, sitting down and flicking out her hair. 'I hope he doesn't think I want him to do something crazy. I just want my boys to be happy.'

'He knows that and that's exactly what he's trying to be.'

'Well, at least you can help him there.' Fenella patted Taylor's hand over her shoulder.

'I'll try.'

She set to work on Fenella's hair, and the time whooshed by. Taylor had just finished fixing her own hair when it was time to leave.

'Gosh, you look incredible,' said Fenella.

Taylor straightened out the dress she'd borrowed from Robyn and glimpsed herself in the mirror. As soon as she put on make-up, the resemblance to Skylar intensified. She swallowed.

Jean grumbled all the way to the Glen Lodge Hotel and Taylor was glad to get out. A chill wind carried off the sea and she shivered. Inside, they made their way to a chamber at the end of the corridor, past the dining room they'd decorated the day before. The space had been set up with rows of seats.

'We have seats near the front,' said Fenella. 'But I see Livvi there if you want to sit with her.'

'Oh, sure.'

At the front of the room was a clear area with a large bouquet of flowers. All three Hansen brothers stood in front of it, dressed in their kilts and formal jackets, chatting and laughing.

'Hi,' said Taylor, shuffling into a seat some rows back beside Livvi. At the front, Fenella hugged her sons and dabbed at her eyes. 'They are three good-looking guys.'

'They really are,' said Livvi, bouncing Polly on her knee. 'I'm sitting back here in case Polly needs to leave. She's at an unpredictable age.'

'She's so cute.'

'She is.' Livvi kissed her daughter's cheek. 'But she can be a terror.' When Livvi looked up, she seemed to notice Taylor in a different light. 'You look great. You remind me of someone, I thought it before, but I can't put my finger on it.'

Taylor pursed her lips, remembering Livvi was part-American. She would have grown up watching the cheesy kids shows Skylar and Taylor had starred in. Skylar appeared in several films and TV shows globally, but her main fanbase was in the US and Livvi was of an age to know about her. Taylor tucked her hair behind her ears, wishing she'd not put on so much make-up.

Seats around them filled up and Taylor caught Magnus's eye. A wolfish smile spread across his face, and he winked, making Taylor giggle. After about twenty minutes, the background music stopped and the doors behind opened. A woman in a trouser suit walked down the aisle, shook hands with all three brothers, then turned to the guests. 'All rise, please,' she said, gesturing with her palms up.

The crowd rose and Taylor joined the sea of heads, peering around as the music started. The doors opened again and Robyn came in with her mother, the short-haired hotel owner.

'Oh, god,' gasped Livvi. 'She is so beautiful.'

In a rustle of satin, Robyn passed by, tall and graceful, her long blonde hair twisted in an elegant half up-do. Her flowing dress gave her the look of a swan. Four bridesmaids followed in powder blue dresses.

'Who's the fourth bridesmaid?' whispered Taylor. 'I'm sure I only met three yesterday.'

'Robyn's sister-in-law,' murmured Livvi. 'That's her brother at the front with the little boy. They didn't arrive until late yesterday.'

Taylor followed Robyn's progress until her gaze flicked to Carl, beaming at the front. To his left, Magnus looked on stoically, his hands behind his back.

Taylor reclaimed her seat. 'It's impossible not to cry at weddings,' she commented, wiping a tear from her eye as Carl and Robyn took their vows.

'I know,' said Livvi, letting her tears fall into Polly's hair. 'It's just beautiful.'

Chapter Eighteen

Magnus

Magnus kept his hands clamped behind his back, hiding his sweaty palms. His heart sped up. Robyn was like an ice princess as she glided down the aisle in a rustle of white. Delicate lace flowers trailed over her shoulders, forming an intricate neckline, dipping to a perfect V. A simple pendant glinted at her neck. Carl was her Prince Charming, a rugged Highlander version with his long trailing plaid pinned to one shoulder. Even combed, his hair looked unruly, but somehow it fitted. Between their smiling faces, Magnus spotted Fenella dabbing her eyes. All made up and dressed in her pink dress and bolero, she looked like a different person. A bit too glam for his mum, the woman who rarely left the house in anything but wellies.

The music faded out and the humanist officiant began to speak, welcoming them with her soft voice and allowing them to be seated. Magnus took his place by the window beside Jakob, on the opposite side from the four bridesmaids. He set his hands on his thighs, rubbing them on the coarse fabric of his kilt. Carl hadn't taken his eyes off Robyn since she'd reached him and Magnus couldn't blame him.

The photographer bustled around, barely noticeable but present, clicking shots here and there. Magnus pulled his knees together. Normally, he didn't sit like that but the photographer didn't seem too scrupulous about where he was shooting.

'Today we will witness the marriage of Robyn and Carl,' said the officiant. 'In the manner traditional to the celts of Scotland a handfasting ritual will take place…'

Magnus wanted to find Taylor in the crowd again but he didn't dare. He trained his focus on his youngest brother. If he saw Taylor now, he would imagine her dressed like Robyn, holding out her hands for him. The vision hit him so hard, he blinked and shuffled in his seat. *What am I thinking?* How could he even consider marrying Skylar Rousse? Movie stars didn't marry pilots and settle down. Christ, his commitment issues were nothing compared to hers. She'd demand so many prenups, she'd probably find someone else in the time it took Magnus to sign them. But none of that fit with Taylor. This alter-ego she'd created was so damned convincing. He'd fallen hook, line and sinker. He was ready to drop to his knees and tell her he loved her. Loved her so bloody much she consumed every piece of his soul.

Inside the thick wool socks which covered his shins almost to his knees, his *sgian-dubh,* pressed against his leg. That little dagger he'd named his *ski-ing-do* ever since childhood could end all this heartache. He could be a proper little Romeo and cast himself on it. He stifled a dry laugh. Madness! Utter madness. He had to get a grip and reroute his brain onto the path of normality. When Taylor had joked the other day about no one ever beating him, had she known this was a game she could win at? Was she waiting for him to confess his love so she could slap him down with her winner's hat on?

His gaze lifted and roamed across the hats, hairstyles and bald heads until it settled on her. A tingle in his shoulders told him she'd been watching him for some time. Her lips curled up and she winked. He maintained eye contact but gave nothing back. How had she conquered him this well? The woman he'd kissed on that balcony in Hollywood five years ago was so far removed from Taylor, it seemed impossible it was the same person. Maybe before he made crazy declarations, he should carry out a thorough investigation. Even Google would serve. He hadn't cared enough to keep track of Skylar's life but perhaps he should check it out. Maybe she was mentally unstable. Perhaps she'd run because she'd been incarcerated for her own safety. But it all seemed too ridiculous. His heart and his gut told him her feelings were real, even if the situation was fake.

A new voice spoke, and he snapped his attention to the lectern. The officiant had moved aside and the bridesmaid with the blonde bobbed hair had taken her place. Magnus scratched his lower lip with his teeth, trying to recall her name. She was a friend of Carl's but Magnus had never really known her. He'd lost touch with the comings and goings on Mull, though at times he missed it more than anywhere in the world.

'This poem was written by my fiancé, Archie Crichton-Leith, for the bride and groom,' said the bridesmaid. Her voice was light and chirpy. Magnus made a concerted effort to focus but it was no use. Taylor, Skylar. Skylar, Taylor. Whichever way he swung it, all he could think about was Taylor and the absurdity of what they were doing. Why had he allowed it? And worse, joined in, enjoyed it? Let himself go.

'Thank you, Georgia,' said the humanist, and the bridesmaid returned to her seat. 'A beautifully written poem. And now for the handfasting.'

Magnus snapped back to Taylor but this time she had craned her neck to get a better view of what was going on. The officiant spoke to Robyn and Carl, explaining the ancient ritual before holding up two lengths of boat rope. Magnus smirked; it was so them. If he married Skylar, would she want this? Perhaps to be bound to him with a pink feather boa or glitter string. But there he was getting ahead of himself again.

Robyn smiled gently as the humanist wrapped the cords around them, speaking gently of the bond of love. The photographer knelt in the aisle, snapping away. Once he had his fill, the cords were removed and they stood to sing. Magnus joined in softly; he had to save his voice for later and this was just a warmup.

Jakob took the lectern next, reading a short verse before Magnus had his turn. He located the rings in his pocket without even the pretence of not being able to find them. Fenella would never forgive him. Summoning his best smile, he flipped open the boxes and presented them to the officiant. Two simple white gold bands twinkled under the lights.

Pressing his lips together, Magnus held his breath as Robyn and Carl exchanged vows. Carl looked like he was only just holding himself together, fudging a couple of lines, as emotion threatened to overcome him. Robyn maintained her calm poise, though her tone was a little higher than usual. As she slipped the ring onto Carl's finger, Magnus pulled his lips into a smile, mocking the little twist in his heart, marking the selfish moment that he officially became the last single brother.

'You may now kiss the bride.'

Carl sealed his lips with Robyn, and Magnus banished the negative thoughts. This day was about love and he clapped with the other guests. The music struck up, and Robyn and Carl broke apart with broad smiles.

The officiant stepped down and held out her arms in the direction of the door. Hand in hand, Robyn and Carl exited, beaming and waving. A jaunty tune accompanied them. Magnus and Jakob waited for the bridesmaids to go before taking their places at the back.

On his way past Taylor, Magnus flipped her a little wink, and she beamed. He needed to go somewhere quiet with her and talk. They had to sort themselves out, but in the middle of a wedding where they still had hours of photographs, speeches and the unexpected singsong to go, it didn't seem likely to happen any time soon.

Chapter Nineteen

Taylor

The music stopped and people started talking and standing. Livvi bounced Polly on her hip as the little girl cried and waved her arms about. 'It's ok,' said Livvi. 'You'll see Daddy in a minute.'

'She's a real daddy's girl, isn't she?' said Taylor.

'Definitely. I thought she might not notice him going past, but nothing goes past you, little one. Does it?' Livvi nose rubbed Polly and she stopped crying for a moment and giggled.

'He must be just out there,' said Taylor, hoping Magnus would be too.

'I'm not sure what happens now.'

Taylor and Livvi joined the throng at the door. Everyone had congregated in the entrance hall.

'Here's Jakob,' said Livvi, standing on tiptoes.

Polly laugh cried. 'Dadda.'

He turned and made his way through the crowd.

'There you are.' He took Polly as she jumped on him excitedly.

'What happens now?' asked Livvi, linking her hand through his arm.

'We're getting some pictures outside. It's family shots first, then Robyn and Carl are getting theirs done together.'

Taylor hovered uncertainly.

'You're to come too,' said Jakob.

'Oh… ok.' Taylor followed. She shouldn't be in the family photos; that was wrong on so many levels.

'Oh, that was wonderful.' A hand landed on Taylor's shoulder and she spun around. 'What a beautiful service,' said Fenella. Taylor nodded in agreement.

Polly pulled away from Jakob, leaning to her granny.

'Oh, hello, little princess. You look gorgeous,' said Fenella, taking her. 'But don't mess Granny's hair today. Aunty Taylor was so good to fix it for me.'

Aunty? Heat prickled up Taylor's neck. That was jumping a million steps and forgetting the pretty huge obstacle that Magnus didn't actually know who she was.

'Hey.' Magnus waved over the crowd as they approached the door.

In a scene that reminded Taylor of days out with Skylar, a clamour of people tried to reach Robyn and Carl. They weren't signing autographs but were shaking hands and accepting congratulations.

'Are the photos outside?' asked Taylor, making her way to Magnus's side.

'Yup.'

'It's freezing out there.'

'Bracing, darling, bracing.'

Taylor forced a smile. 'Listen, I shouldn't be in the photos.'

'Why not?'

'I'm not family.'

Magnus put his arm around her shoulder and moved back from Jakob and Livvi. 'You don't have to be in the photos, but I'd like it if you were. And…' He glanced around. 'If you refuse, my mum will force you.'

Taylor laughed. 'Yes. I expect she will.'

Maureen clapped her hands and called for order. 'If everybody except the wedding party would please move into the lounge area. The bar is open and we'll reconvene at five o'clock for the speeches and the meal.'

'Are you doing a speech?' asked Taylor.

'Oh yes. Both Jakob and I are doing something. So is Carl, and I guarantee it'll be like nothing you've ever seen before.' Utterly intrigued, Taylor followed him into the freezing air outside.

*

After attempting another protest, Taylor realised Fenella wouldn't let her sit out the photographs. Even as she smiled her biggest, most Hollywood smile, she wondered if somewhere down the line, she'd have to be airbrushed out. Her head ached as she tried to unravel all the possible connotations of what they would think once they found out her true identity.

'There, that didn't hurt,' said Magnus. He rubbed his palms up and down her bare arms. 'Though the cold might.'

The photographer left with Carl and Robyn for their couple pictures and Magnus took Taylor back towards the hotel. 'Magnus, I'm scared.'

'Of what?'

'That this is all going to go horribly wrong and I'm stuck in those photos forever.'

'Hmm. I guess there's the chance the paparazzi get their hands on them. I should have thought about that. I don't suppose Carl wants his wedding featured in *Hello* magazine.'

The entrance area was quieter. 'Look, Magnus, I have to tell you something.' Drumsticks were attacking Taylor's heart like Animal from 'The Muppets'.

Magnus lifted his hands and clamped them to her cheeks, then leaning in he kissed her. 'Ok,' he whispered. 'Tell me.'

Taylor could hardly breathe; now was the moment but what was he expecting? Did he think she was about to say she loved him? 'I… eh…'

The front doors opened and Jakob came in with Livvi and Polly. 'Magnus,' he said, and Magnus dropped his hands from Taylor.

'Yes, brother dear.'

'I think we should practise our speech one last time. It could go badly wrong.'

'Ok, fine. We'll be twenty minutes or so.'

Taylor watched him go. 'What are they doing?' she asked Livvi.

'Wait and see, it'll be brilliant. These guys are so talented.'

*

Taylor slipped off her shoes under the table and flexed her toes. Beside her, Livvi organised Polly into a highchair. The four men at the table were the bridesmaids' partners. Robyn's brother settled his son into a highchair next to Polly and Livvi giggled as the two toddlers gave each other the daggers before starting to laugh.

'They're doing the speeches before the meal,' said Livvi, resuming her seat. 'Which is a great idea, because when it's after, everybody falls asleep.'

In front of the large windows at one end of the room was the top table – twinkling strings of lights and delicate lanterns hung above them. Magnus and his family took their positions. Taylor sipped her champagne as an expectant murmur rippled around the room.

'Ladies and gentlemen,' called a loud voice. 'Please, will you all rise for the bride and groom.'

A high wail of bagpipes skirled into full glory and chairs scraped back as everyone got to their feet, clapping. Some cheers and wolf-whistles sounded through the rousing pipe music as Robyn and Carl made their way in. Two balloons popped above and confetti sprinkled down, showering them. Robyn held out her palms like she was in a rainstorm and Carl laughed. He took her hand and held it high as they made their way to the top table.

Magnus clapped and grinned as they approached. Taylor kept him in her sight. As he pulled out his chair and sat, his expression dulled. Taylor sucked her lip, taking her own seat. When Magnus checked up again, his smile was back and he said something to Maureen, who was sitting on his left.

The chatter died and servers came around topping up champagne glasses. Taylor put her hand over hers. She needed to stay focused for the singing later. At the top table, Magnus raised his spoon and pinged a glass with a cheeky but charming smile. Maureen cast him a bit of a dirty look as she got to her feet and put on a pair of glasses.

Unfolding a piece of paper, she cleared her throat. 'Thank you for coming, everyone. Of course, it's traditional for the bride's father to make a speech. You'll know, however, that we sadly lost Robyn's father. So, I hope I can do this justice.'

Taylor's gaze flickered around from Maureen to Robyn, to Carl, Fenella and Per, Jakob, the bridesmaids, then Magnus. He had lounged back and steepled his fingers, his chiselled jaw raised to look at Maureen, but something in his eyes gave him away; he'd zoned out. What was he thinking about? As she stared, he slowly shifted his focus to her. With a tiny lift of his eyebrow, he met her look, before flicking back to Maureen.

'Robyn's independent spirit is a force to be reckoned with,' Maureen continued and Taylor forced herself to listen. When the speech was done, Maureen sat back down and her shoulders dropped. She turned to Magnus and whispered something to him.

Carl stood next. Taylor jumped as a man at their table wolf-whistled. Cheers and claps followed. Carl raised his hands for quiet, his broad smile splitting his face.

'On behalf of my wife and I—'

The words were barely out when the cheering and clapping started again. Taylor shared a grin with Livvi as little Polly bashed her highchair and giggled like she agreed with everyone.

Taylor pressed her fingers to her lips as Carl spoke. Would anyone ever say such beautiful words about her? She almost didn't dare look at Magnus, but when she did, his focus was trained on his brother.

'I'd like to finish with something a little different,' said Carl. 'And my brothers are going to help me out.' He stepped back and walked along behind the table.

Taylor furrowed her brow and a few people whispered curiously as Magnus and Jakob got to their feet. In the corner, close to a curtain, was a white piano. Magnus sat at it. Carl lifted a guitar and stood behind a microphone. Jakob also had a guitar and sat on a stool close to the piano. 'This is a song that Robyn and I call our song. I'd like to dedicate it to Robyn, my beautiful wife.'

Magnus opened on the piano with the introductory chords to the song, 'You're Beautiful'.

Carl's voice was mellow with a slightly rough edge but he didn't crack or well up, unlike everyone else in the room. Rapturous applause and profuse nose-blowing followed its final note, and when Carl returned to the table, he hugged Robyn for a long moment. After the clapping died out, Magnus lifted the microphone. 'Ok, thank you, everybody. And, Carl, that was beautiful. It's a hard act to follow and, as the eldest brother, I don't like to follow my little brother into anything, but in this case, I'll make an exception. You might be wondering why Jakob and I are still over here rather than back at the table, pulling out our speech notes and making you all laugh with some witty repartee about our baby brother Carl. Well, we decided we'd shake things up a bit and instead of a stuffy speech, we're going to give you our very own composition about Carl.'

Carl covered his face and shook his head.

Magnus returned to the piano and struck up a jaunty chord that reminded Taylor of *Cabaret*. He started to sing a funny little song and Jakob strummed along, adding asides as though correcting his brother. After the first few lines, everyone was in stitches.

'They should be on the stage,' said Taylor.

Tears rolled down Livvi's cheeks and she shook with laughter. 'They really should.'

As they concluded, everyone cheered and laughed. Taylor grinned at Magnus and he sent her a little wink. This was what it meant to be in his world and she didn't ever want to leave.

Chapter Twenty

Magnus

Sitting at the top table gave Magnus a great view of the room, but nothing caught his eye more than Taylor. He sipped his champagne, watching her laughing with Livvi and some guys at their table. She looked more like her old self with the make-up and the fancy dress. Was he insane? He'd asked her to give it a shot. Could Skylar Rousse ever date a 'normal' guy like him? Had her saying yes been an act? Was the whole thing part of the act? When they sailed away from the island, would she turn on him, laughing her head off? A victory smile replacing the Hollywood pout. Surely she wasn't that good at faking it? Or was she? The glass rim touched Magnus's lips and he held it there. Was he being played for a fool?

After a brief recess, while the tables were moved aside to make way for the dance floor, Magnus and Taylor made their way back into the main function room with a large group including Jakob, Livvi, Polly, Fenella and Per, plus Jean, a group of cousins and various aunts and uncles. The lights were low and twinkling, casting stars around the room.

'I have to dance the first dance with the head bridesmaid,' said Magnus, rubbing Taylor's hand between his forefinger and thumb. 'After that, I'm all yours.'

'And I suppose you'll turn out to be Fred Astaire.'

'What are you talking about?'

'After your little stint on the piano, you should be on the stage. A change of career is what you need.'

'I told you before, that's never going to happen,' he said.

'Did you, when?'

'Five years ago.' Maybe he shouldn't be surprised she'd forgotten. He'd been one tiny moment in her colourful life. Funny though, how selective her brain could be. After claiming all these feelings she'd retained for him, only to forget the details.

'Oh…'

Maybe all the stints in rehab had addled her memories. A twinge of uncertainty tugged at his gut. The same thought he'd had earlier returned. What if she was unstable? Could she be trusted? 'I guess you've forgotten. You suggested I appear in some movie with you. One where I didn't speak but there were plenty of naked shots.'

Taylor's pupils flared and she opened her mouth and closed it again before saying, 'Yeah, about that… I think we need to—'

'Ladies and gentlemen,' announced the MC over a microphone. 'Can we put our hands together for the bride and groom?'

'Shit,' said Magnus, the word drowning in the applause. 'I need to find the bridesmaids. I'm supposed to join the dance.'

Leaving Taylor, he jostled amidst the crowd to get to the collection of blue dresses he spied on the other side of the dance floor. A low chord rang out and Robyn and Carl hit the dance floor, looking every inch the perfect duo as they waltzed closely, Carl's large hand splayed on Robyn's back.

Magnus had been through this a few years back with Jakob. That had been hard enough, seeing his younger brother so obviously in love, now Carl. The baby, the one they 'knew' would never settle let alone get married, but look at him now. No matter how often Magnus told himself he was ok being single, he wasn't sure it was true anymore. The life of a free agent had certain perks… and downsides. Especially at his stage of life. But dating Skylar Rousse didn't exactly tick boxes on the steady relationship front. *Jeez. Who am I kidding?* If they agreed to it, what would the reality look like? Her in Hollywood, him in Glasgow flying the short haul. He'd made a conscious decision to leave the long haul just over a year ago. And although he'd reasoned with himself it was to have a better quality of life and less disruption to his circadian rhythm, he wondered now if deep in his subconscious he'd done it to give himself a chance to settle, if the right person came along. But if that person turned out to be Skylar, he'd have to rejig his life all over, and he couldn't be sure it was worth it. Despite how much it seemed she'd changed, he knew her reputation. She didn't settle at anything for long.

Magnus reached the bridesmaids just in time. He took Beth McGregor to the floor. She was equally as tall as him, slim and elegant, and definitely not a pushover. No way would he be leading her; she was leading him. His head was so full of fuzz, he let her, spending the few minutes trying to figure out a sensible next move. It had to be tactful in case Skylar's feelings were genuine, but not too heartfelt in case it was a play. He harrumphed and Beth looked at him. 'Sorry,' he said. 'Just thinking.'

'Right,' said Beth.

When the dance finished, he handed Beth over to her boyfriend, a tall guy who looked like a model but had an expression like he might murder Magnus. Obviously, he didn't appreciate anyone dancing with his girlfriend. With a quirk of his eyebrow, Magnus went searching for Taylor. She found him first and dragged him straight back to the dance floor. Despite the Hollywood in her veins, her dancing was subdued. Gone was the Skylar who danced on tabletops in LA and was photographed at drunken raves in her youth. This Taylor version of Skylar was more refined and their dance was such an act of beauty Magnus lost the ability to speak or think. Just slowly revolving together, taking an occasional twirl and gazing into each other's eyes was all that mattered. Nothing about this seemed fake.

After a couple of gentle waltzes, the music's tempo picked up, and Taylor shook her head. 'I need to get on the stage, I've got my live section next.'

Magnus rolled his shoulders. 'Can we get the duets out of the way first before I get too drunk?'

'Yes.' Taylor's pupils dilated and she clung to his arm, her other hand at her throat.

'Are you ok?'

'I… I just…'

'Hey.' Magnus steadied her with a hand on each arm.

'I haven't done this for a long time. What if it's a disaster?'

'Done what?'

'Sung live to an audience.'

'Oh.' Magnus frowned. 'You were awesome in the car. And if some idiot somewhere has told you they need software to enhance your voice, then the world is beyond fucked. Believe in yourself. If anyone should be cacking it, it's me. This is way out of my zone. Singing a jokey little skit is one thing but a full-on duet with a Hollywood superstar, quite another.'

'Yeah, but I know how incredible you are too.'

'So, let's give it our best shot.'

She nodded and he led her to the podium. They chatted to the band about the songs they'd agreed to, old favourites Magnus had belted out at karaoke nights and a healthy bit of songs from the musicals. Keeping Taylor's hand in his, he approached the mic, smiled at her, and tapped his thigh, encouraging his inner calm to come forth, the one he summoned every time he landed a plane.

A few groans and chuckles rang out as the opening bars of 'People Will Say We're in Love' rang out. Magnus winked at Taylor.

As he sang, he looked her in the eye, keeping his mouth to the mic. *'Don't praise my charm too much.'*

She folded her arms and pulled a face. The guests laughed, but Magnus ignored them, focusing on the song with only brief glances at the lyrics on the stand in front of him.

As Taylor belted out, *'Let people say we're in love,'* she held his gaze and the message struck him so deep, he almost missed his cue.

The power in Taylor's voice was astonishing and he released his inner showman to match her as they powered their way through 'The Time of My Life'. Every damn line in the song seemed to apply to them. He'd never felt this way, ever. Her expression told him she was thinking exactly the same.

As they wound up, he blanked out the cheers from the dance floor, dipped his head, and kissed her cheek. 'You're amazing,' he whispered. 'Now let them have it.'

He hopped off the stage while Taylor geared up for 'Girls Just Want to Have Fun'. Already a groove was going and people were letting their hair down, including rather embarrassingly, Fenella and Joanne who looked like they were at a rave gone wrong. Aunt Jean was in a world of her own, boogying with her two sticks and two young men laughing their heads off as they did some kind of conga around her.

Magnus strolled to the bar and got a drink. Taylor was winding up the song as he took a seat next to Jakob, who was bouncing little Polly on his knee. 'Well done,' said Jakob. 'That took some balls.'

'Thanks.' Magnus sipped his beer.

As Taylor finished, Livvi erupted into applause with several other people. 'She's utterly brilliant.' Livvi jumped up and down as Taylor started another song Magnus didn't recognise. Her voice soared around the ballroom like the pro she was. So much for requiring software to enhance her voice. Who needed that kind of criticism?

After more raucous applause, she left the stage doing a good impression of looking bashful, keeping her head down. Well-wishers accosted her and people clapped her on the back, congratulating her as she moved towards the table, her cheeks very flushed.

'That was brilliant,' said Magnus, jumping up to hug her.

'Amazing,' said Livvi. 'And look, you've inspired Polly. She's found her dancing legs just as she should be going to sleep.'

Magnus grinned as Jakob twirled the tiny little girl on the dance floor beside the table, her frilly dress puffing out as she giggled and squealed. Magnus didn't let go of Taylor but closed his eyes and splayed his fingers on her bare back. An ache for something he couldn't reach tugged his heart.

'She's such a cutie,' said Taylor, patting Magnus's back then fanning her neck. 'I'm roasted. That was nerve-racking.'

'I'll get you a drink,' said Magnus.

'I'll just have water,' said Taylor, pouring some from a jug on the table.

Livvi placed her glass down, still beaming at her daughter. As she turned back to the table, her face lit up. 'Oh, my goodness.' She banged the table, a triumphant gleam in her expression.

'What is it?' Magnus peered at Taylor. Livvi was staring at her in such an odd way. Was she about to faint or something? But apart from her rosy cheeks, she looked a picture of health.

'It's just come to me who it is you look like,' Livvi said.

'Oh?' Taylor glanced sideways at Magnus, running her fingers around the low neckline of her dress.

Shit. Had they been rumbled? Magnus adjusted his tie and tried to keep his expression even.

'There's an American TV star, Skylar Rousse. You probably won't have heard of her,' Livvi said to Magnus. 'She makes these girlie type films, romcoms and the like. Taylor, you are her double. She has different hair and stuff obviously. I could google her and show you.'

'Na, it's ok,' said Magnus. 'We know about that. Everyone says it.'

'Do they? Wow, I know why. I used to watch this show she did when I was a kid. She was only like five or six when she was in it, but she was so sassy.'

Magnus sipped his drink, raising his eyes over it, trying to send Taylor a telepathic message that everything was still ok. But his heart was drumming. If they were going to make a go of this, the truth would come out anyway. Should they make it now?

'I was so disappointed to find out years later,' Livvi went on, 'that it wasn't always her. Apparently, she had a twin sister and they both did the part because of the child acting law. I loved that show,' said Livvi, gazing into space and taking another drink.

Music pounded in the background but the thumping of his pulse in his ears deadened it.

'And she can sing,' Livvi said, 'though I think you sound better. I saw her in a musical and her voice was that fake way like it's been put through a computer.'

Livvi's words got lost. *Skylar has a twin sister.* Magnus shifted his gaze to Taylor. She was staring forward, her jaw set. Slowly, her face turned to him, and his heart flipped over. It wasn't her. Of course it wasn't. No wonder she'd seemed so changed; she was a different person. Standing up and cracking his thigh on the table, Magnus growled and bundled his chair out of the way, then stormed towards the bar.

'Is he ok?' he heard Livvi say as he strode forward, flicking the lapels on his jacket, barely able to string a cohesive thought together.

As he joined the queue for drinks, a hand tapped him on the shoulder.

'Magnus, please.' Taylor stared at him with pleading eyes.

'Please what? Am I about to discover that Skylar's twin sister happens to be called Taylor?'

Taylor covered her mouth and looked away. 'Yes.'

'And who are you? Actually Taylor? Or Skylar pretending to be Taylor in the old twin double, treble, quadruple bluff?'

'I'm Taylor. I told you I was Taylor.'

'And that makes it all fine, does it?' Ringing and pounding clamoured in his ears. How had he been so stupid?

'I wanted to tell you, I just thought—'

'Thought what? Thought I might not feel the same if I realised I'd been sleeping with a perfect stranger for the past few days. Ugh!' He tugged at his hair.

She nodded, still covering her mouth. 'Exactly.'

'Spot on then. How did you know who I was when I bumped into you?'

'I met you… fleetingly. It was me you spoke to in the bar on the day of our party.'

'Jesus Christ.' Magnus rubbed his hand down his face. 'I don't know what to say. I can't begin to describe what this feels like. I'm beyond anything.' Bile rose in his chest.

'I'm sorry, I really am.'

'Whatever. Because we're done. You've played me good and proper. There's no way anything is happening now. After tonight, you're gone. In fact, I'm going to sleep on the sofa when we get back. I don't want anything else to do with you.'

She sniffed back a tear and Magnus looked away, his head pounding. When he turned back, the crowd had swallowed Taylor.

He banged his hand on the bar, ordered a double whisky and downed it. Everyone else was using this as an excuse to get drunk, so he had the perfect cover. He wanted to erase all memory of this evening and cursed the day he'd crashed into Taylor Rousse.

Chapter Twenty-One

Taylor

Taylor ran down the wide steps at the front of Glen Lodge Hotel straight into a gust of icy wind. Cinderella had nothing on this. If Taylor lost a shoe on the stairs, she wouldn't even notice. *Why am I outside?* Pain splintered through her chilled veins, stabbing her so deeply she almost doubled up. *What have I done?* Since her last breakdown, she'd tried to detach and disassociate, blank out the hurt and lack of fulfilment in her life. Now the full weight of her insignificance clobbered her with crushing strikes. She held her chest. Air. She needed air.

Leaning over, she braced herself on a hefty balustrade. Slowly and steadily, she forced herself to inhale, then exhale until her lungs expanded. She straightened up and shivered, rubbing her arms, trying to awaken something other than the desire to fall on the cold hard ground and give up. Taylor Rousse didn't need to stoop this low because of some guy. She was her own person, wasn't she? Blinking fast, she pressed her lips together, denying the tears; she'd brought this on herself. Falling so deeply for Magnus was never part of the deal. A bit of harmless deception had turned into full-blown betrayal because she'd given emotions airtime.

Now he hated her. How could she explain the feelings were real? Everything had been real. Except she wasn't the right person. She couldn't because she'd never see him again. She had to get away. How could she face him? Face his family?

Tears clouded her vision and she gave up trying to stop them from spilling out. They trickled down her cheeks. Despite being made from the same genetic material as her sister, she was lacking. Even when she'd been considered the more promising actress, her confidence had failed her. Skylar was the one born to be seen and loved, Taylor to sink into the background.

Voices made her look up and she pushed her palms across her stinging cheeks. The tall bridesmaid Magnus had danced with was walking towards the door, laughing with a sexy-looking guy in shirt sleeves; his kilt-suit jacket was slung around the shoulders of the bridesmaid and he was talking with his lips close to her ear. Taylor froze, needing to move but seeing nowhere to go.

'Oh, hi,' said the bridesmaid. 'Are you ok?'

Taylor didn't meet her gaze, hoping to hide the panda eyes which might show up even in the artificial outside light. 'Yeah, sure.'

'Aren't you freezing?' said the man. Taylor glanced up, remembering he'd been at her table during the meal.

Taylor's bare arms glowed under the Victorian-style lamp. Goosebumps erupted all over her, she trembled and her teeth chattered. 'I need to get back.'

'Where to?' said the man.

'Back to LA.'

Taylor caught the two exchanging a glance. *Yeah, I know it's crazy, but I want to go home.* 'Can you give me a lift to Tighnatraigh or tell me who to call, taxis, minicabs, anything.'

'Should I get Magnus?' said the bridesmaid.

'No,' Taylor replied sharply. His name brought her to her senses. She had to be sensible. 'He can't drive, he's had a lot to drink. I have to go somewhere quiet and deal with some business. It's really important.'

'I can drive you,' said the man. 'It's only a few minutes up the road.'

'Would you?' said Taylor. 'That would be great. I'll message Magnus.'

'I'll come too,' said the bridesmaid. Taylor barely heard whatever they were saying after that. She pulled out her phone but no way was she really messaging him. In the backseat of the smart blue Audi, she scrolled through Google browsing for hotels on the island within walking distance of the ferry. In the short drive back to Fenella's house, she made a plan.

'Thanks so much,' she said, jumping out. 'And enjoy the rest of your night.' Fenella had told her people on the island rarely bothered locking doors, especially when they owned as many dogs as her. Taylor patted the big softies briefly as she entered the cottage. 'You'd make useless guard dogs. Get back to your beds, go on. I know you've been walked, Fenella told me she'd arranged it. I'm not sticking around. I need to make a few phone calls, then I'm out of here – forever.'

She changed out of the dress, folded it up and left it on the bed in the little room she'd shared with Magnus. *Don't look around. Don't think.* She mustn't let it affect her. None of it was real. She'd stolen a week of love but now she had to let go and leave it behind.

Packed and changed back into her normal clothes, she rang a hotel she'd ear-marked and tapped her finger as she waited for the call to connect. Reception was dodgy but the call connected. The person who took the call didn't mask their incredulity, but Taylor didn't care.

'Yes, a room for tonight.' Or what was left of it. 'Also, do you have a shuttle service that could pick me up from a house in Salen?' The silence on the other end told her that was a categorical no. 'So, a number for a local taxi then please.'

As soon as she discovered they had a room, she ended the call and rang the taxi company. Even with an hour's wait that was fine. She wanted to write a note. In fact, three. The first one she left with the dress for Robyn. The second a heartfelt thank you to Fenella and Per for having her. Her eyes swam with tears as she wrote Fenella's name. She wiped them away and glanced heavenwards.

The third was to Magnus. She only had a small notebook but by the time she got the words right, she'd wasted several pages. Eventually, she ripped out the sheet and placed it on the bedside table, slipping it under the lamp. Then she stood in the entrance, waiting. After what felt like an age, lights flickered in the distance. *Please god, let this be the taxi, not one of the family.* Her prayer was answered and a few minutes later, she was in the backseat, whizzing down the crazy little roads. When they passed the entrance gate to the Glen Lodge Hotel, Taylor put her head down and didn't look up until the light changed. They were in a village, windows illuminated the buildings around a curved bay.

When the taxi rocked up in front of a two-storey white house, Taylor realised this was the hotel. Not the way she'd planned to spend her last night on the island, but here she was.

She paid the driver, collected her case and staggered to the door.

Chapter Twenty-Two

Magnus

Someone was talking. Who? Who cared? Magnus downed another glass of whisky and banged it on the bar. He didn't look around from his bar stool. When a hand touched his shoulder, he wrenched it away, his vision swimming. The hand didn't move. When he finally glanced up, it took him a few minutes to work out whose face was spinning before him.

'There you are. Do you want some of the cake?'

'What?' Magnus blinked. His mum came into focus. The jaunty sound of Scottish dance music pounded inside his head like a mallet on a string.

'The cake, they've just cut it. Where's Taylor?'

Magnus rubbed his forehead. 'Somewhere about,' he muttered.

Fenella frowned and put her hands on her hips. 'What is going on? Have you fallen out?'

'Yeah.'

'Oh, Magnus. Livvi said she thought something was up. What happened?'

'Don't wanna talk, Mum, ok? I'm good.'

'And Taylor? Where's she? Is she ok?'

He cinched his shoulder blades together. 'Who knows? But she won't have gone far, it's not like she can, is it?' He lifted his glass and stared into its emptiness. Before he could raise his hand to order another, Fenella took hold of his wrist.

'You've had enough.'

He looked away. *I'm too old for her to order me about,* his fogged brain protested. But he slammed the glass down and squared his jaw. 'Whatever.'

'You should go and get some fresh air. I'm going to look for Taylor. What's her number?'

Magnus got off the barstool, managing to stay upright despite the world spinning before him. 'I'm not giving you her number. She'll be somewhere, I'll find her. But whatever hopes and plans you had for us, you can forget it. We're finished.'

*

Magnus's eyes didn't want to open. His mouth was the opposite. Eventually, he forced it shut and peeled up his eyelids. Where was he? Fragments came back, jabbing like broken glass against his forehead. He groaned and laid his hand on his temple.

Something dug uncomfortably into his back. Fumbling around, he found soft covers. He was still in his kilt. He yanked at the sporran chain, pulling it out from under him. The motion induced a wave of nausea and he shut his eyes. More memories dripped into his subconscious.

They hadn't found Taylor. Beth McGregor and her boyfriend had said they'd given her a lift back to the house. Fenella had been relieved and as the wedding party dwindled, she'd decided to take Magnus home. *In case I ruined the day for my little brother.* Which was likely. Jean had been snoring beside him on the drive back. Daylight threatened him through the gap in the curtains, but everything else was dark and obscure.

Where was Taylor now? She hadn't been in the house when they came back. Had the police come hammering on the door and he'd missed it in his stupor? *Jesus, I'm an irresponsible brat.* Heaving himself into a sitting position, it took all his strength not to throw up.

He tugged off the wedding outfit, pulled on a robe and slogged towards the bathroom. He needed to wake himself up and lose the contents of his stomach before facing his family. When he'd drowned himself in hot, then cold water, he pulled the robe back on. Padding over the soft carpets in his bare feet, he checked every room, finding no one except Jean sleeping in the old armchair. The last room was the kitchen. Fenella had her back to the door, stirring something on the hob.

'Oh, there you are.' She barely looked at him as she referred to a page in a cookbook. 'We're heading back to the hotel in an hour to wave off Carl and Robyn on their honeymoon. It's a surprise. Come if you like. I'm making a pot of soup for later. I thought I'd try this new recipe.'

'Mum.' Magnus ran his fingers through his hair. 'Where's Taylor?'

Fenella turned and shook her head; her pupils flashed red. 'Now you ask.' She returned to the book. 'Well, in your own time.'

'Ok. So, she's not here, and as you're not calling out the cavalry, I assume you know she's safe.'

'No, I don't know for sure, but as she's an intelligent young woman, I'm sure she's done everything she can to have a safe journey.'

'Dare I ask you what she told you?' Magnus bit his bottom lip, digging his teeth into it.

'The truth, and the only part of it which makes me question her intelligence, is taking up with you.'

'Oh, bloody charming,' he muttered, throwing his hands in the air. His head reeled.

'She acted with her heart, which was silly, though she wasn't to know.'

'Wasn't to know what? She didn't act with her heart. If you knew the truth, you'd understand exactly what she did.'

Fenella turned around and folded her arms. 'Then tell me.'

'The whole thing was fake.'

'She said.'

'Did she?' He ran his fingers through his hair and twisted his lips. 'And did she tell you about the part where she thought it would be fun to pretend she was her twin sister?'

'Yes, all of that.'

'And you think that makes her intelligent?'

'Why do you think she did it?'

Magnus frowned. 'How the hell should I know? She must be unstable.'

'And if she is, she needs more compassion than this.' Fenella glared. 'I wouldn't be at all surprised if she's unbalanced, not after the life she's had.'

'You do know she's not Skylar?'

'Yes. I do. She left me a note, telling me everything. She's lived in the shadow of her sister for years. When she met you, she saw a chance to get one over on her sister but mostly it was a chance to escape to a different world, to be free, have some fun and let go of herself.'

'Then why not tell me?'

'Yes, that was naïve. But by the time she realised she wanted you to know, it was too late. She'd fallen too hard.'

'Seriously,' Magnus mumbled. 'You believe that?'

'Yes, Magnus. I do. And I know she lied to you, but really, you lied to all of us. She wasn't your girlfriend at all.'

'Yes, I know, but I hate…'

'Hate what?'

'Feeling left out.'

'Taylor felt the same. She's always overlooked for her sister. After she arrived here, it was easy to forget she was lying because the two of you had grown so close. She found something in you she admired and she thought you felt it too.'

'I did,' said Magnus, clenching his fists. 'But that makes it worse. It was all based on a lie.'

'Does it change how you feel?'

'Yes!'

'So, if she really was the twin sister, do you think the week would have played out like this?'

Magnus snorted. *No. Of course it wouldn't.* None of it would have happened with Skylar. That seemed obvious now. 'Why didn't I click right from the start? She was so different. I didn't even know Skylar had a sister.' He frowned. He'd met Taylor first. Skylar must have seen their encounter and sought him out later. Why? Was she jealous of Taylor? What twisted world had he got himself mixed up in? 'I thought she'd changed.'

'Into someone kind, sweet, fun—'

'Yeah, ok. I get the message.'

'Just twelve hours too late.'

'Oh, whatever.' Magnus sighed. 'So where is she?'

'Gone. She booked into a hotel so she could get the first ferry out.'

'Right.' He rumpled his hair. 'Maybe it's for the best.' Taking a few wide steps, he crossed the kitchen and embraced Fenella, planting a kiss on her head. 'I'm sorry, Mum. I'm no good at this.'

Fenella patted him on the back and while his mum's hugs were always comforting, it didn't come close to mending the gash in his chest. 'You have to find a way to get better then.'

'Yeah. But not with Taylor. It's too late for that.'

'It's never too late, Magnus.'

He returned to his little bedroom and tossed off his robe. What an amazing few nights they'd spent here. And so much more. Grabbing a pair of boxer shorts, he tugged them on.

If he'd crashed into Skylar, she'd have sued him for every pound of flesh on his body and every penny in his bank account, assuming he'd got out the airport alive and her bodyguards hadn't murdered him.

He'd thought she'd changed and loved her for it. He frowned. Taylor was… tailormade for him. She'd never been Skylar. She'd always been Taylor, and he'd fallen for her. They'd hatched crazy plans that had seemed too huge, but if he removed the movie star, they didn't seem so impossible anymore. Except, of course, Taylor was gone, and he'd told her he never wanted to see her again.

The edge of a piece of paper on his bedside table caught his eye. He slid it out from beneath the lamp and read.

Magnus

I will never be able to put into words how I feel right now. My heart is crushed. Not by you but by my own stupidity. I don't know why I ever thought this could work and I have no excuses. I will never forgive myself. When I saw you again, I was in a rage with Skylar, and saw a chance to get back at her. It wouldn't have worked. She wouldn't have cared. But my idiot-self decided to do it anyway. I believed if I could win you over, I'd have won against Skylar. But after only a few hours, I realised you were so much more than a good-looking guy. That's when I made the big mistake. I fell for you for real and I couldn't stop falling. Maybe I won't ever stop. Everything we did was amazing and I cherish the feelings we shared because I meant every single one. I can't bear the idea that I put you through this. I toyed with a living, breathing, feeling man in order to satisfy a need in myself. The desperate need to be valued and to feel loved. For a few days you gave me that and I've honestly never felt that way before. Thank you.

I won't trouble you again. I wish you every joy in the future.

I love you.

Taylor Rousse

Magnus furrowed his brow, his eyes roaming over the last few words. The characters blended into a blur of grey and crazy thoughts trumpeted in his ears like a brass band booming. He dropped his head into his hands. His body slumped forward. How would he ever get over this?

Chapter Twenty-Three

Taylor

Skylar's voice rang out loud and clear from the back of the limo. Taylor sank back into the leather couch as her father reached for a bottle of water from the ice chest.

'Try it again,' he said. Skylar's eyes flashed with annoyance, twinkling in the reflected glow of the track lighting.

'Just once more,' Skylar said. 'I know it.'

'Once more, only more convincing this time.'

Taylor lowered her gaze, scrolling through an iPad and breathing sharply as they jerked around a corner.

'Watch it,' muttered Skylar to no one in particular before resuming her speech.

Four weeks ago, a giant hand had plucked Taylor out of her world and thrown her into a completely different one. Now, just as suddenly, she was back where she belonged, keeping her head down, pretending she didn't exist, but this time always under the watchful eye of her parents. As soon as she'd arrived back on mainland Scotland, she'd been dragged back to reality.

Unable to think about where to go, she'd messaged Liesel. Within a few hours, Liesel and an army of bodyguards arrived to retrieve her.

'My god, we thought you were dead,' Bianca had said. 'This is exactly the reason we don't like you going anywhere alone. You're a danger to yourself.'

'I wasn't in any danger.'

'Taylor, this is so like you. Only thinking of yourself. Didn't you stop for a second to think how Skylar felt when you just vanished? She was beside herself. We thought you'd stopped all this. You should start considering other people, and if you can't, it's time to go back to therapy.'

Yes, my fault. Wasn't it always? Skylar's words were like a dull chant in the background, blending with the music, the horns honking and the rush of traffic outside.

Skylar had lapped up the poor wounded sister attention with quips like: 'You terrified the life out of me. How could you? You wrecked my time in London. Where did you even go? Some drug den? And here we were thinking you were clean.'

Taylor didn't reply to any of it. None of them knew where she'd really been. The countryside was as vague an answer as she could muster. Mull would have been lost on them completely. Mull? Even the name sounded like something from a distant memory. Was it even real? Or somewhere she'd dreamed up? The memories were like something that had happened to someone else. They were slipping away like sand through her fingers.

Without the messages, she could have been persuaded that none of it was real. She woke her iPad, barely hearing what Skylar was talking about. The message thread that kept her going flashed up and Fenella Hansen's little round profile picture smiled from the page top. She'd changed the picture to one from the wedding. A little jolt of pain struck Taylor in the chest. Skylar's cloying perfume was nauseating and Taylor took a moment to lay back her head, catching the cool swell from the A/C before rereading the messages for the umpteenth time.

She skimmed over them. What did she expect to find? Nothing from Magnus. Fenella's words over the past few weeks had been comforting but didn't indicate any change in her son. Just swapping chats with someone from that world gave Taylor a flicker of joy in these otherwise dark days. Fenella skirted neatly around the Magnus subject, telling Taylor more about the dogs, Aunt Jean, Robyn and Carl, or her granddaughter. And while loving it all, Taylor wondered more and more if keeping up the friendship made sense – for Fenella. Surely she had more important things to do?

Skylar's voice sang out as she practised her speech for the opening of a charitable foundation. She should have it off-pat by now but other things were always more important: hair, nails, make-up, a spa therapy session. Taylor almost choked at the thought of the foundation. Skylar and charity couldn't be used in the same sentence as far as she was concerned, but it was part of the new image, the all-American girl who'd pulled herself out of the black hole of child stardom, the addictions and the rehab to become a squeaky-clean icon.

All fake. Taylor's insides contracted at the word. If anyone was the queen of fake, it was her. Maybe it ran in their family. With both parents being actors, the gene was there. The one which caused the desire to be someone else and the desperation to be noticed. Skylar achieved it by acting and being famous. Taylor didn't. And when she'd tried to act and get someone's attention, it backfired.

'Was that better?' asked Skylar.

'Excellent, you nailed it,' said her father. 'You're a natural.'

'Great.' Skylar squinted at Taylor. 'Why are you here? You should have stayed with Mom.'

'Mom's busy,' said her father. 'Taylor's got some work to be doing.'

Oh yes. Taylor had work. A bit of lip service to PR that they paid her for, but it was nothing except an umbilical cord keeping her attached to them. Whenever she suggested moving on they reminded her how her life was secure and safe here. How she would always have the help she needed – whether she wanted it or not. She got to share in a life of luxury. Who would object to so much spending money, designer clothes, fast cars, private flights, luxury hotels, poolside parties and all the trappings of a Hollywood star? And they had control. They didn't want Taylor out in the world being 'a danger to herself' or risking any damage to Skylar's precious career.

Taylor's glimpse into a different world had been cut short. As she skimmed the messages, she smiled, thinking how much Magnus's world would have petrified Skylar. She may preach charity but to see life in a world so much humbler than her own would freak her out. The glimpse into a new dimension had fascinated Taylor, surrounding her with people who cared and where caring didn't mean overspending just so the leash could be tightened. She couldn't leave because she 'owed them'. Magnus's family had accepted her without question, taken her in and valued her. Her family wouldn't do the same for him. He'd be an outsider and they'd only look at him with suspicion.

The limo ground to a halt and Skylar peered out the window, the corners of her mouth turned down. Taylor didn't need the twin bond to read her sister's mind. With Skylar being so used to rolling up outside grand hotels, exclusive clubs, casinos and movie theatres, this had to be the biggest comedown of her life.

Her focus flicked from the window and she gaped at her father. 'I can't go in there.'

Taylor took in the worse-for-wear building and liked the way they had decked it out for the occasion. The residents and staff at the Holdbane Shelter for the homeless had made a genuine effort. It wasn't every day a celebrity turned up, especially one as young and glamorous as Skylar. A gang of photographers and reporters waited around on the sidewalk, desperate to get the best shot of Skylar. At the bottom of the steps was a little podium decked with posters. Taylor had arranged for it to be as picture perfect as possible. One of those little jobs she got to do and was expected to be delighted about.

Their father gave a sharp shrug. 'It won't take long, just get out, shake some hands and make the speech.'

'Think of the Instagram photos,' said Taylor.

'Oh god.' Skylar threw her head back. 'You're loving this, aren't you?'

'Not really.'

'Of course you are. You deliberately set me up in the most dreadful area of town.'

'I just arranged the stand. The idea wasn't mine. And anyway, you don't exactly get homeless shelters in the best parts of town.'

'Sometimes I wish you still looked like me,' said Skylar. 'Then you could do all this shitty stuff for me.'

Taylor shifted in her seat. She looked enough like her; Skylar just didn't want to see it. 'I do enough of your shitty stuff already.'

'You have no idea how easy your life is,' said Skylar.

'Seriously? Anyway, I thought impersonating you was a criminal offence these days.'

'Girls, don't start,' said their father.

'Well, she doesn't have a clue,' said Skylar. 'All she does is mess around on that iPad, lives on my money and gets the best of everything without having to do anything.'

Taylor flashed her the daggers. 'If I do nothing, then I'll quit.'

'Empty words,' said Skylar. 'You're the leach twin. You can't live without feeding off of me. And when things go wrong, you make up lie after lie.'

'No… I don't. You—'

'That's enough from both of you,' said their father. 'Now come on, Skylar, they're waiting.'

Two bodyguards flanked the outside doors of the limo as Skylar stepped out. Their father hopped across to the couch on the other side for a better view as she shook hands with the shelter owner.

'Dad, I'm serious, I want to quit. I don't want to do this anymore,' said Taylor. 'I'll sign a disclaimer or whatever. I won't impersonate Skylar, I swear.'

'Look, honey.' He barely took his eyes from the window. 'I wish I could believe that. Trouble is, we can't trust you. All these stories you've made up about your sister over the years, they're not real. It's all in your head. All of it. No one wanted to tell you and, even with the therapy, you don't seem to have come any further forward. This all kicked off when you were fourteen and you missed getting the *Girls get Gritty in the City* part. I know it cut deep. After that, you were never the same.'

'Dad, I told the truth about that. It's not me making up the stories. I didn't tell the producer I'd give up the part. It must have been Skylar dressed as me.'

He gave her a sad smile and Taylor's mouth fell open. He thought she was making it up, even now… Was she? Had she warped the memory in her favour? No. No. It was true!

Her father's focus returned to the window. Skylar was at the podium, smiling and gesticulating as she made her speech, looking like a Barbie doll version of Eva Peron.

'You don't believe me? The producer had already decided I could have that part. Skylar couldn't stand it.'

'Yeah, honey,' her father replied. 'We heard. But that's not what happened. It was a long time ago. Let's drop it. You're a good girl and you're good at these admin type things, so it all worked out for the best, didn't it?'

Taylor knew he didn't require an answer. His gaze locked on Skylar and he smiled an indulgent smile, his white teeth sparkling and contrasting to his heavily tanned skin. Here was Taylor back in the cage, the padlock bigger than ever and the hope of escape non-existent.

As she looked on from the limo window, her iPad pinged and she woke it to check the message. Her heart skipped a little when she saw Fenella's picture. Even if it was just a new recipe she'd tried, or a photo of her dogs, it was like a little bit of gold dust to sprinkle on dull days.

FENELLA: Hey! You won't believe this. I've persuaded Magnus to come to LA. We're all coming! I've always wanted to visit Hollywood and they've agreed to take me for my sixtieth! Magnus wasn't keen, he thought it was a setup, and between you and me, it is a bit. As soon as I have concrete dates, I'll let you know. I don't want you to worry about it, but please meet us while we're there.

Taylor bit into her lower lip. She didn't want Fenella wasting a once in a lifetime trip on her. No wonder Magnus was against a setup. What could she say that she hadn't said already? Her crimes were unpardonable.

Chapter Twenty-Four

Magnus

Getting air miles wasn't a problem. Getting annual leave only a little. But getting through to his mother that nothing she said would make him meet up with Taylor was impossible.

Magnus's connections helped him get the whole family on first class. As he took his seat, he gave a resigned huff at no one in particular, but the scene was all too familiar. His mum and dad in their booth together, checking out all the mod cons, Robyn and Carl getting comfy and making eyes at each other, and Livvi and Jakob settling little Polly with doting voices. Magnus crossed his ankles, checked his phone and twiddled his thumbs. He wouldn't be the stick in the mud who spoiled his mum's birthday treat, but he couldn't help feeling he was missing out on so much. Watching these scenes for the next seven hours would be like watching a slow-motion film of his spleen being removed with a cheese knife.

'This is wonderful,' said Fenella, beaming at him.

'Are you glad not to be piloting?' asked a flight attendant.

'I'm not sure.' Magnus ran his hand down his cheek.

'Just relax and enjoy it,' she said. 'Would you like a drink?'

'Not yet, thanks.' Flying and drinking didn't marry in his mind, even when he didn't have to worry about communication breakdowns, the angle of the sun or suspicious fuel smells in the cockpit. But it might help him blank out.

He flipped on the air-con and lay back in his seat. The plane filled around them, mostly with businesspeople on laptops. Magnus rolled his head away and gazed at the tiny window. Fenella had done her best to convince him this was all for her benefit and, yes, she'd always wanted to visit Hollywood, but he wasn't a fool. His mum was still in touch with Taylor, though she didn't let on much about what they talked about, and he guessed his mum lived in hope of some reconciliation. Maybe Taylor did too. Deluded as ever then. She'd scammed him and the worst part was she'd made him care. Forgive and forget? No chance.

*

After a reasonably uneventful flight, a quick changeover and a smooth landing at LAX, they made their way to the apartment. They'd hired two cars and seemed to think Magnus the most likely to find the way, so he drove off first with Robyn and Carl in the backseat. Should he wear a cap and expect a tip? Livvi was driving the car behind with Jakob, Polly, Fenella and Per.

'Does Mum know these cars have Satnav?' said Magnus.

'She likes to think we're in the most capable hands,' said Carl.

'Thanks. I feel like a cab driver.'

After almost two hours in nose to tail traffic, they reached the apartment. It had amazing views over the city. Fenella was in her element making sure everyone was happy, and Magnus cracked open a beer and sat by the window in the living area, ankles crossed, soaking in the scene. If this was all he had to do to make his mum's birthday a success, so be it. But nervous tension crackled around him. He loved his mum and would trust her with his life… just not his love life. He couldn't be sure even now she wasn't cooking up some plan to get Taylor here.

Livvi's mother, Trix, joined them the following day. Her usual residence was in New York but she'd flown over to see her daughter and granddaughter. Although Polly was now eighteen months, Trix had only seen her once. Magnus grinned at the contrast between her and Fenella. He wouldn't swap his mum for anyone and this woman was as un-mum-like as he could imagine. She was every cent the glamour queen and though she must be at least fifty, she looked twenty years younger and in the bloom of health with her glossy auburn hair and tanned skin. After she'd given him the once over, Magnus made himself scarce. His brother's mother-in-law giving him the eye was verging on new levels of creepy.

The apartment contained a small gym at the back and Magnus worked off his pent-up energy. When the door opened, he swallowed a moment of panic. He didn't like the idea of Trix seeing him dressed in his gym shorts – he hadn't bothered with a top.

'There you are.' Fenella slipped in the door and closed it quietly.

'Mum. Seriously. What is it?'

'Oh, don't be silly. It's not as if I haven't seen you like that before. I need to tell you something and I want you to listen without going off on one.'

Magnus folded his arms across his bare chest. 'Don't tell me you've set me up with Taylor. I wasn't born yesterday.'

Fenella cocked her head. 'It does have something to do with Taylor, that's why I want you to listen.'

With a grunt, Magnus sat on the bench and lifted a dumbbell. 'I made myself clear, Mum. I won't change my mind.'

'I still want you to listen. I have invitations for us to attend a red-carpet event at the Goldcrest Hotel. It's in aid of a charity foundation set up by Taylor's sister.'

Magnus plonked the dumbbell on the floor. 'You have to be kidding. You have no idea, do you?'

'Yes, I do. And I'd like you to come too.'

'So I can meet Taylor and do what? Talk about all the lies she told and drag it all up again?'

Fenella sat down, her expression filled with concern. 'I know this is difficult. Taylor got these tickets for me because I asked her to. She's well aware you don't want to see her and I don't think she really wants to see you.'

'Right. So, why bother?'

'In truth, it's not for you, it's for her.'

'I don't follow.'

'I want to see her and check she's ok. From her messages, I get a weird feeling. If you don't want to come tonight, I'll understand, but I'm going and I want to see her. I hoped, yes, that the two of you could at least be friends, but if not, I respect that.'

Fenella stood up, walked over and placed a kiss on his forehead. 'I only ever wanted you to be happy. Stay here, if you'd rather. Trix will be here looking after Polly, but I'm sure she won't bother you.'

After she'd left, Magnus knocked the punchbag for six.

Was it her words? Or maybe the threat of being left with Trix? Whichever, that evening he showered and groomed himself to red-carpet perfection. With a little tweak of his cufflinks in the mirror, he gave himself a visual appraisal. Not bad. Good enough for whatever his mother had planned.

Their cabbie dropped them off close to the grand entrance of the top-class hotel. Limousines and flashy vehicles lined the street closest to the door. Adjusting his heavily starched collar, Magnus climbed the white stone steps onto the red-carpeted entrance behind the others. Everything enraptured Fenella, and she pointed out cars, clothes and minute details on the ornate doorframes like she was guiding a class trip around a historic house.

Two bouncers the size of bears flanked a woman in a stunning long purple dress with a perfect blonde up-do. She stretched out her arm and greeted Fenella with a dazzling smile. Outsized jewellery glittered on her ears and around her neck. More sparklers gleamed at her wrist and on her fingers. The slight creases on the back of her hand were the only giveaway the woman was older than she looked. With the botox, guessing her age was almost impossible, but Magnus recognised her as Skylar and Taylor's mother.

A bizarre collision of two worlds played out before him. Fenella wouldn't know who she was shaking hands with, unless she recognised her from a film. Mrs Rousse still went by her acting name of Bianca Kain, but she'd never been A-list. As Magnus approached, he took Bianca's hand, listened to her prepared speech and swiped a glass of champagne from a nearby flunky.

Magnus moved into the main chamber, taking in the opulent surroundings, glittering chandeliers, and white-clothed tables decorated with floral centrepieces and crystal dishes. His reflection smirked at him from one of the enormous mirrors; he could pass for a single billionaire – though he didn't quite have the bank balance.

Fenella was still chirping excitedly about everything as they mingled in their group. Livvi looked most at home and spoke of similar events she'd been to, but Magnus was edgy. Too many awkward possibilities jostled ahead. He listened to the soft classical music in the background, and the laughter and chatter, while sampling the hors d'oeuvres from passing silver salvers on the arms of black-clad waiters.

Close to an open window with chiffon curtains fluttering gently, a group of women chattered. Immaculately dressed in shapely black dresses, killer heels and gravity-defying hairstyles, they sipped from highball glasses and laughed.

Magnus broke away from his party without anyone noticing and strolled towards the window.

'Hi,' he said, pulling out his most charming smile.

'Hey,' said one of them, eyeing him from top to toe.

'It's hot in here,' he said, keeping up the smile. 'You ladies have the best spot.'

'We do,' said the woman. 'Do you wanna share?'

'Can I? I could do with some air.'

'Sure.' They parted and let him move closer to the window. 'Your accent is adorable. Where are you from?' said one woman. Ice clinked against her glass as she sipped slowly.

'Scotland.'

'Oh, my god,' said another woman. 'I have Scottish ancestors.'

'Do you?' said Magnus.

'Yes. They came from the cutest little village called Dunkeld. I visited it last year, it's gorgeous. Have you been there?'

'No,' said Magnus, 'Tell me more.' She didn't need further invitation. None of them did. Under the cover of pleasant chat and as much champagne as he could drink, Magnus whiled away the minutes.

'So, do you know Skylar Rousse?' Magnus asked.

'No, but we all work for a regeneration initiative downtown and this foundation marries well with what we're doing.'

'So, we're hoping for some back scratching.'

'I get it,' said Magnus.

'What about you? Do you know her?'

Making a slight adjustment to his collar, Magnus nodded. 'A little.'

'Oh, wow, awesome. Are you an actor?'

'No.' He paused for a moment. 'I used to be a pilot for Courtney Hines. Skylar moved in the same circles.'

'Seriously? You're a pilot?'

'Yeah.' He waited for the awe to die down, though his ego swelled under their wide eyes.

'Did Courtney treat you like one of her family? I heard she's very generous.'

'Yeah, she was good to work for.'

'Bet you're glad it wasn't Skylar you worked for. I've heard she's dynamite and blows up at the slightest thing. I'm terrified of meeting her.'

'She sure has a reputation,' Magnus agreed.

'Well, if you get a chance to talk to her, give her a push in this direction, will you?'

'Yeah, sure, though getting close to her will be like storming the Bastille.'

They laughed and Magnus excused himself as he saw Fenella drifting around. 'Where have you been?' she asked.

'Mingling. Why?'

'I had a message from Taylor.'

Magnus turned away, clenching his jaw.

'Stop that,' said Fenella. 'I'm worried about her. I'm not sure she's here. She said she couldn't make it. I tried to call her but she's not picking up.'

He rubbed his forehead, deliberately trying not to heed the worry in his mum's voice. Wasn't it more likely it was just another of Taylor's stories? 'Why trust her?'

'Because I do.' Fenella poked him. 'Have a heart. Remember how you felt when you were together.'

'I do, that's the problem.'

'Then remember, that's how she feels too. She only lied about her name. Everything she said and did towards you was real. Now she's rotting in a pit of misery.'

'Cut the drama, Mum.' But deep inside, he wanted to see Taylor. To know she was ok.

'I mean it. At least do her the service of acknowledging she has feelings just as big as yours.'

'Jesus, Mum,' he muttered. 'I bet she's hurting, but how can I change that?'

'By doing her the common decency of talking about it, rather than giving her the cold shoulder and demonising her because she wounded that great big ego of yours.'

A gong rang and the sound stopped Fenella. *Thank Christ*. The heat of her lecture was scalding him.

Fenella checked her watch. 'I think that's the first keynote speech. I'm not sure if we'll bother with it.'

'I'll go,' said Magnus. 'I promised the ladies over there I'd do something for them.'

'Who?' Fenella frowned at him. 'Honestly, sometimes I don't know where we got you from.'

Magnus gave her a quick peck on the cheek. If he got an audience with Skylar, he would speak up on the women's behalf, but something else stirred in him. Where was Taylor? He could understand her not wanting to see him but knowing she wasn't here made the dull ache in his heart grow heavier.

He joined the queue for the antechamber and after a few minutes, took his seat. His first glimpse of Skylar came as she marched onto the stage, head high, hair tumbling behind. She gave a wave and a big smile as people applauded. Magnus watched her sitting on a clinical white chair on the stage, her long glamorous legs crossed in front of her. As the speaker carried on, Skylar leaned forward, her cleavage showing as she nodded in agreement. Plastic beauty radiated from her heavily made-up face. How could he ever have mistaken Taylor for her? Even when Taylor had been dolled up, she was more natural. If only he'd had that much insight when he first met her. Even Skylar's voice sounded fake. Maybe it was the microphone, but the words were harsh and brassy compared to the soft sounds of Taylor whispering in his ear or singing her heart out.

He got to his feet before the applause was finished, ready for a quick exit. As he withdrew, he tried to keep an eye on Skylar but she was whisked off the stage at the back.

More champagne flowed and Magnus found the group of women. He stuck with them until he spotted a huddle in the middle of the room. Two enormous men, looking totally out of place, stood menacingly with their arms folded, pushing in earpieces and speaking into walkie-talkies.

'That'll be Skylar.' Magnus sipped his champagne, browsing the crowd.

'Oh, jeez, we're never gonna get close.'

Magnus dropped his empty glass on a passing tray, swiped another, and tossed it back. 'I'm going to try.'

'You go.'

'Yeah, you're awesome. Get in there, man.'

Egged on by the women's cries, he edged his way through the crowd, closer to the throng in the middle. Quicker than expected, he came eye to shoulder with one of the giant bodyguards.

'Hey, mate,' said Magnus. 'Any chance of me talking to the princess?'

The guard folded his arms and glared down his thick nose.

'We're old friends,' Magnus continued. 'Just let me a bit closer so I can say hello. She'll be mad if she finds out I was here and you kept her from seeing me.'

The guard's nostrils flared and he glanced around. He shifted slightly and Magnus saw long blonde curls bouncing around a perfectly made-up face, pink lips glittering like they were encrusted with diamonds and eyelashes like black widow legs. What a phoney. Her whole existence was fake. Her body, her face, even this foundation – all an act.

But Taylor. When she'd been faking, she was real. The real deal and a deal Magnus had grown so attached to his heart wanted to crack open. Seeing Skylar now was like looking at a grossly overdone caricature of someone he wanted so badly. Damn his mother for being right, as always. As he funnelled his brain into remembering this was not Taylor, despite the likeness, Skylar looked up with a pout so big it could rival Mick Jagger. Her expression changed rapidly when her eyes landed on him.

'Oh, my god.' She raised her hand to her throat, lowering it over the bare expanse of her chest to rest on the low-cut edge of her black off-the-shoulder dress. Her trout pout had morphed into a gape. 'Well, I never. Is that Handsome Hansen?' she said in a loud, carrying voice.

The large guard glowered at Magnus.

'Yup. That's me,' he said to the guard with a wink. 'I told you she'd want to see me.' The crowd parted like the Red Sea before Moses, and Skylar snaked towards him, prowling like a catwalk model in her killer heels. He'd seen this move before. The last time it was followed by her arm swooping around his neck, her lips crashing against his, her tongue in his mouth, and her body all over him. What would she do now? His hand leapt to his black tie and he straightened it compulsively. Surely she'd behave herself; she was in public – not that it had bothered her before – but this time she was trying to show off a new squeaky-clean image.

Two perfectly manicured hands gripped his arms. 'Handsome Hansen, of all the people.' She reached up and air-kissed him. First on the right cheek, then on the left. Before she pulled away, she whispered, 'Hot as ever.' As she drew back, she beamed. 'Can y'all move back? I need to talk to this old friend of mine.'

On cue, the two large men moved into position, folding their arms and the crowd melted back.

'What are you doing here? It's been too long.'

'Has it? I think we met what? All of twice.'

'Sure. I've missed you every day for nearly three years,' she said, the pout back in place.

'Five years. And no, you haven't. Quit the bullshit.'

'Is it really five years? Oh my god. But you're so wrong. You're like the hottest guy I ever had the pleasure of not getting it on with.'

He smirked. 'Don't believe you.'

'Tell you what.' She moved closer, licking her lips. 'Why don't you and I get together later when this is done? We can play some catch-up.'

'Hmm,' said Magnus, pinching his lips together and staring at the gilded plasterwork on the ceiling. 'I've come to beg a favour,' he said.

'Oh?'

'Where can I find Taylor?'

'Who?'

For a split second, his heart stopped. 'Your twin sister.'

Skylar beamed and Magnus's pulse hammered in his ears. She did have a sister, didn't she? Then the corners of her lips fell. 'Wow, you know about her.'

'I met her before I met you.'

Skylar's eyes narrowed. 'But—'

'Just tell me where she is.'

She frowned and arched one perfect eyebrow. 'How do you know her?'

'I need to talk to her.'

'What's going on? Has she sent you here to spy on me or play some kind of trick on me?'

'No, of course not. I just want to talk to her.'

'About me? Please don't tell me she spun some lies about me and how misunderstood she is?'

'I can't say what it's about.'

'You've been pulled onto the Taylor sympathy bus. This is exactly why… Oh, never mind. She's a danger to herself; she has been for years. We have to keep a close watch on her.'

Magnus weighed the information but didn't speak. He stared into the eyes that were so similar to the ones he wanted to be gazing into. Believing this act would be easy. Skylar was a seasoned pro. But he knew now which sister he trusted. Taylor's lie had come from the heart; Skylar's was malicious. 'Just tell me where I can find her.'

'Will you kiss me?'

'What?'

'If I tell you?'

The chattering crowd seemed to close in as though they sensed something about to happen. Magnus scanned the faces and ran his hand over his cheek. 'Seriously?'

'Why not? For old times' sake.'

She had to be kidding, right? Her hard look said she wasn't. 'Now?'

A man tapped Skylar on the shoulder. 'Fifteen minutes until the next keynote.'

'Oh, hell.' She glanced at Magnus. 'We have a deal,' she said. 'Don't run off. I'll be back for my payment.'

'You haven't told me anything yet.'

'After the speech, thirty minutes.'

Magnus let out a protracted breath as Skylar regrouped with her bodyguards and disappeared. Why was everything with her such a drama? A gentle touch on Magnus's arm made him jump. One of the women in the regeneration group beamed at him. 'Hey. Did you happen to mention us?'

'Sorry, I couldn't get an answer to anything; she just railroaded me. She has her own agenda, and I'm not sure how to get through to her.'

Going through with her little game was a small price if she kept up her end of the bargain. If she didn't, he was ready to blow his top. Despite his qualms about seeing Taylor again, a primitive urge was telling him to find her. She needed him and he needed her.

Chapter Twenty-Five

Taylor

Taylor's suite was so huge the whole of Fenella's house could fit inside it. Taylor sat cross legged on the enormous bed, tapping her iPad. Fenella was here downstairs with Magnus. *So close! Ugh.* Taylor flung herself onto the pillow. What could possibly be different from before?

Her father was on high alert and she was under house arrest. This was her reality and it sucked. There was no escape from the misery. Twelve years ago when Taylor had been offered the part in *Girls Get Gritty in the City*, it had started. Skylar told a different version of the story and everyone had believed her. *Have I kidded myself all these years? Made up a story and clung to it until it became my truth?* Even her therapist had suggested it. Maybe she'd never been the more talented actress. She just wished for it. And if she made out Skylar had scuppered it for her, then she had a crutch, something to blame for her failings.

She covered her face and held her hands over her eyes. She couldn't be clear on anything. When she'd been with Magnus, she'd been whole and real, but under a cloak of lies. A resounding thump on her door made her jump. 'What the hell?' She moved her hands, revealing the giant satin bed canopy above her head.

More pounding. 'Open the goddamn door,' shouted Skylar.

Taylor sighed and hopped off the bed, padding across the floor in her fluffy slippers. Seeing her sister all dolled up while she was in her pyjamas always made her feel like a second-class citizen. But what was new?

'Something very interesting just happened,' said Skylar, marching straight in, crossing to the window and closing it.

'You crossed the million-dollar mark?'

'How should I know?' She spun around from the window. 'This is much more interesting than that. I met someone.'

Taylor waited, her heart pumping fast. 'Who?'

'Someone who knows you.' Skylar put her hands on her hips and stared. 'It shocked me. A lot.'

'Who?'

'I didn't think he'd even worked out you were a different person. I thought I'd fooled him.'

'Who?' she repeated, but she knew.

'Handsome Hansen, the sexy pilot.'

Taylor walked backwards until the soft bedcover brushed her skin. She sat, placing her hands on either side of her and gripping the blanket. 'You saw him?'

'Yes, goddammit. Why the hell does he want to talk to you?'

Taylor didn't reply. How could she? If Skylar knew the truth, what the hell would she make of it?

'Oh, god.' Skylar slapped her forehead. 'Don't tell me! You met him somewhere and you've told him a pack of lies about me. Is that where you went when we were in Scotland? What have you done?'

'Nothing.'

'I don't believe you. Everything you ever do is to scupper my career.'

'It wasn't like that.'

'Wasn't it? Oh, god. You slept with him, didn't you? And pretended you were me.'

Taylor crossed her feet, matching the love hearts on her slippers. Shit was about to hit the fan. All of Skylar's worst suspicions were about to come true. Taylor almost laughed. This was what she'd wanted: to get one over on Skylar, and it was exactly what her sister dreaded.

'Tell me!' demanded Skylar. 'Or did you try to get him into bed and he guessed you were a fake? Is he blackmailing you? Does he want our silence?'

'Yeah, fifty million dollars.'

'What?'

'Each month for the rest of your life.'

'Are you serious?'

'No, of course not. But you're making up some crazy story of your own, so I figure you're not interested in the truth.'

'Then tell me,' said Skylar, pulling a goofy face as though Taylor was witless. 'And hurry up, my speech is in five minutes.'

Pinching her lips together, Taylor rocked on the bed. 'You were almost right.'

'What?' Skylar's eyes blazed with shock.

'When I "disappeared",' she air-quoted, 'he crashed into me at the airport.'

'Jesus.' Skylar raised her hand to her forehead.

'He thought I was you and I played along.'

'You did what?'

'It was your fault. You ran off with the guy I'd arranged to meet.'

'Oh, here we go,' she said. 'The fairy tales begin.'

'Seriously, you know it's true. I'd been messaging Alex for months.' Taylor ignored Skylar's headshake. 'So, as I was saying, he knocked me over and—'

'This is far-fetched even for you.'

'It's the truth. I let him think I was you and we… went off together.'

'Jesus bloody Christ. How could he think you were me? He knows I don't travel alone.' She stamped her foot. 'Ugh!'

'He asked why no one was with me. I said I needed alone time.'

'What the hell were you thinking?'

'I wanted to piss you off.'

'And you slept with him! While pretending to be me. That is despicable.'

Taylor shrugged half-heartedly. 'Why? It's not like we shared him. The two of you never got that far. And he liked me—'

'Because he thought you were me!' Skylar screamed.

'No. He thought you'd changed. He liked the new you better, the new you who wasn't you at all. It was me. Me that he liked.' Tears welled and Taylor sucked in her lips and stared at the canopy.

'There is something far wrong with you.'

Taylor couldn't reply. If she'd told Magnus the truth from the start, she could have avoided all this and maybe he would still have taken her with him. If she hadn't been so hellbent on revenge.

'So what does he want to talk to you about?'

'I don't know,' said Taylor. The expression on his face when he discovered the truth would haunt her forever. He wanted Skylar. Maybe he wanted her to have changed, but at the end of the day, Taylor was the wrong twin and always would be. Even Fenella's kind words wouldn't change that.

Skylar left the room with a slam and Taylor flopped back on the bed. Tears rolled down her cheeks as she remembered those nights she'd slept next to Magnus, when they'd told each other all the things they loved about each other. It had taken place under a fake pretence but Taylor had meant every word. She'd made herself believe he had too.

She swiped away the tears and sprang up, grabbed her case from the floor and raked through it until she found something semi-respectable. Throwing off her pyjamas, she dressed inattentively. She had to talk to him before Skylar got her claws into him again. The door opened silently. *Phew.* The bodyguard had his hands in his back pockets and was pacing the hall at the far end, looking out the window. Taylor slipped behind him, ran around a corner and through the door to the main stairs without looking back.

Stopping on the landing, eye-to-eye with the enormous chandelier that hung from a double-height ceiling through the centre of the hotel, she peered into the grand lobby. A few people milled around but the main sounds were coming from a room on the left. Heads turned and eyebrows raised as Taylor shuffled past, feeling like Cinders again, only this time, the naughty Cinders who hadn't escaped before midnight and was at the ball in her rags. With a deep breath, she straightened her black sheath dress and entered the main room. Most people were too busy talking, drinking or eating to notice her, but one or two people glanced up quizzically. She must look a fright with her hair pulled back into a makeshift up-do; the teeth of the crocodile clip bit into the back of her scalp. A gong sounded, and people started moving into the antechamber. Taylor flicked her family pass and nipped in, standing at a window, making sure the large swooped-up drape screened her.

The room filled with people. Finally, Taylor saw someone who made her heartrate skyrocket. Magnus, looking utterly glorious in his tux. Memories of what they'd done in Carl's spare bedroom flooded back. Then more images of how they'd cuddled on the beach and written those words in the sand. But they were transient. Magnus couldn't love Taylor forever.

Skylar emerged from the front of the crowd onto a podium and started her rehearsed speech.

Taylor kept her eyes on Magnus. He seemed to have taken up with a group of women and was whispering to them quite at his ease.

Loud applause broke out and Skylar stepped off the podium into the crowd. Magnus made his way to the front until he was beside Skylar. She beamed at him and Taylor balled her fists as he spoke to her, his hands gesticulating. He pointed at the group of women; they grinned and waved at Skylar who gave them a condescending raise of her hand in return.

Magnus smiled and closed in on Skylar, as though saying something more private. Taylor moved closer. Skylar was whispering something in Magnus's ear. He nodded triumphantly before Skylar glanced up, her fluttering eyelashes provocative and alluring. She clutched him by the lapel and tugged it. With an oddly quick movement, like time had speeded up, Magnus slid his hand around Skylar's waist, dipped his head and kissed her. Taylor stopped dead. Maybe her heart had stopped too. No, it was beating, pounding in her ears, deafening, but everything else went silent. Skylar had moved in for the full Hollywood, and Taylor couldn't watch any more. Bitter bile burned in her throat.

Turning around, she tried to run from the room. People blocked her everywhere and she dodged them. Now or never. It had to be. She couldn't wait any longer. For years and years, she'd suffered this. Every time she'd tried to escape, they thwarted her, every time she had something good, Skylar stole it. No one ever saw her, believed her, listened to or recognised she had worth in herself. No one except Magnus and the people in his life. Now he was here in Skylar's arms, and Taylor's phoney dream was blasted out of the water.

Chapter Twenty-Six

Magnus

Wolf-whistles rang out and Magnus yanked himself out of Skylar's clutches. As the consummate Hollywood actress, she knew how to put on a good kissing display but, despite going through the motions, Magnus felt nothing other than the physical touch of Skylar's lips on his.

She pouted, looking annoyed he'd stopped her just as she was getting into it. Which was exactly why it had to stop. 'Why'd you stop?'

'Remember where you are,' he said. 'It's not a club or a private room.'

'Oh, yeah.' She straightened herself out and beamed around. 'I love this guy,' she told the onlookers.

Magnus grimaced. Those words meant nothing from her.

'I haven't seen him for such a long time, excuse me for getting carried away.' She turned back to him. 'At least there's no paparazzi here, or you and I would be all over the internet.'

'Anyone here could have been filming that.' Magnus didn't give a shit if every website on the planet displayed the footage. He had an address for Taylor. Now he needed to get out and find her.

'Would you like to meet me upstairs after?' asked Skylar. 'We have a lot to catch up on and there's no point in you going to Taylor's apartment. It's out of town and too late to call now. Taylor's a sad little puppy who goes to bed very early.'

'Is she?'

'Well yes. Obviously, you don't know her that well.'

'Did I say I did?'

'What happened when you met her? I suppose she pretended to be me.'

Magnus frowned and fiddled with his cuff. 'What makes you say that?'

'It's what she always does. She's totes insecure and pretending to be me makes her feel better. Everybody knows about me and the problems I had growing up. I'm in the public eye, I can't hide. Everything I'm doing here and now is because of that. But it's just as well people don't know about Taylor. She's a hundred times worse.'

'How so?'

'I'm not sure I have time to tell you, right now. It started when we were fourteen and we both auditioned for the same part. She made up all sorts of lies about why she didn't get it and then went totally over the edge. She's been a liability ever since. My parents don't let her get too far, she's a danger to herself. But sometimes it happens; she runs off, pretends to be me, leads some kind of double life for a few days, then comes back, or my parents find her and drag her back. I guess that's what she did to you.'

Magnus didn't reply. His brain was whirring around like it was on a rollercoaster. Was any of this true? Taking Skylar with a pinch of salt seemed wise. But some of this rang true and it made sense. It explained why Taylor was so lost and uncertain. 'Hmm,' he muttered.

'And she can be so convincing,' said Skylar. 'Pretending she's me, but I've changed and become so grounded. She's a good actress, you know. If she'd carried on with her career, she could have been almost as good as me, only she didn't have the confidence. She always bottled it at the last minute.'

'Look, I need to go.'

'And meet me later.'

'I'll think about it,' said Magnus with no intention of doing it. Skylar let him go with a serenely unconcerned expression as she moved into the throng of waiting onlookers. Magnus stopped by the group of women he'd met earlier.

'That was some kiss,' said one of them.

'Was that you whistling?' asked Magnus, grinning, despite the heat rising in his neck.

'Guilty.' Another woman raised her hand.

'Yeah, well, the lengths a guy has to go to these days to get an answer. Anyway, I told her about your venture and she seemed interested. If you join the queue, she'll get round to you. I need to go, but thanks, all of you. You've really helped me tonight.'

After some pats on the arm and a couple of air kisses, Magnus left the hotel, jumping down the white stone steps onto the pavement. He needed air before the meal. No doubt Fenella would be fussing and wondering where he was. Passers-by chatted in the evening buzz under the streetlights and horns honked. The ever-present hum of traffic filled the air and Magnus pulled out his phone. Skylar had told him where to find Taylor but he hadn't written it down or tapped it into his phone, he'd committed it to memory and was desperately trying to remember it the whole time Skylar had been talking to him. Opening Google maps, he put in the address. It was some distance away. Maybe he and Fenella could go the next day. He tapped out a quick message to his mum, saying he'd nipped out for air.

Slipping his phone into his pocket, he strode along the road. Walking around the block might air his brain after that encounter with Skylar. He'd not gone far when he passed the entrance to an alley. Its near wall was the hotel side and a door was open. Smoke and cooking smells wafted from it. He scrunched up his nose. If Skylar knew her dinners were made in a place that smelled like that, she'd have Gordon Ramsay called in.

A scream split the darkness further up the alley and Magnus stopped dead. Some kind of struggle was taking place, not the kind of thing he wanted to get involved with, but now he'd seen it, he couldn't stand back and pretend he hadn't. A head poked out the smoky side door and peered around.

Magnus jogged up the alley. 'What's going on?' he shouted.

The man at the kitchen door, dressed in chef's overalls, stepped out and yelled, 'Hey, leave her alone.'

A woman was struggling against two men. One of them was big and beefy and looked like one of Skylar's bodyguards. The other man was older and a shock of white hair fell around his face as he tried to restrain the woman. She kicked and flailed. Her foot jerked, connecting with a suitcase. The huge guy snatched it and launched it behind him. Magnus dodged it.

'Hey,' he shouted, putting up his hands. His heart hammered as he got closer and saw the woman clearer. It was Taylor. And the man restraining her was her father. Magnus recalled meeting him once when he'd worked for Courtney and knew his formidable reputation.

A cold sweat broke out on Magnus's forehead. He wouldn't put it past Sammy Rousse to be armed, and surely the bodyguard would be. Was this where he met his maker? In a back alley in LA. Jeez, what would his mum and dad make of this?

'Stand back,' said the bodyguard.

'Taylor,' said Magnus.

She looked up mid-kick and stared.

'Who are you?' said Sammy Rousse.

'A friend,' said Magnus.

Sammy frowned, still trying to hold on to Taylor. 'A friend? Of who?'

'Taylor.'

'You know Taylor?'

'I do. Can you let her go, please?'

'This is none of your business. I don't know who you are, but I want you to leave.'

'Taylor knows me,' said Magnus. 'Let me talk to her.'

'No,' Sammy said.

'Please,' Taylor whimpered, making a weak attempt at breaking free. 'Let me go.'

'No.'

'Why not?' said Magnus.

'You're a danger to yourself,' Sammy said to her, ignoring Magnus. 'It isn't safe for you to run off again.'

'It's up to me. I don't want to hear any more lies. Skylar's lies, your lies.'

'No, Taylor,' said Sammy quietly. 'It's you. This is projection and false memories. We've been through this with your therapist, remember?'

Desperation flashed in Taylor's eyes, and she didn't meet Magnus's gaze. She shook her head, tears welling. Her arms were locked behind her back as her father held them.

'Why don't you at least let her go,' said Magnus. 'Holding on to her like that can't be comfortable.'

'Will you get out of here?' said Sammy. 'I told you already. Your help is not required. Now scram or Jackson here will remove you.'

'Look.' Magnus threw up his hands. 'I don't want to interfere, but I really need to see Taylor. Could we maybe go inside and talk?'

'No one's gonna be talking to Taylor tonight. Least of all you. I don't know who you are, but I can smell trouble a mile off.'

'I don't want any trouble.'

'Then get away from me and Taylor. And if you're some kind of pap, there'll be hell to pay if any of this is reported.'

With a quick flip of his palms, Magnus shook his head and drew back. 'I'm just a friend.'

'Taylor doesn't have any friends. Now scram before I have to make you.'

Magnus backed off and left the alley. As he reached the pavement and the bright street, a surreal feeling crept over him. Taking his life in his hands, he glanced back into the alley. Taylor was slung between the two men like a corpse; they bundled her in a side door.

'Fucking hell.' Magnus ran his hand down his face. He was out of his depth. This world didn't belong to him. An overriding desire to put as much distance as possible between himself and this family gripped him. But what about Taylor? Maybe keeping her out of his life was the best route. What would Fenella make of this? This was the kind of place Taylor Rousse came from – a different dimension.

He started to walk, but all he could think of was the expression on Taylor's face. Her tormented soul. Those eyes that had once looked at him with such love and admiration were now full of terror. He couldn't leave her there alone. He just couldn't.

Chapter Twenty-Seven

Taylor

Taylor lay on the bed, shaking and sobbing. Her head ached, her eyes stung, her heart was raw and naked and had been ripped so thoroughly from her chest it could have been lying beside her on the bed, bleeding out, staining the pristine white sheets.

She'd seen Magnus again and he'd seen her. Witnessed her reality. What must he make of her? Why had he kissed Skylar? He'd claimed to be her friend but what was he doing now? Was he in the bar with Skylar while she filled his head with her lies? Carl and Robyn's wedding was playing out all over again with renewed keenness. If someone had attacked her with a knife, it wouldn't have hurt this much.

All the fight had ebbed out of her. Had they injected her with some sleep-inducing drug during the struggle? Because she felt listless and apathetic. Outside the world was happening, but what did it have to do with her? She was a stranger to it.

Her door opened. She didn't look up. Something thudded on the floor.

'That's your case,' said her father's voice. 'And let's not pull any more tricks like that one.'

'Hey, honey.' Bianca's soft voice spoke as if from a dream. With a waft of Chanel, the bed dipped and a hand landed on her back. 'We've been talking and we've agreed the best thing would be for you to go back into rehab.'

'What?' Taylor sat up, rubbed her eyes and hugged herself. 'I don't need rehab. I just need my freedom.'

Bianca cocked her head with a sad smile. 'If only that were true. You're so agitated, we can see the signs.'

'There are no signs. I'm clean, I have been for years. I just want to lead my own life.'

'But, honey, every time you go AWOL, you do something crazy. This latest thing tells me you need help. If it's not rehab, then we'll get you back to therapy. We have to do something because you simply cannot keep impersonating your sister like this. It's not right.'

'Ugh.' Taylor balled her fists. They would never get it, would they? It would always be her fault.

'Skylar told us…'

Of course, how it always begins.

'That you'd been off with some man, claiming to be her. It's dangerous, Taylor. You might not always appreciate it, but she's in the public eye and as her sister, we expect you to help maintain her image. We can't afford to have you going off like that doing whatever you were doing and blackening her name in the process. This man might end up selling the story. He might have photographs.'

Taylor pressed her palms into her cheekbones, massaging her sinuses. 'So, unless I have surgery to make me look different, you're keeping me locked up?' said Taylor.

'Locked up?' said her father. 'You have everything you could ever want and more. It isn't exactly a hardship.'

Taylor's heart sank to her feet. There was no way out. There never was.

'Listen,' said Bianca, 'you need to have a good night's sleep. Gather yourself. Tomorrow we'll take you to rehab and you can sign yourself in. We'll get you the best care possible.'

Her father stepped forward, took Taylor's face in his hands, and kissed her forehead.

'Sleep well, baby girl,' said Bianca, giving her a peck on the cheek. As they left the room, the lock clicked with ominous finality.

Great. Just great. Would anyone anywhere ever believe her? She slumped back on the bed and got lost in the luxuriously soft pillows. She'd much prefer to be back in that little room in Fenella's house, wrapped in the warmth of love and acceptance. When she closed her eyes and pulled the duvet tight, she could reclaim those feelings in her mind. And the heat surrounding her came from Magnus's strong arms, not the plush duvet cover. His lips kissed her cheeks. *I love the new you.* The words had come from his heart. *But it wasn't the new me. Just the person I want to be.*

An abrupt knock made her sit up. Rolling over, she frowned at the door. The knock came again. She got up. Who would knock? Her father would have a bodyguard standing there vetting anyone.

She pulled open the door and her jaw dropped. Magnus. He didn't hang about, almost pushing her out of the way as he shut the door behind him.

'What are you doing? How did you get in here?'

'My mum's chatting up your bodyguard.'

'Oh Jesus.' Taylor massaged her temple.

'Look, what is going on? I feel like I've arrived in LA and gone straight onto the set of a movie.'

244

'You won't believe me if I tell you.' Taylor walked to the window, not wanting to look too closely. The sight of Magnus could reduce her to tears. If she'd been real, he'd comfort her now, let her know things were ok. But she wasn't the right woman. 'No one ever does and with my track record I can't blame you.' The city glittered beyond the window.

'Taylor, I want you to come with me.'

She spun around and stared. 'Why?' Her shoulders trembled and her chest constricted.

Magnus walked slowly towards her. As he drew level, he ran his thumb from the corner of her eye across her cheek, taking a tear with him. 'Because I love you,' he whispered.

'Me?' she said, her voice barely above a whisper.

'Yes. You.'

'Not Skylar?'

'No.'

'But I saw you.'

'I don't follow,' he said, adjusting his cuffs.

'I saw you kissing her.'

He stared out the window and shook his head. 'That was part of the deal.'

'You made a deal with her?' Taylor's insides turned to ice.

Magnus let out a little snort. 'She said she'd give me your address if I kissed her, so I did. We didn't think you were here.'

'What address did she give you?' Taylor's mouth dropped as he told her. 'I don't live there, she was messing with you.'

'Jesus Christ. Fooled again. I'm a real sucker.'

'But you wanted to find me that bad?'

'Yes, I told you. I fell in love with you.' He peered up at her. 'You know I did. I wrote it on the beach. I meant it. Everything that happened was real for me.'

'And me… But I messed up. I wish I'd been truthful from the start.'

He put his hands on her arms. 'I do too, but I understand better now. And what I understand most is how I feel when I'm with you and how I feel when I'm not.'

'I'm sorry.' She looked up, willing the tears back.

Strong hands gripped her shoulders, his thumbs gently stroking her. 'My ego took a hit. But I'd be stupid to let it get in the way of how I feel.'

She stared at him. His pupils dilated in his icy blue gaze. Taylor clamped her arms around his back at the same time as he took her face in his hands. Their lips sealed and he groaned as she poured everything into the kiss. No apology was spared, no secret hidden. She laid herself bare and he stepped in, tilting her back towards the window to claim her with a deep and engulfing kiss.

'Come with me,' he said, lacing his fingers into her hair and pressing his forehead against hers.

'Now?'

'Yes.'

'What if my bodyguard's back?'

'We walk past him and leave.'

Taylor stared into his eyes; her breathing matched his: erratic and ragged.

'I can't leave tonight,' she whispered. 'They'll drag me back. You saw what they're like.'

Magnus drew his fingers down her cheek. 'But we're not letting them do that again. We can be strong together. Get your case.'

'Are you serious?'

'Of course. Unless you don't want to.'

'I do. I really do. I don't even care where we go. I just want to go with you.'

He dipped his head in and kissed her cheek. 'Me too. Just be with me.' He slipped his palm up her back and rubbed gentle circles on it. 'Where we belong. Together.'

'I don't know how. I can't.'

'Stand up for yourself. Be you. Let them see Taylor. It doesn't matter what Skylar did to hurt you in the past. Drop it and let it go. Let her go. Set yourself free.'

'But, Magnus, they never believe me.'

'You don't need to make them believe you, just show them someone they can believe in.'

She inhaled a long shaky breath as his hand stroked, calming her right down. This was almost a return to perfection. Getting out of this room with him was another matter entirely. How could she make them listen? But Magnus was right. She had to at least try.

Chapter Twenty-Eight

Magnus

Magnus opened the door. The bodyguard crossed his arms and frowned. 'What are you doing in there?' he asked.

'Coming out,' said Magnus.

'You're not allowed out,' the bodyguard said to Taylor as she slipped out behind Magnus, pulling her case behind her.

'Yes, we've seen what you did to her the last time,' said Magnus. 'Try that again and I'll report you for assault. You've got no grounds to keep her here against her will.'

'How do you know what grounds we have?' The bodyguard growled. 'Taylor, you know your father's rules.'

'I do. But I'm also twenty-six and quite capable of deciding for myself. I'm just not strong enough to take you on.'

'And she shouldn't have to,' Magnus added. His height matched the bodyguard but he was nowhere near as brawny, and violence of any kind was the last thing he wanted.

'I'm going to have to call Sammy,' said the bodyguard.

'Right,' said Magnus. 'You get on with that and we'll leave you to it.'

The bodyguard gave him a filthy look and pulled out his phone. As they started down the stairs, Magnus was aware of him not far behind, talking urgently. 'Yup, she's coming down the stairs with the guy from the alley.'

Taylor glanced at Magnus. 'This won't work. I can't walk out, they'll hound me and you. And your family.'

'You have every right to leave if you want to.' In the throng at the bottom of the stairs, Magnus spotted his parents. Per's fluffy hair stood out amidst the Hollywood perfection. 'Mum,' he said as they drew closer.

Fenella spun around. 'There you are. And Taylor.' She opened her arms and welcomed her into a massive hug. Taylor's shoulders shook as Fenella held her. 'And here's my friend.' She looked over Magnus's shoulders and he followed her sightline. They still had the bodyguard.

'Ma'am,' he said. 'I didn't realise you were part of this.'

'Part of what?' she asked with wide innocent eyes. 'I'm not part of anything. I just want everyone to be happy.'

'Where is she?' A voice boomed behind the bodyguard and Sammy Rousse pushed his way through the crowd with Skylar close behind.

Taylor pulled away from Fenella and adjusted her hair, recreating her messy up-do with her crocodile clip.

'Taylor,' said her father, coming closer and speaking quietly, putting his shoulders between them and the growing crowd. 'You need to get back to your room.'

She shook her head. 'I'm leaving.'

'Yes, so we heard,' said Sammy. 'That's why I brought Skylar with me. I thought you'd try this.'

'Try what?'

'She said that'd be your next thing. Running off with this guy, pretending to be her. Well, you can see for yourself, you've failed.' Sammy frowned at Magnus.

'Failed?'

'In your attempt to kidnap my daughter.'

Magnus put his hand to his forehead and ran his fingers across it. 'Right. I'm not trying to kidnap anyone. I'm well aware this is Taylor.'

'Are you?' said Skylar, swirling a cocktail and sipping it slowly. 'You weren't the last time you were with her.'

A slight scuffle stopped her in her tracks, and Bianca pushed her way forward. 'What is going on?' she muttered.

'I'm leaving,' said Taylor.

Skylar stared; her lips formed into a thoughtful pout. 'You know, handsome,' she said, approaching Magnus and running her finger down his lapel. She leaned up and whispered in his ear, 'You can have me right now. Let's just get the hell out of here. Let Taylor go back to her room.'

'Why would I do that? It was never you I liked.'

She narrowed her eyes and drew back, pure hatred glinting in her face. 'Go to hell.' She tossed the contents of the cocktail glass at him.

'Seriously?' He jumped back, holding out his arms. The front of his dress suit dripped with sticky liquid.

'What are you doing?' Taylor stepped forward.

'That's a bit childish,' said Fenella.

Skylar's mother squinted at her.

'And you think Taylor is unstable?' said Magnus, shaking out his jacket.

'What is it with you?' snapped Skylar. 'And, Taylor, you're…' She seemed to be searching her repertoire for a suitable putdown.

'Skylar,' Sammy warned. 'Let's stay dignified.'

'Taylor made an impression on me somewhere you never will,' said Magnus.

'Oh gross. Just gross. You make me sick.'

'I'm talking about in here.' He rapped his chest and looked at Taylor. She smiled back at him, her eyes watery.

Behind her, lit up by the bright lights, stood Fenella and Per. What were they making of this? Was this the evening Fenella had imagined? It certainly wasn't how Magnus had seen things playing out. And they weren't out of the water yet.

Chapter Twenty-Nine

Taylor

Taylor straightened the front of her dress and blinked at the glaring faces surrounding her. Being with them was all she'd ever known, except that brief stint with Magnus. There were no guarantees. She could take off with him and he might grow tired of her in a week, but whatever the future held, she couldn't sit back and do nothing. Opportunities had been ripped from her too often in the past and whether it had been through her own fault, bad luck or sabotage, she couldn't let that affect her now.

She twisted her hands and looked at her father. 'I'm leaving.'

'Taylor, we've been through this. If you leave—'

'Let me try,' she said. 'Instead of locking me up, give me a chance.'

Skylar and Bianca exchanged glances. They were so alike, blonde, bronzed skin, and impeccable dress sense.

'Taylor,' said Bianca. 'You've had chances, lots of them.'

'No. I haven't. Not really.'

Skylar had her eye on Taylor and when Taylor glanced at her, she smirked. 'Here we go with the accusations and the denial.'

'Shut up and let her speak,' said Magnus.

'Magnus.' Fenella half frowned at him.

Bianca pursed her lips. 'I think Taylor should go back to her room and we can talk about it there. This is not appropriate.'

'Yes, back you go,' said Skylar. 'You weren't dreaming of a handsome prince riding up and rescuing you, I hope.' The sparkle in her eye froze Taylor's blood.

'Come on, Taylor,' said Bianca, stepping up, pinching both her cheeks and beaming as if Taylor was a newborn baby. 'You be good. At least we'll know you're safe then.'

Skylar wiggled her eyebrows.

'She'll be perfectly safe with me,' said Magnus.

'And who are you?' said Bianca Rousse. 'Some mad abductor?'

'He's definitely not the mad one around here,' Fenella muttered.

'That's true,' said Skylar with a wicked glance at Taylor.

'Can everyone stop?' Taylor held up her fists and screwed up her face. 'I'm leaving right now. I'm going with Magnus, and I want you all to hear this. I am not running away because I'm unhinged. I am not dangerous, and I know exactly what I'm doing. So, don't bother calling out the search parties or trying to make me and everybody else believe I'm insane.'

'Taylor, we have never—' began Bianca.

'Let her finish,' said Magnus and Bianca stepped back, placing her hand on her neck, looking horrified.

'I'll keep in touch,' said Taylor. 'But I'm not coming back unless it's to visit.'

'You think you're so smart.' Skylar tossed her hair.

'Because she is,' said Magnus. 'She's really smart, but she's been trapped.'

'Trapped?' said Sammy. 'Safe more like.'

'You'll never be as famous as me,' muttered Skylar, stepping closer to Bianca.

'Good,' said Taylor. 'I'm real glad. I don't want that kind of fame. I just want to be free. I know what happened when we were fourteen.'

'Taylor, not this again,' said Bianca.

'Yes. And for one last time, I'm going to say it. Skylar, dressed up as me, went to the producer of *Girls Get Gritty in the City* and claimed I didn't want the part because of my anxieties. Then he upped and offered it to her. It was not me!'

Skylar looked away, picking her nail. 'So you keep saying.'

'All the lies you've told in between are irrelevant,' Taylor added. 'I don't need to hear you defend yourself. We both know the truth and that's all that matters. My therapist once told me just because I felt something, I didn't have to act on it. But this time, I am. It feels right going with Magnus, and I'm going to give it a try.'

'Well, whatever,' said Skylar. 'So what if I spoke to that producer? You were always a terrible actress. Really, you only got what you deserved.'

Taylor quirked a half smile and nodded. The truth at last. Maybe, in her own twisted way, Skylar was right. 'Let's hope that's true,' said Taylor. She'd got a whole new life – and Magnus. If that was what she deserved, she'd take it.

Skylar narrowed her eyes and opened her mouth, but before she could speak, Taylor pulled away from Magnus, stepped towards her and gave her a quick kiss on the cheek. She then turned to her mother and did the same. Bianca briefly took her arms while Skylar stood plank straight with her mouth hanging wide, clutching her cheek as though Taylor had given her the kiss of death. Inhaling deeply, Taylor turned to her father. He grimaced.

'I know you've been trying to protect me, but I don't need you anymore. I can fend for myself.' She leaned up and kissed his cheek.

Magnus stretched out his hand. She took it and he led her through the front doors into the evening air outside. Fenella and Per were beside them as Taylor glanced around the street, an odd open sensation filling her chest. She could do anything, go anywhere, but she didn't know how.

'Well,' said Fenella, placing her arm around Taylor's shoulder. 'That has been one of the strangest evenings of my life.'

'I'm so glad you came,' said Taylor.

'Our pleasure.' Fenella kissed her on the cheek.

'Listen, Mum, can I have a minute with Taylor?'

'Of course, Dad and I should find the others. They won't believe what's happened.'

Magnus took Taylor by the hand and led her towards the alley where a couple of hours ago, she'd been apprehended. Taylor stopped and looked at him as soon as they turned the corner. Struggling to hold back the flood of emotions bubbling inside, she gazed into his ice-blue eyes, glinting in the dim light.

'You did it.' He smiled.

She let go of her case and flung her arms around his neck. He wrapped her in a tight embrace. 'I just panicked it was all going to go wrong.'

'Life has no guarantees.' His fingers splayed on her back and he kissed her forehead, long and tender. Their bodies moulded together and Taylor slipped her hands under his arms, pulling him even closer. Their eyes met, and for a long time, they just looked. Then, as if it were slow motion, their faces edged closer and their lips met with the gentlest touch. Normal speed resumed as their mouths played catch-up, getting to know each other all over again. Taylor closed her eyes, welcoming his need for her and matching it with her desire.

Breathing heavily, they pulled back and Magnus clamped his hands on either side of her head. 'Let's go home.' He winked.

'Where's that?'

'Wherever we like.' He smiled like a shrewd wolf. 'We've got each other. The world's our oyster.'

Chapter Thirty

Magnus

A week after Taylor's 'escape', Magnus arrived in Glasgow in the early evening. His apartment was freshly cleaned and, as always, had the air of a holiday home. His chest tingled as he smiled at Taylor. She beamed and Magnus realised they'd spent the last few days doing exactly that, grinning and making eyes at each other.

Essentials such as organising a food shop hadn't occurred to him. His brain had been on a detour, trying to function in the bizarre world of Hollywood. Things like going to the supermarket seemed to be part of a completely different world. Now he had to reconcile himself to some semblance of normality – almost.

'This feels a bit surreal,' said Taylor.

'It does, doesn't it?'

'I've never lived with anyone other than my family, and here I am about to move in with a guy I hardly know, in a different country.'

Magnus dropped his bags and locked the door. 'I've never lived with anyone either. Except that week with you.'

'Everything in my heart was real. I just wish I'd gone about it in a better way.'

'It was partly my ego. If you'd told me who you were at the start, we'd probably have had the same outcome. I couldn't stand the idea I'd been played, and I couldn't make myself see the bigger picture. Thank goodness for my mum.'

There might always be cracks between Taylor and her family, but Fenella had hatched a plan which even Taylor's parents had agreed to – once they'd realised Taylor was set on leaving. A reporter was due the following day for a shoot and short interview. Sammy was arranging to have it incorporated into a press release about the sisters. Fenella's logic seemed sensible: if Taylor's story – a glossed over press-friendly version – was known, she couldn't be caught so easily impersonating Skylar, which appealed to her family, but it would also give her a chance to say her piece and take some credit for her achievements.

Taylor bit her lip and blinked. 'Oh, god.' She held her chest. 'What will I say to them? I haven't got much to be proud about.'

'Hey.' Magnus took her hands. 'You do. Talk about your early career if you like, just keep the bits about Skylar vague. Tell them how you struggled with fame. It's ok to admit to it. People will admire your bravery for speaking out.'

Taylor's breathing was short and raspy.

'Talk about your plans. Tell them you've had training in PR and you're going to make it a career here.'

'But that's just it. What if we go through with this, then you and I split up?'

Magnus took Taylor in his arms, remembering the curves of her body and how well she fitted with him. 'I wanted to prove to my family I could have a normal relationship, but at the same time telling myself I didn't want one.' He smoothed his palm down her back, stroking her until she became putty, yielding to his touch. 'But now I know I did. And I do. I don't want to be alone anymore and it's you that made me realise that. Who knows where we'll go in the long run, nobody can make predictions like that, but I want to give it our best shot.'

'I loved you almost from the start. That day you crashed into me, you were so nice.'

'And you were so surprising, but even if we hadn't met in LA five years ago, I'd still have liked you.' Magnus kissed her forehead. 'You belong with me and me with you.'

Taylor looked up and smiled.

'Let's go bag some kip so we're ready for tomorrow.'

'You want to sleep?' she said.

'Don't you?'

'Well.' Taylor stepped back and slipped her jacket off. 'I'm still on US time and as far as I'm concerned, we've got hours before bedtime.'

Magnus raised an eyebrow. 'Really? I've been looking forward to bedtime all day.'

'Ok, a compromise. Bed, first. Sleep… after.'

'Deal.' Magnus pulled off his jacket, tossed it aside, and pulled Taylor close.

Epilogue

Taylor

Taylor nipped up the ferry's internal stairs behind Magnus, excitement bursting from every pore. The chill she'd experienced on her previous journey was no more. Sun split the sky, dazzling them as its reflection bounced off the sea.

She wrapped her arms around him as the ship sailed out, powering west through Oban Bay towards the open sea and Mull. Somewhere waiting was Fenella, and Taylor couldn't wait to see her again. Since the stress of leaving LA and the shock of arriving in a foreign country, Taylor had spent the previous three months pulling the strands of her life together, analysing her priorities and putting together a plan of how to get herself on track and make a new start. With work permits in place, she'd taken a job in PR and was getting there slowly. Tuning into the Glaswegian accent was a skill in itself.

The interview had gone well, and though Skylar would never be happy with Taylor getting any attention, she was far enough away for Taylor not to care. Taylor had no intention of returning to that world anytime soon. Skylar was welcome to it. But Taylor missed family interactions. Weird relationships aside, they'd always been there. Now, she was adjusting to more time alone, days in the office, and the best days – when Magnus was home and they could spend time together.

'I wish you'd let me book a hotel,' said Magnus. 'Do you remember what it was like staying with them?' The corner of his mouth quirked up.

She prodded him in the midriff. 'I liked it there. Your family are kind, and that room was—'

'Tiny?'

'Small but cosy.'

'And Aunt Jean?'

'She was funny. Now stop being a killjoy.'

He laughed and held her close. 'Ok.'

*

Fenella burst out the door, waving as they pulled up. Taylor leapt from the car and hugged her before Magnus had stopped the engine.

'You're back,' said Fenella, crushing her with a hug.

'And it's really me this time.'

'Oh, Taylor.' Fenella pulled back, anchoring her hands on either side of Taylor. 'You're always welcome here. Now, in we come.' Fenella hugged Magnus before the three of them trooped inside. 'I'll make some tea. In you go, I think Jean's asleep. Give her a poke if you like.'

'Or not,' said Magnus.

Taylor crossed the room and sat at the table by the window, admiring the sea view and smiling. After a few minutes, Fenella came in with a tea tray and placed it on the table. 'So, how are things with your family?' she asked.

Taylor let out a sigh. 'They haven't much choice but to accept it. And the interview cleared the air.'

'Wonderful,' said Fenella. 'It looked super. I told all my friends to buy the magazine. You two are so gorgeous together. Magnus has always been a handsome boy, not that I'm biased, of course.'

'You're right.' Taylor smirked.

'Will you two get a grip,' said Magnus.

'I think they're right too,' said Jean. Taylor jumped, not realising she'd woken. 'But you shouldn't puff him up like that.'

'For once, I agree with you,' Magnus muttered.

Fenella winked at Taylor. 'And you're settling down in Glasgow ok? Not too much of a shock to the system?'

'Maybe a little but I'm enjoying it. I've got some new friends, I love the apartment, and I'm getting used to Magnus's weird hours.'

'At least I'm not on long haul anymore, that really messed with my circadian rhythm.'

'He keeps trying to explain this to me,' Fenella said. 'I'm not much of a traveller, so it doesn't mean much to me. I'm just so glad you're settling in. I knew you were good news for each other.' She glanced between the two of them, with her eyebrow sitting high in a know-it-all expression.

'I should know by now to listen to my mother,' said Magnus, lifting Taylor's hand and squeezing it. She beamed at him.

*

With the sun high in the sky and not a cloud to be seen, Taylor and Magnus walked to the shore later in the afternoon. Per's little boat was moored close by and they strolled towards it.

'Champagne aboard the *Clunie Lass*?' asked Magnus, pulling a bottle from the cool bag he was carrying.

'How can I refuse… Are you going to drive the boat?'

'Sure, it's a doddle compared to the plane. That leaves the whole bottle of champers to you. I don't want to be under the influence.'

Taylor stepped in front of him and held up her hand. She brushed it slowly from side to side in mid-air.

'What are you doing?'

'You're already under the influence.' She flicked him a little grin. 'My influence.'

He chuckled. 'Yeah, I know that and I don't need the wonky hand signals to prove it.' He placed the bag on the pier, walked forward, and threaded his fingers into Taylor's hair, melting into her for a warm, slow kiss. 'Now let's have some fun.'

Before she could say a word, he swept the feet from under her and carried her to the end of the pier. 'Oh, my god… Do not throw me in. I won't let go if you do, I'll pull you in with me.'

He laughed and swung her around, walking back towards the boat. 'I wasn't going to. Honestly, as if I would. I was just helping you onto the boat.' With a grunt, he set her on her feet and helped her aboard. 'There.'

Taylor shaded her eyes from the glinting reflection of the still sea.

Magnus leapt on board. For a few moments he stood quite still, then he placed the cool box on the deck with a clink.

'I have something for you,' he said.

Taylor moved closer. Without dropping her gaze, she took his hand. 'And I have something for you.'

'What?' His pupils pierced hers.

She leaned in, stroked her fingertips over his rough cheek and gently raised her lips to him. 'This.' Her heart almost leapt from her chest, blood rushed to her head and surged through every part of her body as she tasted his lips, soft with Burt's Beeswax. He slipped his hands around her waist and pulled her closer. The kiss deepened. He groaned and pushed her gently; she stumbled back against the wall of the boat. He pinned her fast, kissing her until she threw her head back.

He released her and lifted his neck to breathe. With his arm still rigid against the boat, he braced himself. 'Thank you.'

The corners of her lips turned up. 'You're welcome.'

'But…'

'What? Not good enough?' she said.

'Definitely good enough, just not long enough.' He leaned in again, and she lost herself in a world where only the two of them existed.

'Magnus,' she whispered, breaking away and catching her breath. 'What were you going to give me?'

'Oh. You distracted me.' He fished in his pocket, withdrawing a little black box.

Taylor gaped at it, her heart hammering. 'This is a bit sudden, isn't it?'

He smiled, still holding out the box. 'You better open it and find out.'

With a shaky hand, Taylor took the box and flipped it open. A silver bracelet twinkled and she tugged it gently. Set in the middle was a pink pebble, polished up and gleaming. 'Is this the little pebble I found on the beach here?'

'It sure is.'

Taylor slipped it onto her wrist. Magnus watched, smiling. The sun sparkled and reflected in his glossy irises.

'It's perfect,' she said.

'It doesn't mean I don't want other things,' he said. 'In the future, when we're ready. I'm happy to go with you wherever you like. I'm in this for the long haul and…' He stopped and took a breath. 'I hope you're with me.'

She flung her arms around his neck. 'Of course I am. I'll be with you as long as you want me.'

'I don't think there'll ever be a day when I don't.' Magnus held her close and she closed her eyes, resting on his shoulder. After years of uncertainty, she finally had something for herself and she intended to make the most of every precious moment.

The End

Share the Love!

If you enjoyed reading this book, then please share your reviews online.

Leaving reviews is a perfect way to support authors and helps books reach more readers.

So please review and share!

Let me know what you think.

Margaret

About the author

I'm a writer, mummy, wife and chocolate eater (in any order you care to choose). I live in highland Perthshire in a little house close to the woods where I often see red squirrels, deer and other such tremendously Scottish wildlife… Though not normally haggises or even men in kilts!

It's my absolute pleasure to be able to bring the Scottish Island Escapes series to you and I hope you love reading the stories as much as I enjoy writing them. Writing is an escapist joy for me and I adore disappearing into my imagination and returning with a new story to tell.

If you want to keep up with what's coming next or learn more about any of the books or the series, then be sure to visit my website. I look forward to seeing you there.

www.margaretamatt.com

Acknowledgements

Thanks goes to my adorable husband for supporting my dreams and putting up with my writing talk 24/7. Also to my son, whose interest in my writing always makes me smile. It's precious to know I've passed the bug to him – he's currently writing his own fantasy novel and instruction books on how to build Lego!

Throughout the writing process, I have gleaned help from many sources and met some fabulous people. I'd like to give a special mention to Stéphanie Ronckier, my beta reader extraordinaire. Stéphanie's continued support with my writing is invaluable and I love the fact that I need someone French to correct my grammar! Stéphanie, you rock. To my lovely friend, Lyn Williamson, thank you for your continued support and encouragement with all my projects. And to my fellow authors, Evie Alexander and Lyndsey Gallagher – you girls are the best! I love it that you always have my back and are there to help when I need you. Thank you also to Mandi Blake for reading this book and checking I got all the Americanisms correct! Much appreciated.

Also, a huge thanks to my editor, Aimee Walker, at Aimee Walker Editorial Services for her excellent work on my novels and for answering all my mad questions. Thank you so much, Aimee!

More Books by Margaret Amatt

Scottish Island Escapes

Season 1
A Winter Haven
A Spring Retreat
A Summer Sanctuary
An Autumn Hideaway
A Christmas Bluff
Season 2
A Flight of Fancy
A Hidden Gem
A Striking Result
A Perfect Discovery
A Festive Surprise

Free Hugs & Old-Fashioned Kisses

Do you ever get one of those days when you just fancy snuggling up? Then this captivating short story is for you!

And what's more, it's free when you sign up to my newsletter.

Meet Livvi, a girl who just needs a hug. And Jakob, a guy who doesn't go about hugging random strangers. But what if he makes an exception, just this once?

Make yourself a hot chocolate, sign up to my newsletter and enjoy!

A short story only available to newsletter subscribers.

Sign up at
www.margaretamatt.com

A Winter Haven

She was the one that got away. Now she's back.

Career-driven Robyn Sherratt returns to her childhood home on the Scottish Isle of Mull, hoping to build bridges with her estranged family. She discovers her mother struggling to run the family hotel. When an old flame turns up, memories come back to bite, nibbling into Robyn's fragile heart.

Carl Hansen, known as The Fixer, abandoned city life for peace and tranquillity. Swapping his office for a log cabin, he mends people's broken treasures. He can fix anything, except himself. When forced to work on hotel renovations with Robyn, the girl he lost twelve years ago, his quiet life is sent spinning.

Carl would like nothing more than to piece together the shattered shards of Robyn's heart. But can she trust him? What can a broken man like him offer a successful woman like her?

A Spring Retreat

She's gritty, he's determined. Who will back down first?

When spirited islander Beth McGregor learns of plans to build a road through the family farm, she sets out to stop it. But she's thrown off course by the charming and handsome project manager. Sparks fly, sending Beth into a spiral of confusion. Guys are fine as friends. Nothing else.

Murray Henderson has finally found a place to retreat from the past with what seems like a straightforward job. But he hasn't reckoned on the stubbornness of the locals, especially the hot-headed and attractive Beth.

As they battle together over the proposed road, attraction blooms. Murray strives to discover the real Beth; what secrets lie behind the tough façade? Can a regular farm girl like her measure up to Murray's impeccable standards, and perhaps find something she didn't know she was looking for?

A Summer Sanctuary

She's about to discover the one place he wants to keep secret

Five years ago, Island girl Kirsten McGregor broke the company rules. Now, she has the keys to the Hidden Mull tour bus and is ready to take on the task of running the business. But another tour has arrived. The competition is bad enough but when she recognises the rival tour operator, her plans are upended.

Former jet pilot Fraser Bell has made his share of mistakes. What better place to hide and regroup than the place he grew to love as a boy? With great enthusiasm, he launches into his new tour business, until old-flame Kirsten shows up and sends his world plummeting.

Kirsten may know all the island's secrets, but what she can't work out is Fraser. With tension simmering, Kirsten and Fraser's attraction increases. What if they both made a mistake before? Is one of them about to make an even bigger one now?

An Autumn Hideaway

She went looking for someone, but it wasn't him.

After a string of disappointments for chirpy city girl Autumn, discovering her notoriously unstable mother has run off again is the last straw. When Autumn learns her mother's last known whereabouts was a remote Scottish Island, she makes the rash decision to go searching for her.

Taciturn islander Richard has his reasons for choosing the remote Isle of Mull as home. He's on a deadline and doesn't need any complications or company. But everything changes after a chance encounter with Autumn.

Autumn chips away at Richard's reserve until his carefully constructed walls start to crumble. But Autumn's just a passing visitor and Richard has no plans to leave. Will they realise, before it's too late, that what they've been searching for isn't necessarily what's missing?

A Christmas Bluff

She's about to trespass all over his Christmas.

Artist and photographer Georgia Rose has spent two carefree years on the Isle of Mull and is looking forward to a quiet Christmas... Until she discovers her family is about to descend upon her, along with her past.

Aloof aristocrat Archie Crichton-Leith has let out his island mansion to a large party from the mainland. They're expecting a castle for Christmas, not an outdated old pile, and he's in trouble.

When Georgia turns up with an irresistible smile and an offer he can't refuse, he's wary, but he needs her help.

As Georgia weaves her festive charms around the house, they start to work on Archie too. And the spell extends both ways. But falling in love was never part of the deal. Can the magic outlast Christmas when he's been conned before and she has a secret that could ruin everything?

A Flight of Fancy

She's masquerading as her twin, pretending to be his girlfriend, while really just being herself.

After years of being cooped up by her movie star family, Taylor Rousse is desperate to escape. Having a Hollywood actress as a twin is about all Taylor can say for herself, but when she's let down by her sister for the umpteenth time, she decides now is the time for action.

Pilot Magnus Hansen is heading back to his family home on the Isle of Mull for his brother's wedding and he's not looking forward to showing up single. The eldest of three brothers shouldn't be the last married – no matter how often he tells himself he's not the marrying type.

On his way, Magnus crashes into a former fling. She's a Hollywood star looking for an escape and they strike a deal: he's her ticket to a week of peace; she's his new date. Except Taylor isn't who he thinks she is. When she and Magnus start to fall for each other, their double deception threatens to blow up in their faces and shatter everything that might have been.

A Hidden Gem

She has a secret past. He has an uncertain future.

Together, can they unlock them both?

After being framed for embezzlement by her ex, career-driven Rebekah needs a break to nurse her broken heart and wounded soul. When her grandmother dies, leaving her a precious necklace and a mysterious note, she sets out to unravel a family secret that's been hidden for over sixty years.

Blair's lived all his life on the Isle of Mull. He's everybody's friend – with or without the benefits – but at night he goes home alone. When Rebekah arrives, he's instantly attracted to her, but she's way out of his league. He needs to keep a stopper on his feelings or risk losing her friendship.

As Rebekah's quest continues, she's rocked by unexpected feelings for her new friend. Can she trust her heart as much as she trusts Blair? And can he be more than just a friend? Perhaps the truth isn't the only thing waiting to be found.

A Striking Result

She's about to tackle everything he's trying to hide.

When unlucky-in-love Carys McTeague is offered the job of caring for an injured footballer, she goes for it even though it's far removed from the world she's used to.

Scottish football hero Troy Copeland is at the centre of a media storm after a serious accident left him with career-threatening injuries and his fiancée dumped him for a teammate. With a little persuasion from Carys, he flees to the remote Isle of Mull to escape and recuperate.

On Mull, Carys reconnects with someone unexpected from her past and starts to fall in love with the island – and Troy. But nothing lasts forever. Carys has been abandoned more than once and as soon as Troy's recovered, he'll leave like everyone else.

Troy's smitten by Carys but has a career to preserve. Will he realise he's been chasing the wrong goal before he loses the love of his life?

A Perfect Discovery

To find love, they need to dig deep.

Kind-hearted archaeologist Rhona Lamond returns home to the Isle of Mull after her precious research is stolen, feeling lost and frustrated. When an island project comes up, it tugs at Rhona's soul and she's desperate to take it on. But there's a major problem.

Property developer Calum Matheson has a longstanding feud with the Lamond family. After a plot of land he owns is discovered to be a site of historical importance, his plans are thrown into disarray and building work put on hold.

Calum doesn't think things can get any worse, until archaeologist Rhona turns up. Not only is she a Lamond, but she's all grown up, and even stubbornly unromantic Calum can't fail to notice her – or the effect she has on him.

Their attraction ignites but how can they overcome years of hate between their families? Both must decide what's more important, family or love.

A Festive Surprise

She can't abide Christmas. He's not sure what it's all about. Together they're in for a festive surprise.

Ambitious software developer Holly may have a festive name but the connection ends there. She despises the holiday season and decides to flee to the remote island of Mull in a bid to escape from it.

Syrian refugee Farid has made a new home in Scotland but he's lonely. Understanding Nessie and Irn Bru is one thing, but when glittery reindeer and tinsel hit the shelves, he's completely bemused. Determined to understand a new culture, he asks his new neighbour to educate him on all things Christmas.

When Holly reluctantly agrees, he realises there's more to her hatred of mince pies and mulled wine than meets the eye. Farid makes it his mission to inject some joy into Hollys' life but falling for her is an unexpected gift that was never on his list.

As their attraction sparkles, can Christmas work its magic on Holly and Farid, or will their spark fizzle out with the end of December

Printed in Great Britain
by Amazon

81146477R00164